A Riveting Reply

Amanda tried to keep herself from asking Lord Ashindon the question whose answer she dreaded. But it was like trying to keep her tongue from probing a tooth that ached.

Finally she surrendered to her need to know. "You've known Lianne for a long time?"

"Almost all our lives." Lord Ashindon faced Amanda abruptly, the glow of candlelight turning his eyes to molten silver. "She and I were to be married," he said harshly. "Is that what you wanted to know?"

Amanda stared at him searchingly. "Are you still in love with her?" she asked in a low voice.

For a long moment he said nothing. Then, in a sudden movement, he grasped her to him and bent his head. "I shall let you be the judge of that," he growled just before he brought his mouth down on hers—in a kiss devilishly well designed to leave her with no judgment at all. . . .

Step in Time

>—•◊•—◊—•◊•—<

by

Anne Barbour

A SIGNET BOOK

SIGNET
Published by the Penguin Group
Penguin Books USA Inc., 375 Hudson Street,
New York, New York 10014, U.S.A.
Penguin Books Ltd, 27 Wrights Lane,
London W8 5TZ, England
Penguin Books Australia Ltd, Ringwood,
Victoria, Australia
Penguin Books Canada Ltd, 10 Alcorn Avenue,
Toronto, Ontario, Canada M4V 3B2
Penguin Books (N.Z.) Ltd, 182-190 Wairau Road,
Auckland 10, New Zealand

Penguin Books Ltd, Registered Offices:
Harmondsworth, Middlesex, England

First published by Signet, an imprint of Dutton Signet,
a division of Penguin Books USA Inc.

First Printing, March, 1996
10 9 8 7 6 5 4 3 2 1

For Rosemary Rozum Yirka,
wise and witty and altogether
a sister-in-law to be treasured.

ACKNOWLEDGMENT

I wish to thank P. A. Zepp
for her medical advice on my heroine's
unfortunate situation.

Chapter One

London, April 14, 1996

"Are you all right, miss? Do you need help?"

Amanda McGovern stiffened at the concern in the elderly gentleman's voice, and the headache that had barely made itself felt a few moments ago phased into a dull throb.

"No," she replied coldly. "I'm fine, thank you." Her voice echoed harshly in the shadowed church as she lowered herself gingerly into a pew. "I just came in to rest for a few minutes."

The gentleman raised his hand. "I did not mean to intrude, my dear, but the way you were . . ."

"I always walk like this," Amanda interrupted, her voice sharp. "It's a permanent condition." Softening her tone, she added, "But, thank you for your concern. I'm afraid I've walked too far today and thought I'd sit for a moment. It's so lovely here." She glanced around the little church, empty except for herself and the old man.

"Yes, it is," he agreed mildly. "I drop in often myself."

To Amanda's dismay, the man entered the pew ahead of hers and sat down, removing his hat as though prepared to settle in for a lengthy chat. Amanda did not fear the man, for a more harmless individual could not be imagined than this bespectacled, conservatively dressed nonentity, so fragile with age that he appeared on the verge of crumbling like old plaster. Still, she had no wish to be buttonholed by an importunate stranger, no matter his state of decrepitude.

"You're an American," the old man stated, beaming as though delighted by this fact. "Is this your first time in London?"

"Yes." She bent ostentatiously to the pamphlet she held in her hand, picked up from a table near the church entry. After a moment's silence, she became uncomfortably aware of her rudeness and added, "My field is English literature, and—and British history." Rather to her surprise, she continued. "Besides London, I want to see—oh, the Lake District."

The man nodded, his faded wisps of hair drifting in the slight current of air that moved through the church. "Of course. Wordsworth and Shelley."

For the first time Amanda smiled. "Yes, and Keats. And, I must go to Chawton to see Jane Austen's home. I have already visited Dr. Johnson's house here in London, and Dickens', too, as well as the new Globe Theatre restoration." For heaven's sake, she thought, startled, she was prattling like an eager guest on *Oprah*.

"All in one day?" asked the gentleman, obviously impressed.

She nodded. "I only have a week in the city before I begin on the countryside, so I have to make the most of every moment." Despite herself, she was beginning to enjoy the ephemeral contact with this endearing old relic.

"But what are you doing in Mayfair?" he asked.

Amanda's laughter sounded loud in her ears. "Oh. Well, I was in a bus and I saw a street sign that said BOND STREET. I couldn't resist the urge to windowshop there." She continued, bewildered at her uncharacteristic chattiness. "And then I decided that I must see Berkeley Square. I was delighted to see that so many of the old Georgian town houses are still here, for the Georgian and Regency periods are of particular interest to me," she concluded.

"I see," said the old man, his spectacles glittering in the waning twilight. "And now you have tired yourself to exhaustion."

A renewal of her irritation swept through Amanda. "I am quite accustomed to walking," she said curtly. "I simply got lost and decided to rest while I—regroup."

In the silence that followed, she squirmed in her seat. "But, yes, I'm afraid I overdid it just a bit. You see," she continued, feeling once more oddly compelled to confide in this unassuming little person, "I was severely injured in a car crash when I was small. I'm all right now—well, not all right, precisely," she said, running her fingers over the familiar twisted contours of her legs, "but, I'm able to function almost normally."

"It must have been—very difficult for you," murmured the old man softly.

"Yes," she said calmly. "It was difficult. But, I survived."

The old man quirked a thread of an eyebrow. "Yes, you have accomplished a great deal."

Amanda started. What an odd thing to say! He could not know about the doctorate—and the rest.

She looked at the old man again, more closely this time. With his high old-fashioned collar, from which protruded a scrawny neck several sizes too small, he resembled something straight out of Dickens. His stiff, black suit was rusty with age. His eyes, behind the wire-rimmed spectacles, gleamed with an eldritch twinkle, and his cheeks were rosy little nobs set on either side of a small, sharp nose, down which the spectacles slid to perch uncertainly at its very tip.

She jerked to attention, aware that he was speaking again.

" . . . and you made the trip alone?"

"Oh, yes," she replied airily. "I—I prefer to travel by myself. I thought of taking a guided tour, but I hate the idea of those things. I'd rather strike out on my own."

"But doesn't your family worry about you—striking out on your own? And your friends?"

An odd, forlorn feeling fluttered in the pit of Amanda's stomach. "My friends respect my desire for independence. Actually," she continued after a long moment, "I don't have many close friends, and I haven't been in touch with any of my family for years. They—they don't understand my particular—problems." She listened to herself, appalled. She could not possibly be saying these things to a total stranger! "I prefer it that way," she added quickly. "I don't need any other encumbrances in my life." She gestured to her legs.

"Encumbrances?" The old man gazed at her with infinite sadness. "You have never let anyone—in?"

Amanda suddenly found it hard to swallow past the painful lump in her throat.

"No," she whispered. "Except . . . No." She clamped her lips shut. She had already spilled more of herself to this peculiar old man than she had to anyone else in her adult life, but she was not, by God, going to tell him about Derek.

The old gentleman heaved a sigh so profound that it seemed

impossible it could have come from that slight frame. He picked up his hat.

"I would love to stay longer, my dear, but I must be going," he said, rising with an audible creaking of joints.

To her surprise, Amanda opened her mouth to protest before arranging her face in a polite smile. "Of course," she murmured. "It's been nice chatting with you."

Moving into the aisle, the old man turned to her and raised a trembling hand to touch her cheek, just above the misshapen line of her jaw. It was like being brushed by a cobweb. He nodded his head abruptly. He took her hand for an instant, staring at her intently, and Amanda was aware of a strange, comforting warmth emanating from his thin fingers.

"Well, well, it appears you are the right one, after all," he said cryptically. He stood back to survey her for a long moment, his head bobbing several times on the frail stem of his neck. "You have a long journey ahead of you. I wish you well," he said simply before turning away to become absorbed into the shadows.

The right one for what? Amanda wondered as the silence of the church settled on her like a heavy blanket. She felt oppressed, suddenly, and was aware that her headache, which had eased during her conversation with the old man, had returned. They were becoming more and more frequent, she noticed distractedly. She'd have to get her eyes checked when she got back home. She really didn't need any more aches and pains.

Unconsciously, she lifted her hand to touch a pendant that hung on a slim gold chain about her neck, and she closed her eyes. Derek. An image flashed before her in swift painful detail of thick, curling golden hair and eyes the color of the sea. She had seen those eyes burn with passion, and later, had watched in misery as they turned cold and flat with disinterest.

She clutched the pendant in her hand, almost welcoming the sharpness of the edges that dug into her palm. Lord, she thought in sudden irritation, she had got over Derek years ago. Why had she clung for so long to this symbol of his fragile devotion? Certainly not as a memento of lost love. She had kept it, she told herself firmly, because it was beautiful—and as a reminder that love was an illusion fostered by the sentimentalists of the world. She dropped it into her neckline and made as though to rise. She'd rested long enough. Up and at 'em, Amanda.

"Damn!" She uttered the word aloud. She should have asked directions of her Good Samaritan. She glanced at the pamphlet in her hand. Grosvenor Chapel, built in 1730. She rather thought she had seen the name in her guidebook. Unfortunately, she'd left the guidebook in her hotel room—again.

Let's see, she'd been on—no, *in*, the English said—North Audley Street. Just before the pain in her hips and legs had driven her to seek haven, she had noticed the chapel, with a lovely park behind it, and the building next door which bore a sign proclaiming it to be the Mayfair Public Library. If she kept on in the direction she had been walking, she would eventually run into Grosvenor Square, wouldn't she? And after that, Oxford Street. She wasn't sure she could face the crowds on that busy thoroughfare just now. Yesterday, she had stumbled and nearly fallen on the corner of one of the huge paving stones.

A memory rose before her, so vivid she almost gasped, of Derek pulling her along a beach just outside San Diego. He had laughed as she lurched clumsily in his wake, but it was a tender sound, one of love and encouragement, and she had renewed her effort, determined not to spoil his afternoon.

She came back to her surroundings, suddenly cold, to realize that it was almost dark. She must return to her hotel—if only she could find the way. Well, she'd just have to take a taxi. As she clutched the edge of the pew in front of her and began to struggle to her feet, she was dismayed to feel tears on her cheeks. She was assailed by another wave of depression and she sank back against the wood. The lovely little church blurred before her, and she turned her face upward.

"Please," she murmured. "Please help me. I'm so lost."

She made again as though to rise, but in that instant her headache suddenly blossomed into a searing vortex of pain. The sound of her gasp echoed in the shadowy church, and the darkness advanced on her until it seemed to cover her, to absorb her into its suffocating depths. The next moment, a shaft of pure, white light that seemed to come from the window above the altar transfixed her, and the pain swelled into a physical assault, almost exquisite in its intensity. With a small moan, she slumped into the pew, giving herself up to the blackness.

London, April 14, 1815

William, the Earl of Ashindon, was an angry man. Ignoring the anguished protests of the woman who sat next to him in his curricle, he drew up with a jerk before the Grosvenor Chapel. Behind him, he heard the sound of another carriage pulling up, but, heedless, leaped to the ground and made his way to the chapel entrance.

"Please, my lord . . . "

He looked down into the pleading eyes of Serena Bridge, wife of Jeremiah, whose pounding footsteps caught up with them at that moment.

"Please, my lord," repeated Serena. "Let us—my husband and I—take care of this."

"That's right," puffed Jeremiah, his thinning hair falling in disarray over broad features. "There is no need to concern yourself with this—unfortunate situation, my lord."

"Oh, is there not?" returned the earl angrily. "It seems to me that under the circumstances, my concern is not only understandable, but required. And cannot you silence that god-awful screeching?" He flung a hand toward the maidservant who hovered nearby, her apron thrown over her head. He turned on his heel as Jeremiah barked an order at the unfortunate girl.

Good God, thought the earl, it needed only this to set the seal on his wretched situation. He had struggled for months against the urgings of his man of affairs to pursue the Bridge chit, and when he finally succumbed, look where it had led him. Cuckolded before he was even wed, for God's sake.

To be sure, his heart was not involved, but his *amour propre* was sorely wounded. The fact that Amanda Bridge had preferred a man like Cosmo Satterleigh to himself was enough to make him a laughingstock in the *haut ton*. He had never cared for the opinion of that body—those self-proclaimed arbiters of custom, but this was the outside of enough. When he had discovered on his arrival *chez* Bridge to make an official declaration that the object of his attentions had apparently eloped an hour earlier, he had almost choked on his rage and humiliation. None of which, of course, he had allowed himself to display. His demeanor remained calm and frigidly correct, and it was he who had conducted the interrogation of the hapless maid, leading to the intelligence that Amanda had fled to a rendezvous with her beloved in the chapel.

It was, he assured himself, the sheer unexpectedness of the situation that had so taken him aback. He had no illusions concerning his personal attributes, for he could by no means be considered personable, and his social skills were minimal. Moreover, his financial situation . . . He snorted. The last time he had stood in the dark, empty Hall of Ashindon Park, he had felt like a ghost presiding over the ruins of a dissipated legacy. There was, however, the ancient and honorable Ashindon title, a commodity highly desired by the likes of Jeremiah Bridge.

Ash had thought his status appealed to Bridge's beautiful daughter, as well. She had seemed to welcome his attentions, fluttering her incredible lashes at him and giggling dutifully at his every pleasantry.

Apparently, he had been mistaken.

He should be grateful, of course, at this excuse to break off the budding relationship, but, no. He had too much invested. He was, in short, desperate. Still, he thought as he moved purposefully toward the chapel, he could cheerfully throttle the silly little widgeon, who undoubtedly waited inside with breathless anticipation for the arrival of her lover.

The Bridges in his wake, he entered the vestibule and pushed through the door that led into the chapel. His gaze swept the interior. Yes, there she was, seated alone in a corner in an attitude of prayerful expectancy. Behind him, Serena Bridge gasped, and at the sound the girl rose. With a rustle of silken skirts, she whirled to face them.

Her mouth was a wide O of surprise and distress, and she raised her hands in a defensive gesture. In the next instant, however, a grimace of pain distorted her lovely features, and her fingers lifted to her forehead. She uttered a soft moan and slumped to the floor.

Ash stifled an exclamation of anger. Did the chit think to escape punishment by feigning a swoon? He knelt to gather her in his arms. He shook her roughly, then his breath caught. Her face was utterly still and slightly tinged with gray. He had seen death many times and knew its aspect well. Suddenly cold, he placed his fingertips at the base of her throat, to find only stillness. He glanced up at Serena and Jeremiah, the bewilderment and anguish in their eyes striking him like a blow. He steeled himself.

"She's—" he began. "Mr. and Mrs. Bridge, I'm afraid your daughter is—"

He felt a stirring in his arms, and looking down, saw to his astonishment that Amanda's eyes were fluttering open.

Amanda's first sensation on regaining consciousness was an unaccustomed feeling of warmth and security. Her second was an uncomfortable realization that she was being cradled in the arms of a strange man. She struggled to a sitting position and became aware with some relief of the presence of a middle-aged man and woman of an undoubtedly respectable mien. She noted, also with relief, that her headache had disappeared. She glanced up at the man who still held her and whose face was disturbingly close to her own. Good heavens, he was dressed in some sort of costume, as were, she realized with a start, the other man and the woman. Oh, dear Lord, had she passed out in the middle of some sort of reenactment?

"Please," she whispered. "I—I'm sorry. I seem to—"

"Amanda!" It was the woman, speaking in accents of severe disapprobation. "Amanda, how could you, you wicked girl?"

"W-what?" asked Amanda in bewilderment. She hadn't spoiled their presentation—or whatever they were engaged in—on purpose, after all. . . . And how did they know her name?

"It's no good pretending you know nothing," growled the older man. "We know what you were up to . . . and you deserve a good thrashing for it."

"What?" exclaimed Amanda again, in stronger accents. "Who the hell *are* you people?"

"Amanda!" cried the woman. "What will his lordship think?"

His lordship? Amanda turned with a jerk to confront the man who still held her gripped in an embrace. She judged him to be tall, and his eyes were of an unnerving steel gray. He could by no means be called attractive, for his features were harsh and irregular, arranged haphazardly around an imposing nose. Yet he was definitely lordly, she admitted, for he was possessed of a casual elegance and an air of command. He appeared to be about thirty years old, and his costume was composed of a pearl gray coat jacket, a silk vest, and a ruffled shirt, completed with an intricately tied cravat that added to the effect of upper-class arrogance. His hair was a thick black thatch that fell over his forehead in disarray.

Hastily, she thrust herself away from him. "I'm sorry," she began again, waving her hands, "if I've spoiled your—oh, my God!" she concluded in consternation as she glanced at her hands. They could not be hers! Her hands were squarish and capable, with blunt, clipped nails. These alien appendages were smooth and delicate, the slender fingers tapering to polished nails. She looked down at herself and almost collapsed into unconsciousness once again. A deep trembling began in her, for her gaze encountered an ankle-length gown of some sort of light cloth. It was pale yellow in color and over it she wore a very short, light jacket with a high neck and long sleeves. With the younger man's assistance, she rose gingerly to her feet. Dizzily she realized that she was moving on legs that were long and straight and strong.

My God, she must have had some sort of seizure! She had gone completely mad! In a blind panic, she turned to rush from the church, only to be grasped roughly by the older man.

"Now then, missy, we'll have no more of your nonsense."

"Indeed, Amanda," said the woman. "You must come home with us. We will—talk about it later."

"The devil we will," snorted the older man. "You'll be spending the next few weeks in your room. Or, assuming . . . " His fleshy lips clamped shut as he shot a glance at "my lord."

"Come along then," he concluded, wrenching her toward the exit doors.

Amanda glanced wildly around the church. It was still empty except for herself and this collection of maniacs. "No!" she cried. "Please! I don't understand . . . "

The younger man spoke for the first time. "Let her go, Bridge." His voice was as harsh as his appearance, but his tone was cool and detached. "She is obviously distraught. I shall convey her home in my curricle. I suggest you save your questions until she has had a chance to recover herself." Taking her hand, he led her along the aisle.

Dazed, she followed him unresistingly until they reached the sidewalk outside the church. She stopped abruptly, her eyes nearly starting from her head. It was broad daylight, and the sun shone on a scene she knew could not possibly exist. Horse-drawn vehicles of every shape and size trundled along the street, and pedestrians, all dressed in costume, jostled about them. Up and down the avenue, vendors pushing carts hawked wares at the top of their lungs. And the buildings! Gone was the Mayfair Public Library. In its place stood a row of small houses. Behind the church, where before she had glimpsed a lovely park, lay a graveyard.

She turned to stare in anguish at the man, who still held her hand in his. His returning gaze was unpromising.

"Come along, Miss Bridge. You must face the wrath of your father sometime, you know. And I am due at Carlton House in less than an hour to meet with the Prince Regent."

Amanda simply gaped. "The—the Prince Regent?" she croaked, just before she fell into another swirling chasm of darkness.

Chapter Two

Amanda woke to find herself nestled in the softness of a comfortable tester bed, hung with a silky fabric of pale pink, matched by the draperies at the tall window that faced the bed. Further inspection of the room revealed a charming dressing table and a graceful wardrobe against one wall. A small desk occupied a nook near the window.

She had no sooner absorbed all this, when the door to the bedroom flew open to admit a dark-haired young woman wearing a plain apron-covered dress.

"Oh, miss!" cried this apparition. "You're awake, then. Oh, I'm that sorry, miss. I couldn't help it—I had t'tell them. Please forgive me, miss. Please!" She hastened across the room to stand before Amanda, her hands clasped before her and her blue eyes wide with apprehension.

For a moment, Amanda could not speak, but as the girl showed signs of bursting into tears at any moment, she said quickly, "Okay, I forgive you. Now, tell me, where am I?"

The young woman stared at her perplexedly. "Why, you're in your own home, miss. In your own bed. Can I fetch you something? A nice cup of tea, mayhap?"

A nice cup of tea! Amanda could have laughed aloud if her situation were not so bizarre. What had happened to her in that little church? She must have passed out from the pain of the headache—and, perhaps her fatigue. Had she hit her head on something? She was obviously hallucinating, but it was sure a damned odd illusion. How could she not know where she was—or who the people were she kept encountering? Particularly since they seemed to know her. This was her hallucination, for God's sake. She should know these things. "His lordship" had spoken of the Prince Regent. An odd shiver passed through her at the memory of those flinty eyes poised so close to hers, staring straight through to her center. No. Never mind that. The Prince Regent. Could she have imagined herself back to Regency London? The clothing seemed right—but—why? She sank back into her pillows. Lord, what a mess. She glanced at the young woman standing before her. This person was not real— she was merely a fantasy created by a disordered mind. Amanda opened her mouth, but was brought up short by the odd certainty that she must not divulge the truth. Smiling tentatively, she turned to the aproned woman.

"Who are you?"

The woman's eyes widened in fear. "Why, I'm Hutchings, miss, your maid. Don't you know me?"

Amanda widened the smile. "No, I'm afraid I don't. I don't re- member anything. I think I must have hit my head when I fell. Hutchings, I don't even know my own name."

At this, the maid gasped. "Oh, dear heaven, miss! What a terri- ble thing." She turned as though to run from the room. "I'd best fetch your mama."

"No!" cried Amanda. "No," she repeated in a softer tone as Hutchings paused in her flight. "Just tell me a few things first. How did I happen to be in that church, and—and who was the man who scooped me up off the floor?"

"Why you slipped out of the house early this morning, miss, to meet Mr. Satterleigh, your own true love! You and him was to elope, miss! It was ever so romantical." Her face crumpled sud- denly. "And I ruined it for you. I'm that sorry for it," she said again, tears beginning to stream from her eyes.

"Yes," said Amanda hastily. "Well, never mind about that now. Is that his name—the man in the church? Satterleigh?"

Hutchings paused in the act of dabbing at her eyes with her apron. "My goodness, miss, you really must be dicked in the nob! No, that were Lord Ashindon, your betrothed."

Amanda brought both hands up to clutch her hair.

"Are you having another one o' your headaches, miss?" the maid asked sympathetically. "They've really been comin' on strong, of late, haven't they?"

"Yes, they have, indeed," replied Amanda hoarsely. "Tell me, er, Hutchings, what is the date today?"

"Why, it's April fourteenth, miss."

"And the year?"

"Lor', it's eighteen hundred and fifteen. You don't even remember that?"

Amanda shook her head numbly. Eighteen-fifteen! Yes. Regency England. Dear Lord, what possible mental quirk could have thrown her back to the early nineteenth century?

"All right," she said slowly. "It's eighteen-fifteen, and my name is Amanda Bridge, and I live in . . . ?" She raised her brows questioningly at the maid.

"In London, o'course," giggled the maid. "In Upper Brook Street," she added, as though indulging a child in a new game. "You're two-and-twenty and your mama and papa are Mr. and Mrs. Bridge—Serena and Jeremiah, their names are. Your mama has been by your bed since they brought you home. Limp as a wet dish clout, you was, when I undressed you. Your papa sent for the doctor and a few minutes ago your mama went to wait downstairs."

Amanda closed her eyes.

"There!" exclaimed Hutchings. "I've tired you out altogether. I'd best fetch your mama now."

Amanda's eyes flew open. "No! No, don't do that. Tell her I'm still sleeping. Please, Hutchings."

The maid eyed her doubtfully. "All right, miss. I expect the doctor will be 'ere soon."

"Very well, but until then, could you please leave me for a few minutes? To sort of get my head back together?"

The maid's expression did not lighten, but she bobbed a curtsy and whisked herself from the room.

Alone, Amanda threw back her covers and slid to the floor, nearly falling on her face from the unexpected height of the bed. Righting herself, she moved immediately to the dressing table, reveling despite herself in her strong, sturdy legs. She peered in the mirror and drew in a sharp breath.

Lord, she was a raving beauty! Golden hair tumbled in charming disarray over her shoulders, and from a piquant little face glowed eyes of a deep amethyst, fringed with a veritable forest of dark lashes. Her nose was short and straight, and her mouth, full and pink, curved charmingly. On second thought, Amanda mused wryly, she looked like a Barbie doll, complete with upthrust bosom and an incredibly tiny waist. Wow, she chuckled, did she know how to fantasize, or what?

For some minutes, she stood very still, contemplating the re-flected vision before her. She marveled at the exquisite workman-ship of her nightgown, a demure concoction of lace-trimmed muslin, embroidered with tiny flowers at neckline and hem. All ac-complished by hand, of course. Still staring, she noticed the slim golden chain that hung about her neck. Hastily drawing it up in her fingers, she gasped. It was her pendant! The one she had examined just last night in Grosvenor Chapel. Or, no—perhaps not last night, but . . . She sank into the little chair before the dressing table, study-ing the pendant in bewilderment. She had not brought anything else of her real life into her hallucination—her purse, or her own cloth-ing—why was she still possessed of this unwanted relic?

She turned the little piece of jewelry over in her hands, remem-bering the afternoon all those years ago when she and Derek had lingered in a little coffee shop in Sausalito. They had relaxed into a moment of reflective silence when Derek reached into his pocket to produce a shiny new penny. Tossing it on the table, he grinned. "Okay, what are you thinking?"

"I love you," she had blurted, and his beautiful green eyes had darkened. He said nothing in reply, but he took her hands in his and pressed them to his lips.

He scooped the penny up in his long, thin fingers, and a week later he had returned it to her, embedded in a delicate lacy filigree of gold he had created himself. On the back, he had inscribed the words, "For Amanda, with my love, Derek," and the date, July 25, 1989.

Amanda smiled sadly. Derek had gone on to great things in the art world, but she had not gone with him. A few months later, their relationship was only a bitter memory of rejection and hurt.

Absently, she allowed the pendant to slide back into its position between her breasts. Crossing to the window, she observed a steady procession of carriages trundling over the cobblestoned street outside. Some were open and rather rakish in appearance, others were closed and more sedate. There were riders on horse-back, too, calling to acquaintances and all but strutting in their saddles. Ladies, obviously dressed in the height of fashion, paced with mincing steps, accompanied by soberly clad maidservants. Others, not so fortunate, made way for these goddesses.

Amanda shook her head in amazement. She had certainly cre-ated a world of precise verisimilitude for her moment of temporary insanity. A sudden chill gripped her. How temporary was the moment to be? She supposed time was a subjective entity in this sort of thing, just as in dreams. In her perception of reality, she had been living in Regency England for two or three hours, but perhaps the actual time elapsed since her collapse in the church was only a few seconds. She was seized by a frantic urge to release herself from this bizarre illusion. Perhaps if she were to go back to bed and fall into a natural sleep, she would awake to find herself back in Grosvenor Chapel in her own time period. Or, better yet, in her own bed in her own hotel room.

On the other hand . . . She grinned, and moving back to the bed, flung one leg up to rest her foot on the counterpane. The grin widened. She'd never been able to do that before without almost falling over.

Well. She'd created a world for herself in which she was whole and strong, and six years younger. To say nothing of beautiful and rich and pampered. She perched on the edge of the bed with her legs extended straight in front of her and wiggled her toes thoughtfully. With any luck, this lovely fantasy would continue until Amanda Bridge was ninety years old, still rich and pampered, hopefully, even if no longer young and beautiful. Amanda McGovern would then awake in twentieth century London with a mere few seconds gone from her life in the real world.

Her smile faded. No, pleasant as it sounded, in that way lay madness. Her life and her responsibilities lay in the twentieth century. After her brief sojourn in London she would return to her position in the English department of a prestigious university. It had taken her a great deal of hard work to reach her present status. She was a good teacher, and her studies on women poets in the eighteenth and nineteenth centuries had achieved a wide circulation in academic circles. She was sought after as a lecturer and had been invited to submit articles to several prestigious journals. It was whispered that in the not-too-distant future she might well become the youngest department head in the history of the university.

She must determine how she had come to hallucinate in the first place, and then attempt to return herself to reality. She cast her thoughts back to Grosvenor Chapel and the strange little man with whom she had held such a strange little conversation. Had she already been on the verge of some sort of stroke, perhaps, when she had experienced her uncharacteristic urge to unburden herself to him?

It must have had something to do with her headache. The episodes prior to last night had been painful, but nothing like—

"Amanda, you have revived!"

Amanda whirled, to be met with the sight of Serena Bridge bustling into the room. She hastened to her daughter and kissed her cheek.

"I am so relieved you are feeling better, dearest." The woman's fingers were busy, patting and stroking as though to assure herself of Amanda's continuing physical presence in the room. "But you must get into bed. The doctor is here." She urged Amanda under the quilt, pulling the sheets up to her neck. "See? Here is Dr. Beddoes now."

Amanda twisted her neck to observe the entrance of an elegantly dressed cadaverously thin gentleman. Placing a small, black bag on the end of the bed, he removed one or two unidentifiable shiny instruments and lay them atop the quilt before bending to his patient.

"Well, now, Miss Bridge, not feeling quite the thing today, are we?" The line of his mouth split in what was no doubt intended as a reassuring smile. To Amanda, it seemed more of a self-satisfied smirk. He seated himself on the edge of the bed.

"Ah—no, we're not," replied Amanda faintly, eyeing the instruments with disfavor.

"Mmm." A bony hand descended on her forehead. "There seems to be no fever. Did you say she was unconscious when you found her in, er, Grosvenor Chapel, was it?"

"Yes," replied Serena Bridge with a quaver. "She had gone there with her maid to . . . er . . . sketch the new altar hangings. It was . . . um . . . an assignment from her drawing master."

"Mmhm," intoned the doctor noncommittally. "Did she hit her head as she fell?"

"I don't know," Serena said. "I did not see her until after she had swooned."

Dr. Beddoes peered into her eyes. "I see no evidence of concussion," he remarked after some minutes. "Tell me, is she still having those headaches?"

At this, Amanda raised herself up on one elbow. "I am right

here in the room, Doctor," she said tartly. "And I'm perfectly able to speak for myself."

The doctor jerked as though she had bitten him.

"And, yes," continued Amanda coolly, "I have been having headaches. In fact, I was experiencing one that was excruciatingly severe just before I blacked out."

"Bl—? Oh," said the doctor, eyeing her warily. "How is your head now?"

"It's fine, except that I seem to be suffering from amnesia."

"Amnesia!" The doctor rose abruptly and stared at her.

"Oh dear," she continued, "you are familiar with the word, I hope?"

"Of course, I am, but I would not expect to hear it on the lips of a person not educated in medicine."

"But, what does it mean?" interposed Serena shrilly. "Doctor, what is wrong with the girl? When she opened her eyes—in the church—she did not appear to recognize any of us."

"Well, yes," the doctor replied in a harassed tone of voice. "That's what amnesia means—a loss of memory."

"What?" shrieked Serena. "Are you saying . . . ?" She swung to Amanda. "Do you not recognize me, my love, your own dear mama?"

"I'm afraid not." Amanda spoke soothingly, as to a distraught child. "It is as though I never saw you before."

"And Papa?" Serena continued faintly.

Amanda shook her head. "And I am only aware of my own name because the maid—Hutchings, is it?—filled me in."

"Filled you in?" Serena asked vacantly.

"Yes—explained," said Amanda. Lord, she was going to have to watch her speech. Although, that was an odd circumstance, now that she came to think of it. She had recognized a difference in the timbre of her voice, but her accent was impeccably upper-class British. Curiouser and curiouser! She forced her attention back to "Mama" and the doctor.

"But this simply will not do!" Serena was saying. "Lord Ashindon will be here soon. Oh, dear Lord, Amanda, never say you do not know who *he* is, either!"

Amanda shook her head again. "To my knowledge, I never saw the man before this morning."

Serena moaned, and began to wring her hands. "Oh, dear, what will Mr. Bridge—" She paused abruptly and stiffened. "Amanda," she said ominously, "are you telling the truth? If you are trying to hoax us in an effort to escape punishment—"

"No, truly, er, Mama. Everything is strange to me—this room, the street outside, everything is as though I had just been born."

"Arrump!" The doctor cleared his throat portentously. "Perhaps," he said with a significant glance at Serena, "we should let our little patient rest for a while. Perhaps some sleep and some reflection will bring her to herself. I think I shall not bleed her just yet," he concluded judiciously, returning the glittering little instruments to his bag. "In the meantime"—the doctor's bushy eyebrows waggled meaningfully—"if I could see you outside, madam."

"What?" Serena said absently. "Oh, of course. Mr. Bridge is waiting downstairs to speak with you, as well."

The two left the room, and Amanda hunched into the quilt. Bleed her! No way, she resolved furiously. She took several deep, calming breaths and closed her eyes tightly, willing herself to sleep. Surely, if she were to fall into a natural slumber she would awake refreshed and rid of this baffling malady. It had been years since she had availed herself of the services of a shrink, but she vowed that making an appointment would be her first priority on arriving back home in the States.

Sleep would not come, however. Which, she concluded, was natural after all she had been through. *I am a cloud.* She formed the words determinedly in her mind. *I am drifting high over the earth, serene and silent. There is nothing to disturb me here. . . .* But the soothing phrases, culled long ago from a magazine article on how to defeat insomnia, failed in their purpose on this occasion.

Amanda tossed restlessly on the puffy mattress and had just punched her pillows for the fifth or sixth time when the bedroom door opened once more, this time to admit the master of the house. Serena trailed behind him, twittering anxiously.

Jeremiah Bridge strode into the room, and to Amanda it seemed less of an arrival than the advent of an elemental force of nature. He was not a tall man, but he was constructed along the lines of a gravel truck and wore an air of power like a medieval warrior might bear his armor.

Continuing his progress, he arrived at Amanda's bed and planted his feet in a wide stance. He bent to grasp her shoulder, shaking it roughly. "All right, missy, what have you got to say for yourself?"

Sitting upright, Amanda, with great precision, removed the man's fingers. "Just what is it you wish to hear?" she asked, unruffled.

As had the doctor before him, Jeremiah straightened abruptly, glaring in outrage as though she had just chucked him under the chin.

"You dare to speak so to your father?" he bellowed in a voice like freight cars derailing.

Deciding on a more prudent course, Amanda tried out a conciliatory smile. "I'm sorry—you must be my father, but I don't know you. I don't know anyone," she said helplessly. "I am so confused—Papa." She shot a glance at him from under the weight of her luxuriant eyelashes. Apparently, she had taken the right tack, for the glare faded, to be replaced by an expression of wary concern.

"Now, don't think to cozen me, missy," he rumbled. "You've really torn it this time, and you'd better be prepared to face the consequences."

"Oh, Amanda, how could you?" moaned Serena in the background.

Hugging her knees, Amanda gazed thoughtfully at her "parents."

"Perhaps if you tell me what I've done, we could discuss the matter more intelligently." She paused as Jeremiah swelled ominously. "Look, sir, I'm as much at a loss as you are. I really, truly, don't know what you're talking about. So, suppose you drop the wounded walrus routine?"

Jeremiah looked as though he might explode.

"Dearest," said Serena to her husband, pulling at his sleeve, "she is not our daughter!"

Amanda gazed at her, startled, but relaxed when the woman continued tremulously. "Can you not see? Her behavior is completely unlike that of our little girl. Her speech, her manner . . . The doctor says he believes she is telling the truth. She has come down with some sort of brain fever, and has lost her memory." Tears sprang to her eyes. "We can only hope it is temporary."

"Temporary?" shouted Jeremiah. "It had better be. What are we to do with her? I tell you, Serena, I'm not going to have every-

thing I've worked for destroyed because your daughter has suddenly taken leave of her senses. What about Ashindon?" He concluded with a furious gesture.

"Oh dear," moaned Serena. "He said he would return later this
afternoon. What are we going to tell him? Oh—ohh—perhaps we
should just pack her away to the country before he gets here. Tell
him she needs to recuperate from her, er, fall."

"Have you gone round the bend, too?" asked Jeremiah crudely.
"The man is on the verge of making a declaration. I'm sure that's
why he came to the house earlier today. No, we'll have to think of
something else."

"We could tell him the truth," interposed Amanda, beginning to
enjoy herself. What a pair these two were! Why, she wondered,
would she dream up parents that were so unlike her own loving
mother and father?

"What!" exclaimed Jeremiah and Serena in unison.

"Well," she said in a reasonable tone of voice, "I don't see how
we're going to hide it from him."

"You could pretend—" began Serena, but was interrupted by
Jeremiah's irritated snort.

"How is she to do that, for God's sake? She can't talk about
any of their acquaintances, or the ball they went to last Tuesday,
or—Oh, God." Jeremiah sighed, sinking down on the bed as the
enormity of the situation descended on him.

"Lord Ashindon is a reasonable man," said Serena at last in a
not-very-hopeful voice. "Perhaps, if we explain . . . "

"Explain that his prospective countess has gone dotty?" Jeremiah produced yet another snort. Then his expression lightened
suddenly. "On the other hand, his precious lordship hasn't much
to say about it, has he? His creditors are yammering at his heels
like a pack of beagles."

Hmm, thought Amanda. Had she created in Lord Ashindon a
typical Regency rake, then? A desperate gambler? A guzzler of
port and brandy and pursuer of unfortunate chambermaids?
Somehow this image did not fit the fleeting picture she retained in
her mind of the cool, self-possessed, prideful aristocrat who had
escorted her to his carriage.

She leaned back against her pillows. She was, she thought,
rather looking forward to another meeting with this enigmatic
peer and his steel gray gaze.

Chapter Three

Refusing what Serena referred to as "a nice tray in your room," Amanda, dressed in a floating muslin gown of pale blue, descended to the dining room for luncheon. She peeked into the various rooms she passed, and again, she marveled at the detail of the setting she had crafted in her mind. Next to her own bedchamber lay another, larger one. This presumably belonged to Jeremiah and Serena. Doors led off to other smaller chambers.

On the ground floor several large rooms gave off to a central entrance hall whose marquetry floor had been buffed to a blinding polish. One of the rooms was a library, and a cursory glance indicated the books therein had been chosen for show rather than for enjoyment. Another chamber was obviously a music room, for it contained a harp and a piano, both of rather overpowering dimensions. Amanda moved delightedly to the piano and ran her fingers over the keys. Perhaps in this most perfect of fantasies she would have time to catch up on her neglected piano practice. Perching on the bench, she flexed her fingers and rippled through a few bars of Eleanor Rigby before rising to continue her exploration. A reception room nearby was furnished rather fussily in Louis Quatorze mixed with classical Regency pieces. It was hung in an overpowering heavy gold damask, and hothouse flowers stood in huge vases on every available surface.

Tiptoeing farther afield, Amanda eventually reached the dining room, a large chamber whose walls were covered with straw-colored silk. Two long windows, facing the street, were hung with matching fabric. A large sideboard occupied one wall, on which stood candelabra and a container that Amanda thought might be a wine cooler.

Serena had arrived before her and was already seated.

"But you needn't have come down, dearest," she said, holding a forkful of salad and cold meat suspended before her. "You should be resting for your interview with Lord Ashindon."

"Nonsense—Mama," replied Amanda briskly. "I feel quite well."

This was true, Amanda reflected in some amazement. She could not remember having felt this good before. She was fairly bursting with vitality and a sense of well-being, and could hardly wait to go outside to explore the London she had created. She was determined to return herself to normalcy, but she could not resist enjoying, for the moment anyway, this delicious imaginary world.

Jeremiah had not deigned to dine with his family, declaring that he would lunch at his club. He promised, however, that he would be home in time to greet Lord Ashindon on his arrival later in the afternoon.

"Now then," continued Amanda, "tell me about Lord Ashindon."

"He is Ash to his friends," said her mother repressively. "To be truthful, they say he's a rude, care-for-nobody who hardly ever smiles and hasn't any friends—but he has always been everything that is most considerate to us.

"Of course," she continued, her color high. "Lord Ashindon's, er, social behavior is none of my concern—and it is certainly none of yours."

"It seems to me, it is very much my concern." Amanda munched on her salad. "I am, apparently, expected to marry the man, after all. Tell me," she asked interestedly, "is this one of those famous marriages of convenience? If so, why are you marrying me off to a poor man?"

Serena spluttered into her wine. "What a question!" she exclaimed when she had mastered her voice. Then, apparently recalling her daughter's "brain fever," schooled her features to an expression of patience.

"It is your father's dearest wish," she said severely, "that you and Lord Ashindon marry. He is titled and possessed of a noble background, even if he is in low water financially—" She stopped short. "That is all you need to know," she concluded with finality.

It was not by a long shot, thought Amanda, all she needed to know. Again, she wondered why things were not clearer to her, if this were all a creation of her own mind. It was almost as if she really had been dropped into an alien situation in another time. She caught herself, a chill settling in the base of her spine. What a ridiculous thought! But perhaps not unexpected. When faced with something one does not understand, she mused wisely, the mind will often supply all sorts of weird explanations.

It was obvious she would get no more out of Serena concerning the mysterious earl, so promising herself a private conversation with her "mother" after luncheon, Amanda tucked into her greens.

Privacy was not forthcoming, however, for the ladies had no sooner retired to the drawing room after their meal—Amanda making a minute, wondering inspection of the room, much to Serena's discomfiture—when a servant entered to inform them of Lord Ashindon's arrival.

"My lord!" cried Serena effusively as he was ushered into the room. "What a happy circumstance. We were not expecting you so early."

"The Regent canceled his appointments for the afternoon," replied the earl with a grimace. "He is closeted with his tailor and cannot be disturbed for something so trivial as negotiations with his allies." His glance swept the room cursorily, coming to rest on Amanda, who stood near the window, watching him in interested appraisal.

She had been correct in her original assessment. He was a very tall man, and he was surrounded with an aura of power, similar to that of Jeremiah Bridge. However, whereas Jeremiah displayed his authority in bluster and swagger, the earl's air of command fitted him as naturally as his superbly tailored coat and pantaloons. He did not conform to anyone's idea of a poor man, being instead the consummate aristocrat, cool, disdainful, and infinitely self-assured. Amanda took him in instant dislike. No wonder Amanda Bridge had fled from him. Who would wish to be married to this long, lean stone effigy of a man?

She met his eyes, and, noting the disinterest in his gaze, lifted her chin and returned his insulting stare. After a moment, his brows rose slightly and a faint smile curved his surprisingly sensuous mouth.

"You seem quite recovered from your earlier indisposition, Miss Bridge," he said, bowing slightly. "The bloom has returned to your cheeks and the sparkle to your eyes."

"Why, thank you," Amanda replied dryly, and once more she caught a flicker of surprise in the earl's gray gaze. "Unfortunately, memory has not returned to my brain—my lord."

"Memory?" The earl's dark, thick brows lifted in puzzlement before snapping together an instant later. "Are you saying—?"

"Precisely," said Amanda, seating herself composedly on a settee of straw-colored satin placed below the window. "I still have no memory of who I am—or who you are, for that matter." Amanda watched him appraisingly as he advanced on her across the room.

From a chair in the corner of the room, Serena whimpered and raised a hand in fluttering protest. "Amanda, dearest, why not wait until your papa . . . ?"

Amanda did not respond, nor did the earl, also seating himself on the settee. "I can't think," he began, "what you hope to accomplish by this charade, Miss Bridge. Or perhaps," he continued in an insulting drawl, "you have succeeded in your purpose? Has your papa forgiven you for your rash behavior?"

"Why does everyone keep talking about Papa and his wrath?" snapped Amanda impatiently. "Is he in the habit of beating me?"

Serena gasped once more. "Of course, he does not beat you! But—but he can be most severe in his punishment, nonetheless."

Amanda did not think she liked the sound of this. She swung to the earl. "Now then, my lo—what do I usually call you, anyway? Have you a first name?"

The earl looked somewhat taken aback. "My given name is William, but you," he said stiffly, as though he were a headmaster chastening a schoolgirl, "as a properly bred young woman do not use it. You have always called me, 'my lord,' or Lord Ashindon. However," he added, as though aware of how pompous he sounded, "my friends call me Ash." He bent an awkward smile on her, tinged with an incongruous sweetness.

In her corner, Serena was twittering again. "Oh, my lord, I hope you will forgive my little girl's forward manner. Indeed, she is not herself, and—"

The earl waved a hand. "There is nothing to forgive, Mrs. Bridge." His glance caught Amanda's again, and she was aware of a disturbing glint deep in their cool, gray depths. "It is expected that her behavior might be a little unusual after such an ordeal," he concluded smoothly.

A little unusual did not cover it by half, thought the earl in some astonishment. This was the first time he had actually seen Amanda behave like a human being instead of a pretty porcelain doll. Could a bump on the head have caused this metamorphosis? Or was this her natural mien and she was simply tired of maintaining her posture of girlish rectitude? Whatever the case, it was a welcome change. He gazed at her assessingly. Her candy box prettiness, he thought, was decidedly improved by that militant sparkle in her eyes.

"I wonder, Miss Bridge," he said smoothly, "if you would care to go for a drive. While the promenade hour is not yet upon us, perhaps a short foray into Green Park . . . ?"

"I'd love it!" exclaimed Amanda immediately, ignoring the succession of gasps and gurgles from the corner. She rose from the settee, her eyes alight with enthusiasm. "Let's go."

She moved to the door and into the corridor, laughing over her shoulder at him.

"But you cannot go without your bonnet and pelisse, my dear." Serena Bridge had followed them, and now spoke rather breathlessly. She was attempting to communicate with her daughter via a series of winks and gestures, and when these failed in their purpose, blurted, "Ring for your maid, Amanda." The older woman gestured toward a nearby bellpull.

"But it's a beautiful day. I don't need a—oh, all right," she concluded at her mother's agonized expression. She strode to the pull and gave it a vigorous tug.

A few minutes later, Ash led a bonneted, coated, and gloved Amanda down the front stairs of the Bridge town house to his waiting curricle. She examined the vehicle in some fascination, and when a diminutive figure took his place atop the rear wheels, she uttered the word "Tiger!" in satisfied accents, as though she had displayed some arcane, specialized bit of knowledge. She seemed to experience some difficulty in mounting the vehicle, even with his assistance, but once seated, she glanced about her with every indication of enjoyment.

For some minutes, she said nothing, but stared as though she had never seen Upper Brook Street before. Her evident fascination with other persons in the street, the various vehicles they passed, and the street names emblazoned on buildings increased with each passing block.

What the devil was going on? he wondered. She seemed as unfamiliar with her surroundings as though she had just been dropped here from the moon. Was she really telling the truth about her loss of memory? If not, she was certainly presenting an impressively de-tailed deception. He rather thought she had not the intelligence to carry out such a complex charade. Or perhaps, he mused sardon-ically, it was her vapid innocence that had been the charade.

Having reached the leafy expanse of Green Park, Ash pulled the curricle to a halt under a spreading linden tree. Instructing the tiger to indulge himself in a walk, he turned to face Amanda.

"You know," he said thoughtfully, his eyes narrowed, "when I was serving in the Peninsula, one of our lads took a crushing blow to the head and suffered a temporary bout of amnesia."

"Good Lord," cried Amanda. "Of course, Napoleon is rampag-ing around Europe right this minute, isn't he? Ash, you were in the war? I should very much like to hear of some of your experi-ences—that is, if they are not too painful to recall."

He was startled, as much by the sound of his nickname on her lips as by her unexpected digression, but he continued smoothly. "Some other time, perhaps, Miss Bridge. To return to our unfortu-nate warrior, the poor fellow could not remember his name, did not recognize the faces of his comrades, and had no knowledge of his family back in England."

This time Amanda made no response, merely inclining her head courteously.

"Oddly enough," Ash went on, "he had no difficulty in remem-bering the ordinary details of his everyday life. He knew that England was at war with Napoleon, and he knew that the Regent is reigning in place of his poor, mad father. The lad had not for-gotten how to ride a horse, and he was able to distinguish English uniforms from those of the French."

Amanda, sensing the direction of Ash's comments, began to squirm in her seat.

"Now you, on the other hand"—Ash's tone contained nothing beyond a bland curiosity—"seem to have forgotten everything that you ever learned in your whole, admittedly rather short, life. You were about to leave the house hatless and coatless, like the veriest hoyden—behavior quite unlike your very proper self, and you seem to have forgotten how to tie a bonnet properly. You are, apparently, totally unfamiliar with the terrain of Mayfair, an area in which you have resided for several years. I am wondering how to account for this."

"How very fortunate," said Amanda in some exasperation,

"that you are so knowledgeable about mental aberration. I know nothing of what I should or should not be able to remember, my lord." How strange, thought Amanda. Calling this man "my lord" was not so difficult, after all, particularly when he phased so beautifully into his stone effigy mode. "It is as I said to my mother this morning, my mind is like that of a newborn child—except of course, that I have not lost the gift of language."

"How very fortunate," murmured the earl.

"Please believe me, Ash, I am not feigning all this. The whole thing is very confusing to me, and a little frightening, as well."

She looked at him straightly, and for the first time, Ash was aware of the beauty of her eyes, for it was the first time he had not thought of china teacups and porcelain dolls when he looked into them. Now, he was put in mind of amethysts and sapphires and tropical skies. Her jeweled gaze was clear and, it seemed to him, honest. He continued to stare, almost mesmerized, and knew an urge to pull her to him, to kiss her until those lovely eyes clouded with passion. Lord, he thought, suddenly appalled, where had that thought come from? It was as though the Amanda Bridge he knew had been stolen away, like a princess in a fairy tale—and now in Amanda's face he saw the gaze of an enchantress. He shook himself at his ludicrous fancy, aware that she was speaking once more.

"Tell me about yourself, Ash. I suppose we must be very well acquainted if, as my father has told me, you are on the verge of asking for my hand. Yes, I know I am being inexcusably forward," she added as the earl stiffened, "but I plead temporary insanity. Please, could you not pretend that we just met?"

For a moment, Ash stared at her. It seemed to him that the afternoon had taken on a dreamlike quality, that he and the magically transformed Amanda Bridge were enclosed in an enchanted bubble that floated, separate and serene, from the rest of the world.

"I'll try," he said, pleased that his voice remained steady, "though you will undoubtedly find my story a dull one." He bent forward in a parody of a bow. "Allow me to introduce myself, Miss Bridge. I am William Wexford, and I am one-and-thirty years of age. My father was the second son of the fourth earl of Ashindon, and when he and my mother died in an inn fire, I was taken by his brother, the fifth earl, to be raised at Ashindon Park in Wiltshire, along with my younger brother and sister. I was four years old at the time, and grew up with my cousin, Grant, heir to the earldom. Grant was two years older than I and we were as brothers. In fact, I rather idolized him." Ash paused for a moment before continuing, and Amanda caught a fleeting expression of pain in those cloud-colored eyes.

"I chose the military as my profession and served under Arthur Wellesley. You have heard of him, I trust—the Duke of Wellington? Yes, well, a year or so before he died, my uncle purchased a captaincy for me, and I rose to the rank of colonel before selling out."

Amanda frowned slightly before recalling that selling out, in this time, did not have an unpleasant connotation, but merely referred to the selling of one's commission preparatory to leaving the army.

"The reason I sold out—just after the Battle of Toulouse, a little over a year ago—is that my cousin died in—in an accident." She really did not need to know the details of Grant's death, thought Ash. "Although I loved the Park more dearly than any place on earth, I had never involved myself in the management of the place. Well," he said, stung a little at the look of surprise and, he thought, contempt, she threw him, "it would have been considered unbecoming in me, since the Park, in the natural order of things, would go to Grant on his father's death.

"When I awoke one morning to be informed that I was the sixth earl of Ashindon, it was as though a weight had suddenly descended on me. In addition to my grief over my cousin's passing, I felt myself completely unequipped to maintain the consequence of a peer." He laughed shortly. "As it turned out, that was the least of my problems. You see"—he reached forward unconsciously and took Amanda's hand in his own—"when I left Ashindon Park, some ten years ago, it was a thriving estate, but when I came home last year, it was to discover the place in ruins." He shook his head in memory. "It was as though an evil fairy had put a spell on the Park. The fields were unkempt, the tenants' cottages were in shambles, and the manor house itself was empty and cold and stark—all the life seemed to have been sucked from it. I could not—" He stopped suddenly, aware that he was saying things he had not spoken of to another human being. "You see," he continued after a moment, "my cousin had a taste for the high life. He bought expensive horses, fine clothes, and the right friends, all with equal abandon. He drank and gambled as though the trees of Ashindon Park showered leaves of gold on him. And, of course there were the—the—"

"Women?"

"Yes, although I should not mention their existence to a gently bred female."

"Just for the time being," said Amanda with a small smile, "let us also pretend that I am not a gently bred female, merely a woman who wants to hear the unvarnished truth."

"There is no such thing," said the earl flatly. "Women like their truth softened and made palatable."

Amanda sat back, startled. The earl certainly had a jaundiced view of the female sex. On the other hand, she mused, from what she had read of this age of arranged marriages and discreet liaisons, perhaps his cynicism was understandable. She bit her lips against the retort she had been about to make.

"But," she said instead, "is your estate very large? Does it produce no income? I always thought that the landed nobility had it made. I mean, every year there are crops, and—"

"If the land has not been properly cared for, the crops will be meager." Ash's voice was harsh.

"My father spoke of creditors," said Amanda in a low voice.

"Did he?" The earl's laugh was little more than a growl. "Yes, Miss Bridge, there are creditors. Now, are you satisfied? Do you know all about me that you wished to know? I certainly would not like to keep any morsels from you."

A sudden thought struck Amanda, and she wondered why it had not occurred to her before. "Jeremiah Bridge is a plain 'mister,' isn't he? I'll bet he isn't even related to so much as a baronet. But he is wealthy, isn't he, Lord Ashindon?"

Ash's lips tightened into a thin line, but he did not answer. Amanda rushed on, aware of a completely unwarranted sense of outrage. "He's wealthy enough to barter his daughter to an impoverished nobleman. Which, of course, is where Amanda comes in. You didn't succumb to Amanda Bridge's blue eyes and golden curls, did you, my lord? You're simply a common, garden-variety fortune hunter."

Chapter Four

On their return to Upper Brook Street, Ash and Amanda found Jeremiah Bridge awaiting them. Ash's mind was still on the bizarre conversation he had held with Amanda in the park, and he was aware of a peculiar churning in his stomach, part anger and humiliation at having given up so much of his private self, and part astonishment at how quickly the chit had drawn it all out of him. Withal, he had the oddest feeling that he had not been speaking with Miss Bridge at all. The woman who peered out from those great blue eyes was so much more of a person than the Amanda he knew. She seemed possessed of a wisdom and maturity far beyond her years, and it confounded him to realize that her expression of contempt had pierced him to a place he had forgotten existed within him.

She had wanted him to talk about the war, for God's sake, when previously the mention of so much as a skirmish would cause her to shudder delicately and ask that the subject be turned to a more diverting topic. Could a bump on the head have produced such a profound change in her? Or, perhaps his earlier surmise was correct. Years of domination by her determinedly proper parents had molded her into a pattern card of simpering missishness, and her loss of memory had released the real Amanda Bridge.

If this was the case, it would be almost a shame, he reflected sardonically, to hope for a complete recovery on Amanda's part. He grimaced. Particularly since he was virtually teetering on the brink of asking for her hand.

He turned to face Jeremiah, who ushered him ceremoniously into a ground floor study.

"I understand you have something you wish to discuss with

me," he said, his mouth spread in a sly, jovial smile. Ash would have given all he possessed—though that was perhaps an unfortunate phrase, given his present circumstances—to turn and leave the room. Bridge knew, by God, of Ash's rage and humiliation at Amanda's recent defection, and he was gloating over the fact that he had his lordship grasped firmly by the throat.

In a few minutes, the interview was over. Ash mouthed the traditional phrases, and Bridge responded in suitable accents of gratification. Settlement arrangements were discussed, and Ash breathed an unconscious sigh as the realization sank in that, though the cost had been almost too great to contemplate, he now had the wherewithal to bring Ashindon Park back to financial stability, and he had assured his siblings' futures. For now, Andrew could pursue his studies, and Dorothea would have her Season.

As prescribed, Ash was then escorted by a servant to the drawing room, where he would wait while Bridge apprised his daughter of her good fortune.

Summoned to her "father's" study, Amanda faced him impassively.

"Have you come to your senses yet, girl?" he asked abruptly, and for a moment she simply stared at him.

"My sen—Oh. If you mean have I recovered my memory, no, I haven't."

"Well, here's something that should bring you round. Ashindon has asked for your hand."

Although the announcement did not come as a surprise, Amanda felt her heart jump.

"H-has he, indeed?" she replied faintly. "How very—nice."

"Nice?" growled Jeremiah. "Is that all you can say? Do you know what this means for us, Amanda?" He smiled suddenly, and Amanda was reminded of the grin of the Big Bad Wolf. "You'll be a lady and you and your ma and me, we'll be received in the finest homes and invited to all the fancy balls and dinner parties."

"My God, is that what you want?" asked Amanda curiously.

" 'Course, it's what I want. Have you forgotten—well, yes, I guess you have, but I haven't—all the snubs and turned-up noses." He turned, suddenly serious, to grasp her arm. "Amanda, I went to work in Horace Fitch's woolen mill when I was nine years old. I worked fourteen hours a day. There was one difference between me and the other lads there—I was a lot smarter."

And a lot more ruthless, I'll bet, thought Amanda—and not too concerned with morality and ethics.

"I worked hard," continued Jeremiah, his voice a flinty rasp, "and I saved every cent I could, so that when the right opportunity came along I was in a position to grab it. After that, I never looked back. Now I can buy and sell most of the nobs in Mayfair, but they're all too good to give the time of day to Jeremiah Bridge. But, now—now things will be different."

Amanda thought privately that hell might well freeze over before Jeremiah Bridge would see the inside of "the finest homes." What hostess, highborn or otherwise, in her right mind would seek his company for so much as a walk across the street, let alone balls and dinner parties? On the other hand, she supposed that money talked as loudly in Regency England as it did in the twentieth century, so, perhaps, once the Bridges got a toe into the filtered waters of high society, they might well find themselves doing swan dives with assorted blue bloods.

Having been dismissed with a wave of Jeremiah's hand, Amanda returned to the drawing room, where Serena and the earl were conversing over tea. That is, Serena was conversing and the earl was listening with an obviously spurious air of attention. Serena smiled in relief as Amanda entered the room.

To Ash's surprise, Amanda appeared composed, indeed, she seemed almost oblivious to the solemnity of the occasion. She greeted her mother, and, with a casual smile at Ash, seated herself before the fire.

"Well, my lord," said Serena breathlessly, "I understand you have something to say to my little girl. I shall leave you two alone—but just for a moment," she added with a coy smirk that set Ash's teeth on edge.

Frowning, he watched her bustle from the room, and crossed the room to seat himself beside Amanda.

"Miss Bridge," he began, taking her hand in his. Her fingers were cool and very soft. "Miss Bridge, I have just spoken to your father, and he has granted me permission to seek your hand in marriage."

Amanda said nothing, but gazed at him in wide-eyed expectancy. Ash ploughed ahead.

"We have known each other only a few months, and"—despite himself, a note of irony crept into his voice—"though you apparently consider your heart given to another, I believe we can deal well together."

Ash suddenly knew a moment of profound depression. As a declaration of undying devotion, his little speech left a great deal to be desired. It should have been different from this, he thought with a pang, but immediately thrust the notion from his mind. Amanda still had said nothing, but was gazing at him with what seemed to him vaguely contemptuous pity. He gritted his teeth.

"Miss Bridge, will you do me the inestimable honor of becoming my wife?" he concluded, the emptiness within him almost thundering in his ears.

Amanda Bridge dropped her lashes before lifting her head to gaze at him for a long moment. "Of course," she replied at last, and Ash was startled at the offhandedness of her tone. Lord, he had just proposed to a woman who had that morning attempted to elope with another man.. Even given that her mind was, theoretically, in total disorder, did she not realize the magnitude of what had just taken place?

"Are you sure?" he asked harshly. "This is your future we are speaking of."

At that, Amanda laughed, an open sound of genuine amusement. "My future!" Her gaze transferred itself to the window. "But the future can be fleeting, my lord."

"I would have thought," Ash replied, "that the certainty of the existence of some kind of future is one of the few constants in our lives, no matter how uncertain the fulfillment of that future might be."

She glanced at him quickly. "I suppose that is true."

"At any rate, you have made me a happy man, Miss Bridge." The words almost stuck in his throat, and under Amanda's disbelieving stare, he flushed. After a moment's hesitation, he grasped her shoulders lightly and pulling her gently toward him, kissed her.

Amanda stiffened in sudden surprise, then relaxed, realizing this must be part of the ritual. His lips were warm against hers, his fingers firm on her shoulders. She found this intimacy oddly unnerving and was relieved when, after only a few moments, he drew back. He took her hand once again.

"Perhaps, we should—" Ash was interrupted as Serena bustled back into the room. Her glance was questioning, but observing the proximity of the earl and her daughter on the settee, she smiled broadly.

"Oh, my lord!" she exclaimed, pressing a hand to her plump bosom. "Is it true what Mr. Bridge just told me?"

Amanda sensed the surge of irritation that swept over Ash at the woman's gaucherie, but he rose smoothly and bowed.

"Yes, Mrs. Bridge, please wish us happy."

"Oh, my dears!" She hastened across the room, embracing first the earl and then clasping Amanda to her like a lifeline thrown to a drowning victim. "Gracious," she continued, sinking into a chair covered in a tapestry silk, "we shall have to start planning our ball, won't we?"

"Ball?" queried Amanda blankly.

"Why, yes, to announce your betrothal. We shall invite only the best people, of course. Next month, I think—on Thursday, the sixteenth. Lady Federsham is holding her soiree that night, if I am not mistaken. *We* were not invited, of course, but I rather fancy that we shall see our rooms full to overflowing, for I shall put about the merest hint that those attending *our* function will be hearing a most interesting announcement concerning the earl of Ashindon and our sweet Amanda." She fell silent, a faraway expression in her faded eyes as though she were immersed in a rosy dream.

Good Lord, thought Amanda, experiencing an urge to rush from the room, what a perfectly ghastly female. She studiously avoided the earl's glance. The next moment she swallowed a chuckle. What earthly difference did any of it make to her? All these people were but figments of her imagination and after a good night's sleep would be no more than an amusing memory.

She turned to face the window. As fascinating as this whole hallucination thing had been, it was more than time to quit it. It had become surprisingly difficult during the course of the day to remember that the Bridges did not exist, nor did the Earl of Ashindon, nor even the little maid, Hutchings. She had found herself caught up in their doings. In fact, during her conversation with Ashindon in the park, she had not once thought of her real life in Chicago, which now seemed as far away as though it were on Mars. For a couple of hours she had become Amanda Bridge, and the earl had been a disturbingly real presence.

She returned to the present with a start, realizing that Serena was still burbling on about the ball. Amanda chastised herself. How absurd she was being—as though these people had a life outside her imagination. She turned to face the group that gazed at her so expectantly. "Do I what?" she asked, realizing that Serena had repeated the same question several times, in growing exasperation.

"Do you think we should invite Charlotte Twining and her mother? I know you and she have been bosom bows, but since your quarrel with her—"

Amanda almost blurted, "What the hell difference does it make who you invite? What difference does any of it make? Tomorrow morning you all will be nothing but shadows echoing in the corners of my mind." Something held her back, however, and she clamped her lips together tightly.

"Have you forgotten, Mama?" she asked instead. "I have no memory of either Charlotte Twining or her mother."

Serena shrugged her shoulders uncomfortably. "Oh, that. Surely you will have recovered your senses by then."

Amanda almost laughed aloud. The woman spoke as though her daughter had broken out at an inconvenient moment with hives. Looking up, she encountered a glance from Lord Ashindon that contained, if she was not mistaken, a hint of pity. He looked away and addressed Serena.

"I shall take my leave now, Mrs. Bridge. I know you have much to discuss."

"Oh, but what about a date, my lord? Did you and my husband—?"

Amanda observed the distaste that rose in him as Serena's plump fingers dug into his arm. "No, Mrs. Bridge, Mr. Bridge felt that the date of the wedding should be left up to Miss Bridge—and yourself, of course."

"How thoughtful," gushed Serena. "I should like to send an announcement to *The Morning Post* right away, but I suppose we should wait until after the ball."

"As you please," replied the earl, a discernable hint of desperation in his voice. Amanda marveled at his smooth courtesy in removing Serena from his sleeve. "I have an appointment elsewhere in a few moments, so I shall leave you ladies to your plans." To Amanda, he said, "I believe you planned to attend the Marchford ball next week, as do I. I shall be pleased to accompany you there, if you would allow me."

"Oh, but you must go, Amanda," interposed Serena. "All the world will be there."

"We'll see," said Amanda noncommittally, forbearing to inform the older woman that by tomorrow night there would be no more Bridges, no more earl, and no more marriage plans.

"You must join us for dinner that night," said Serena hastily as Ashindon turned to leave the room. Thanking her with grave courtesy, the earl made his departure. Amanda accompanied him to the door and glanced up at him from beneath her luxuriant new eyelashes.

"Earlier, you asked me if I was sure I wished to accept your proposal of marriage, my lord. Now, I ask you, are you still willing to go through with it?"

The earl turned to look at her, a startled expression crossing his harsh features.

"Your mother's, er, emotional response to the betrothal of their oldest daughter is quite what might be expected," he said coldly. "It is my earnest desire, of course, that I shall measure up to her expectations."

"Of course," murmured Amanda.

"Until next week, then, Miss Bridge." The earl bowed and descended to his waiting curricle. Amanda watched him for several seconds before turning in to the house.

An hour or so later, Ash lowered himself gratefully into a chair at White's. Near him sat James Wincanon, good friend and former comrade-in-arms, who gazed at him intently.

"It's done then?"

"Oh, yes, old friend. Behold me betrothed." He took a long pull at the brandy that rested on the table by his side.

"You needn't sound as though you'd just been convicted of murder."

Ash laughed shortly. "Sentenced without parole, more like."

"But the Bridge chit is a beauty, and even if her father is a Cit—well, you hear of more and more marriages in the *ton* that—"

"I realize that I should count myself fortunate. Miss Bridge is, indeed, a diamond of the first water, and a perfectly decent young woman, I daresay, when one comes to know her. However, I have always hoped that I would someday choose my own bride."

"But, Ash," said his friend plaintively, "you're forgetting your exalted status. A man in your position don't choose his own bride."

Ash smiled sourly. "My exalted position? I've hardly a farthing to my name!"

"Ah, but the title—goes back to the Conqueror, doesn't it? You've had advisors to kings in your family, to say nothing of warriors of the realm and all that."

"That was a long time ago."

James glanced at him shrewdly. "But, the pride remains, doesn't it, my boy? I've always said you had enough of that commodity to outfit two or three fellows. Do take care you don't choke on it."

"Oh, for God's sake. I—"

"To return to my main thread, the glory remains. And there's the Park, don't forget. One of the great houses of the kingdom—once it's restored. Reason enough why many a maiden of the *ton* would gladly aspire to be Lady Ashindon. Unfortunately, there aren't any around at the moment with enough brass to compensate for your own lack thereof."

"Too true, Jamie." Ash contemplated his long legs, stretched before him. "But would it make any difference? Marrying a maiden of the *ton*, I mean."

"As in 'All cats are the same color in the dark'?"

Ash grimaced. "Something like that."

"Perhaps you're right—but—there's cats and then there's cats. The Bridge kitten is, you must admit, an extraordinarily attractive example of the species. Being leg-shackled might not be such a wretched fate, after all. I'm not suggesting a love match," he added hastily, "but you might grow fond of her, don't you think?"

"Love?" Ash snorted. "Merely a rosy fantasy promulgated by the writers of bad novels. The most one can expect from marriage is an amicable arrangement between a man and a woman that will let each go his or her own way in reasonable harmony. As for growing fond of her . . . "

He trailed off. Her strange behavior today notwithstanding, he supposed he must admit he beheld the fulfillment of his dreams in Miss Bridge. Her lovely face would decorate his home and her lovely money would keep that home from the auction block. The next moment, his thoughts drifted unwillingly to Amanda's enticing form and the golden curls that tumbled carelessly above mysterious, bottomless blue eyes.

"You may be right, Jamie," he murmured thoughtfully. "You may be right."

James took another pull at his drink and fiddled with his quizzing glass for a few minutes. "By the by," he said finally, "I heard this morning that Lady Ashindon is in town."

Ash jerked upright. "La—you mean Lianne? Good God, I had heard nothing of this."

"Thought you might not have. She's staying at her parents' town house."

For a long moment, Ash sat in rigid silence. Since Grant's death, his cousin's beautiful widow had remained in virtual seclusion on the estate belonging to her father. The estate that marched with Ashindon Park. The thought brought a tightening in the pit of his stomach, and memories of the laughing girl with whom he'd grown up filled his mind. No! His hands clenched into fists. It had taken him three years to rid himself of those memories—and she was as unattainable now as she had been the day she had married Grant in the manor chapel at the Park. He turned once more to his friend.

"Ah. Well, I expect I shall be called to wait upon her sometime soon."

"Yes, I expect so." James eyed his friend apprehensively before addressing himself once more to his brandy.

Dinner at the Bridge home that night was, as might be expected, a fairly festive affair. Contributing to the lighthearted atmosphere, thought Amanda, was the absence of Jeremiah, who was again dining elsewhere. At the foot of the table, Serena babbled happily about The Wedding, which, so far, was taking second place to The Announcement Ball.

"I saw a gown in *La Belle Assemblée* last week that will be perfect, Amanda," she said. "It features a slip of royal blue satin with a tunic of silver net. You will look magnificent!"

"Well!" said Amanda, for want of anything more intelligent. She sat back in her chair, reflecting again on the complexity of the dream she had concocted. First, the seeming authenticity of early nineteenth century Mayfair, and then a family whose members might have stepped from a TV soap opera.

Silence reigned in the dining parlor for several moments before Serena, her sunny mood continuing, swung to another subject of importance, The Trousseau.

"I suppose his lordship did not make any suggestions as to where you might go on your wedding trip?" she asked brightly. "No, I suppose not," she said, answering her own question with an airy wave of her hand. "Much too early for that. But be assured, dearest, Papa will stand the ready for a trip to Rome or some such. We must begin planning. We shall start with your underclothing, for those garments will remain the same in almost any climate."

Amanda passed the rest of the interminable evening with teeth clenched. The sky outside had barely darkened when she pled a headache as excuse for an early night.

"Of course, pet," said Serena with a soothing smile. "I shall instruct Hutchings to bring you up a posset. I'm sure that by tomorrow you will be very much more the thing."

Amanda rather thought so, too, and she sought the tester bed with a sigh of relief. Silently, she allowed Hutchings to assist her into another nightgown, this one of pleated lawn, embroidered with small birds and flowers. Thank God this whole nightmare would be over soon. A good night's sleep would surely restore her to sanity. She would accomplish some serious knitting of the raveled sleeve of care, and in the morning—or whenever, she would be back in twentieth century London, and the persons she had encountered today would become merely the remnants of a fast-fading dream. One face, she rather thought, would linger for a longer time than the others, but she purposefully shelved this notion and settled into the downy pillows heaped under her head. She had anticipated some difficulty in getting to sleep, given the bizarre occurrences of the day, but whether from exhaustion, or the ingredients in Hutchings' posset, she soon fell into a dreamless slumber, from which she was wakened some hours later by the sound of birdsong and a cacophony of voices raised in indistinguishable but loud supplication.

Cautiously, she opened one eye and was met immediately by the appalling sight of pink silk hangings catching the glow of the morning sun from where they hung in graceful festoons over her tester bed.

Chapter Five

Amanda sat bolt upright, gazing wildly about the room. The dressing table, the wardrobe, and the little desk were all right where she had seen them for the first time yesterday.

"No!" she screamed silently. This couldn't be happening! Had she truly gone mad? Was she to be trapped here in this pink silk cocoon for the rest of her days? Throwing aside the coverlet, she ran to the window and flung it open. Outside, an army of street vendors made their way along the cobblestoned pavement, each calling out his or her wares. A knife grinder jostled a milkmaid, causing her to spill a few drops of her wares from the buckets that hung from her shoulders. A man balancing a stack of rush baskets sidestepped another man, bent almost double from the weight of the tools he carried in leather bags on his back and tied to his waist. A seller of hot cakes swatted angrily at a crowd of young boys who were obviously attempting to help themselves to some freebies.

The noise was deafening. Good Lord, how did anyone get any sleep in London past sunrise? she thought distractedly. She raced to the dressing table and in a futile gesture traced the outline, reflected in the mirror, of young Amanda Bridge's flawless cheeks. The hallucination remained complete. Dear God, what was she to do now?

She made her way back to bed and sank against the nest of pillows. Her thoughts scrabbled frantically, like rabbits pursued by hounds, trying without success to find a thread of logic in her predicament. Was there some other explanation that she was overlooking? Was it realistic to hope that whatever the aberration she was suffering from, she might still find her way back to her proper milieu? Perhaps her disordered brain merely needed more time in which to heal itself. Or—She sat up with a jerk. Perhaps she herself needed to provide the push that would restore her to normalcy.

The chapel, she thought desperately. She must return to what was it?—Grosvenor Chapel. She would sit there by herself, in the quiet and the dark, and concentrate herself back to where she belonged. She had no reason to hope this plan would produce the desired results, but she strove to take comfort in the fact that she had decided on a course of action, however tenuous.

She snuggled into the pillows and, closing her eyes, gave her thoughts over to the inhabitants of her dream. That was another curious thing. Why had she peopled her fantasy with such an odd assortment of characters as the Bridges? And Lord Ashindon. If she were to be brutally honest with herself, she might admit that his lordship might be the fulfillment of some sort of deeply buried wish fulfillment, though he was not the sort that usually appealed to her. She was not given to adolescent fantasies, but if she were, they would probably center on the Mel Gibson type. His lordship definitely did not fit the requirements, being a few inches too tall and several degrees too arrogant. To say nothing of the nose.

She sighed. How long was she going to have to deal with these people? Her hallucination had already lasted longer than she had expected—though of course, placing a time limit on a hallucination was probably an exercise in futility. Another theory—one that had occurred to her before—snaked through her mind to be squelched yet again. The idea that she had somehow traveled through time to land in the body of young Amanda Bridge was too ludicrous to contemplate. She was not, by God, living within the pages of some lurid sci-fi thriller. No, sooner or later she was bound to return to her senses, and she would do everything in her power to see that it was sooner.

She turned restlessly. It was no use. The din outside seemed to be increasing, and she was not going to get back to sleep. Before she could arise once more, however, a soft knock sounded at the door, followed by the entrance of Hutchings bearing a cup of steaming liquid on a tray, along with two cookies on a plate.

"What's this?" asked Amanda, sniffing suspiciously as Hutchings placed the tray on her bedside table.

"Why, it's your morning chocolate and biscuits, miss."

Amanda lifted the cup to her lips and after the first cautious sip
bent an accusing stare on the maid. "This? This is chocolate?"

Hutchings bobbed her head nervously.

"You are in error, Hutchings. This is not chocolate. It smells
like chocolate, and it looks like chocolate, but it tastes like sh—
that is, it tastes god-awful. What's in it?"

"Why, it's made up with chocolate shavings and water and
milk, miss, and a little sugar—just how you like it."

"Wrong again, Hutchings. I do not like it. Are you sure there is
milk in here? And the sugar content is way below FDA standards."

Hutchings merely bobbed her head again, uncomprehending.
Amanda sighed.

"Well, never mind that. Tell me, how far is Grosvenor Chapel
from here? I wasn't paying much attention when I was brought
here yesterday."

"Grosvenor Chapel, miss?" asked Hutchings, misgiving writ
large on her plain features. "Oh, miss. You aren't planning—?"

"Yes, I want to go back there."

Hutchings moaned faintly. "Miss, you can't! Your
papa . . . Your mama . . . They'll lock you up till you're thirty—
and I'll lose my place!" Her words ended on a rising note of hys-
teria.

"No, no," said Amanda reassuringly. "I have no intention of
meeting what's-his-name there. I just want to go to the chapel. I
want to—to, er, meditate."

"Meditate!" Hutchings repeated the word as though her mistress had just stated her intention of stripping to the buff in the
church's center aisle.

"Yes." Amanda tried to infuse a few more ounces of reassurance into her voice. "I just want someplace peaceful and quiet to
think. I am still very confused, Hutchings," she continued as the
maid remained, seemingly rooted to the floor, staring in bewilderment. "I have not regained my memory and I'm trying very hard
to sort things out." She tried out a wistful smile, and was relieved
to see Hutchings relax—a little.

"Oh, you poor dear. I s'pose—under the circumstances,"
Hutchings began doubtfully. Her face cleared almost immediately. "But, you can't just go into the church, miss," she said in
some relief. "It'll be locked."

"But, how did Aman—how did I get in yesterday?"

"Oh, that was Mr. Satterleigh's doing. He paid the verger to open the door for you."

"Mr. Sat—oh, yes, the boyfriend. Where has he been, by the way? I don't recall his being in the church, and he hasn't been here. Has he?"

"Oh, no, miss. Mr. Satterleigh wouldn't dare show his face here. Your papa forbade him the house some weeks ago—right after he was here asking for your hand."

"Ah," said Amanda. A pair of star-crossed lovers, no less. This whole scenario was beginning to sound like an old-fashioned "mellerdrammer." The golden-haired heroine, forced into a love-less marriage, while the wicked father cracked his whip and the evil villain snapped his teeth and twirled his moustache. Except that Amanda's father proclaimed himself all fatherly devotion and Lord Ashindon, whose dark, harsh-visaged face could easily get him cast as the villain, had no moustache, and had so far refrained from snapping his teeth.

"Well, never mind all that," said Amanda briskly. "We'll just have to get the, er, verger, to unlock it again."

Hutchings frowned doubtfully. "Your mama isn't going to like this."

"Mama doesn't have to know, does she?"

"It's my belief, miss, that after yesterday you'll be lucky to make a trip to the necessary house out back without her knowing."

Amanda sighed in exasperation. "Well, how about a shopping trip? Does Aman—do I like to go shopping?"

Hutchings snorted. "Like a fish likes t'swim, miss, but—"

"Well, there you are. You and I will leave the house, and if Mama intercepts us, we'll just say we're on our way to—to—?"

"Oxford Street. But it isn't all that easy, miss. You'll have to eat breakfast first—downstairs. You'll have to call for the carriage, and you'll need t'send a footman on ahead to roust out the verger."

"Fine. You take care of all that and meet me in the downstairs hall in an hour."

Hutchings had more objections to the plan, but by the time she had assisted her mistress into a gown of pale blue lutestring, embellished with rows of lace ruching at neckline and sleeves, Amanda had managed to stem the flow.

Obtaining, at last, a grudging agreement to her plan, Amanda descended the long, curving staircase to the dining room, which, to her vast relief, was empty. A footman stood at the ready near a sideboard laden with steaming breakfast delicacies, and after she had loaded her plate, the young man poured coffee from a silver urn and placed it reverently by her side at the table. She ate in thoughtful silence, and at the prescribed hour hastened into the hall to be met by Hutchings with pelisse, bonnet, gloves, and reticule. Hurriedly donning these articles, she moved to the door, and had almost made good her exit when a shrill voice from above caused her to falter.

"Amanda! What are you doing? Where do you think you're going?"

Amanda swung about, a bright smile pinned to her lips.

"Why, good morning, Mama. It's so lovely today, I have decided on some early shopping today."

"Shopping!" Her eyes narrowed in suspicion. "Now, see here, Amanda, we will have no more of your tricks. You will march right back up to your room, this instant. I want you well rested before we start receiving calls."

"Calls?"

"Well, of course." Serena sighed in exasperation. "The servants will probably have been talking already, and news of your—indisposition will have spread all over Mayfair. We shall no doubt have a steady stream of visitors, and you must be ready to receive them."

"How am I to do that when I don't know any of them?"

"I'm sure you will recall their faces when you see them—and I shall be here to give you countenance. You can't hide away forever, after all."

Amanda placed little reliance on the benefits of Serena's support, but the woman was right. There was no telling how long this hallucination thing was going to last, and she might as well face up to whatever—or whoever—it would bring. "Very well, Mama, I shall return shortly, and present myself at—what time can we expect the onslaught?"

"Not until after luncheon, but—"

"Well, then, I have plenty of time, haven't I?" She waved a cheery hand and turned to depart.

"Amanda, I insist that you return to your room!"

But she spoke to the empty air, for Amanda had pushed Hutchings outside and, exiting herself, shut the door firmly behind her. As the waiting carriage pulled away, Amanda turned her head and waved cheerily to Serena, who stood on the steps, frustrated affront apparent in every line of her plump body.

Some minutes later she stood before the Grosvenor Chapel. It was rather unimpressive, as London churches went, being foursquare and built of brick, with a tall, spare, New Englandish steeple. Inside, the chapel was not dark at all, the walls being painted white and spaced with a profusion of windows. It reminded her a little of the interior of Bruton Parish Church in Williamsburg. As before, she was alone in the church, except for Hutchings and the footman who had accompanied them. Instructing these persons to wait outside, she moved to the pew in which she had been seated at the moment of her remarkable—episode. That's what they called it in medical terminology, didn't they? She sat down gingerly and, leaning her head against the smooth, dark wood of the pew she closed her eyes.

All right, now. Relax. Make your mind go blank. Think only of returning to your proper place in time and space. You are a cloud. You are—

She opened her eyes with a jerk as a door slammed behind her, followed by the sound of a long stride up the side aisle.

"Now, what the devil are you up to?"

She swung about, her mouth dropping open.

"Lord Ashindon!"

"You must know it will do you no good to play the innocent with me." The earl glanced around the church. "Been stood up again, have you?" he inquired nastily.

Amanda had been about to favor him with an amiable greeting and the explanation she had earlier ladled out to Hutchings, but at his words she shot to her feet. "Don't you dare talk to me that way, you overbearing oaf! You have nothing to say about where I go or why. Now, why don't you buzz off?"

If she had dashed a cup of coffee in his face, his expression could not have been more startled. It took him only a moment, however, to recover.

"I have every right to talk to you like that. We are betrothed, and—"

"The fact that we are betrothed does not give you the right to rag at me like a disapproving parent. What are you doing here, anyway?"

He smiled unpleasantly. "Why, I was carrying out my obligations as a devoted fiancé, presenting myself for an early morning call. Imagine my surprise when I observed my betrothed leaving her house at an exceedingly fast clip. Imagine my further surprise to find her apparently embarked on another assignation."

"Don't be ridiculous," said Amanda coldly. "I am not here to meet anyone. I merely wished to medi—that is, to find a little peace and quiet in which to heal my, er, disordered mind."

Lord Ashindon's dark brows slanted upward in disbelief.

"Ah-huh. One would, of course, choose for such a purpose the inconvenience of a distant church over the solitude of one's bed-chamber, or even an early morning stroll in the park."

"Yes, one would," snapped Amanda. "Particularly if one were trying to create the same set of circumstances that led to one's brain disorder in the first place. Now, if you'll go away and let one alone, one would very much appreciate it."

To her surprise, the earl loosed a bark of laughter. "Oh, no, I don't think I can do that. Judging from your mama's display of indignation on the front steps of your house as I passed, you will be in for a severe hair-combing when you get back. Much better if you arrive at the old homestead in my company." Without waiting for a response, he slid a hand under Amanda's elbow and lifted her, without effort, to her feet. "By the by," he continued, his tone all bland innocence, "was the treatment efficacious?"

"Effica—Oh. No, of course it wasn't. As you must know, I had barely sat down when you barged in. And, thank you, I do not wish to return home just yet. Oh, very well," she conceded, noting the unpromising set of his jaw. "I can see that I shall get no peace here. I shall leave, but not with you, thank you. I—I want to do some shopping."

"Excellent. I shall accompany you."

Without giving her a chance to utter the protest that boiled visibly on her lips, Ash steered her out of the church and into his waiting curricle. Instructing Hutchings and the footman to return to the Bridge residence and to inform Mrs. Bridge that her daughter was in the unexceptionable hands of her betrothed, the earl set his horses in motion.

"Where to?" he asked.

"I haven't the slightest idea," responded Amanda with some asperity. "You know, of all the high-handed jerks I've ever known—and I've known quite a few—you really top the list, my lord."

"Jerks?" repeated Ash. "The term is unfamiliar to me, but I think I would be deluding myself to consider it in any way complimentary."

"You would," said Amanda shortly.

Having swung from North Audley Street into Oxford Street, Ash brought the curricle to a halt. "Since you have nothing specific in mind, I propose that we stroll for a bit. We shall peer in the windows like bumpkins just up from the country, and if you see anything that strikes your fancy, we can then consider a purchase or two."

"Fine," responded Amanda dispiritedly. "Only, I have no money."

Ash eyed her languidly. "How can this be? The daughter of the Brass Bridge without funds?" He stopped abruptly in the act of assisting her from the curricle, so that her hands remained imprisoned in his. "Please forgive me," he said, his voice harsh. "That was inexcusable. I do not know how I came to be so maladroit."

Ash realized that it was his own self-loathing that had given voice, but that did not make his words any less hurtful. To his surprise, she displayed no discomfiture, merely shrugging her shoulders as she attempted to disengage her hands from his tightly clenched fingers. With an exclamation, he released her.

"Is that what they call him?" she asked, her voice a cool shower on his seething emotions. He nodded reluctantly.

"How very apt," was all she said, and Ash stared at her. The Amanda he knew would have been swooning at his feet by now in outraged indignation at this vulgar insult to her parent.

He drew her toward a building that proclaimed itself to be Pickett's Gold and Silversmith. "Not precisely a genteel establishment," he said, "but perhaps you might see something to please you. At the risk," he added, driven by a scarcely acknowledged desire to throw her off stride, "of further descending into gaucherie, I do have money with me—my own. I have so far not availed myself of your papa's largesse."

Her eyes lifted to his, startled, before she relaxed into a warm chuckle in which he joined her a moment later. He noted with some bemusement that this was the first time he had been able to look at his predicament with even the faintest touch of humor.

Inside Pickett's establishment, after a judicious perusal of the wares, Amanda selected a necklet of beaten gold inlaid with pearls. They continued their stroll, and it was not until she found herself in additional possession of a charming porcelain shepherdess, an airy zephyr scarf, and a box of comfits that they made their way to the curricle, which had trailed behind them in the capable hands of Ash's tiger.

As Ash put out a hand to assist Amanda into the vehicle, a small personage bustled up to them.

"Vi'lets, guv'nor? Vi'lets for yer lydey?"

Ash gestured impatiently, but the flower woman was not to be put off.

"Come now, guv. Ye mustn't take yer lydey home wivout a token o'your affection." She thrust her bouquet under Ash's nose. Amanda, watching the proceedings with some amusement, started suddenly. She was sure she had seen the old lady somewhere before. She looked at her intently, noting the drifts of gray hair that escaped her shabby head covering, the cracked spectacles, the cheeks, round and red and hard as little apples. My God, she was the spitting image of the old man in the chapel!

Chapter Six

"Please—" Amanda choked, clutching the old woman's sleeve.

Ash glanced at her, his brows lifted in surprise. "Would you like some violets? Truly?" He fished in his waistcoat pocket for a coin, and, plucking the flowers from the woman's veined hand, proffered them to Amanda with a flourish. She grasped them absently without looking at them. Her whole being was focused on the flower woman, who cocked her head with an impudent smile. Her eyes, clear and youthful and black as coal chips, twinkled mischievously.

"How yer gettin'on, then, dearie?" she asked in a voice like a creaky hinge. "Don't yer look loverly, though, in yer new togs."

My God, thought Amanda, excitement surging through her. She knows! She knows who I am, and that I'm . . .

"Please," she said again. "Tell me—"

But the flower woman shook her head, and with another insouciant smile turned to hobble away.

"No!" cried Amanda. "Don't go."

"Hang in there, dearie," the old lady called over her shoulder. "It'll get better." With a wave of her hand, she disappeared into the crowd of pedestrians thronging Oxford Street.

Amanda felt as though her legs would no longer hold her up and she swayed against the earl's tall form.

"What is it, my dear?" he asked, catching her in his arms. "Are you unwell?"

"Yes," she whispered. "I feel sick. Could you please take me home now?"

Without another word, he lifted her into the curricle and in a few moments they sped along Oxford Street in a westerly direction. Amanda's thoughts whirled in chaos. Who was that old woman? And what was the significance of her appearance? Was she the physical manifestation of some deep-seated unpleasantness in her brain? She had to be connected somehow with the hallucination. Yet—she had not yet entered her hallucination when she met the old man in Grosvenor Chapel, and, surely, his resemblance to the woman she had just seen could not be coincidental.

She looked up to find Ash watching her with some concern, and she essayed a not entirely successful laugh. "You must think me a complete ninny."

"Of course not." He smiled crookedly, and her heart gave an unexpected lurch. "Although, I have never before observed such a startling aversion to violets."

"Oh, no," she said quickly. "It was the flower woman. She—" Amanda clamped her lips shut. Lord, how she wished she could confide in him. She very badly needed some input into her predicament beyond her own demented reflections, but he would think her completely bonkers. "She reminded me of someone," she finished lamely.

"I see." His expression gave away nothing of his feelings, and to her relief he changed the subject. "We spoke yesterday of the Marchford ball. Do you still wish to go? I had the idea that your mother was forcing your hand. If you still have no memory by that time, perhaps you will experience some difficulty with such a social occasion."

Amanda's heart sank. When the ball had been discussed yesterday, she was sure she would be herself by now and returned to her own time. Lord, she couldn't possibly go to a party. Not only would she make a complete fool of herself with young Amanda's acquaintances, but she didn't know how to dance the minuet, or whatever was in vogue right now. Was the waltz in yet? She could probably manage that, but anything that involved changing partners and dosey-doe-ing, or whatever, would be far beyond her.

On the other hand, she had already decided to receive visitors this afternoon, so by the time the day of the ball arrived, she would either have been accepted as the young Amanda, or she would be considered a candidate for the looney bin. She'd better get herself back to the Bridge menage for some serious coaching. She thought for a moment before straightening her shoulders.

"Of course, I plan to go to the rout. Mama would be seriously disappointed if I did not. I'll just have to manage, somehow."

Sometime later, Amanda stood in her room facing Hutchings, whom she had just summoned to her presence.

"Hutchings," she began, "it is time to rally round your poor demented mistress. I am scheduled to make a personal appearance this afternoon in the drawing room, where, so Mama informs me, I shall be receiving visitors. I need your help." She continued hastily in response to Hutchings' unpromising stare. "My memory is still among the missing, and if I am not to make a complete fool of myself, to say nothing of Mama and Lord Ashindon, I need some serious coaching."

"I see," said Hutchings slowly. "You want me to tell you the names of your friends?"

"Yes. I am going to limp along with my tale of a bump on the head and my subsequent loss of memory, which, I devoutly hope, will help explain most of my lapses, and I figured that if you could provide me with descriptions, personal habits, and that sort of thing, I might be able to muddle through."

"I'll try, miss," said Hutchings dubiously. "First, there is Charlotte Twining."

Amanda frowned. "That name sounds familiar. Oh—is she the one I'm feuding with?"

"Yes. Two weeks ago, the Viscount Glendenning danced twice with you at Lady Beveridge's ball and only once with her. She is your age, a little taller than you. She is a blonde, too, but her hair is lighter—and frizzier, and she is not nearly so pretty as you.

"Your next best friend is Cordelia Fordham. She is plump and has a long pink-tipped nose that makes her look a little bit like a nice white rat. She thinks you are quite wonderful, and in her eyes you can do no wrong. You and she shared a drawing master last year and Miss Cordelia fancied herself in love with him. Her mama and papa, of course . . . "

The lesson went on at length, until Hutchings, glancing at Amanda's bedside clock, declared it was time for her mistress to dress for luncheon.

Amanda had decided by now that if she truly had the designing of her own fantasy, she would have eliminated the necessity of being dressed by another person. She found the whole process distasteful in the extreme, even given the fact that the gowns she wore were apparently fashioned so that one could not possibly climb into them alone. Each had a number of fastenings, mostly in the back and mostly inaccessible.

Hutchings helped to choose a gown of pomona green French cambric. It had short puffed sleeves, as did most of her garments, and was lavishly embroidered in a floral motif. When she was dressed, Hutchings, perhaps feeling that her mistress needed additional fortifying, devised yet another hairstyle, this time parting Amanda's hair smoothly in the middle and allowing a cascade of curls to fall on either side of her ears.

"There, miss, if you don't look a treat," breathed Hutchings worshipfully. Amanda thought the hairstyle made her look like a simpering Victorian, but forbore to mention this, particularly since the phrase would mean nothing to Hutchings. Aside from that, she was forced to admit once more that this new Amanda was an absolute knockout. The color of the gown brought out the satiny cream color of her skin, and her curves were artfully delineated by its slim design.

"Tell me," Amanda said thoughtfully, "if my daddy's rich, and I'm so good-lookin', why am I not married at the ripe old age of twenty-two?"

"Well, you could have been married any number of times, miss. There was Henry Tuttle, when you were eighteen. He wrote poems about you."

"And, did I return Henry's affection?"

"Oh, yes. You would have married him in a minute, for he was ever so handsome, but your papa wouldn't have it."

"Ah, Henry lacked a title, I take it."

"Yes, miss, and he was poor as a churchmouse, besides. A few months later, you met Andrew Mortimer, and you was real taken with him. I thought maybe your papa would relent this time, for Mr. Mortimer had plenty of brass. His father was a mill owner. But, no, your—"

"But, Papa held out for a title," finished Amanda. "Even so, surely Lord Ashindon can't be the first peer to fall for Amanda's—that is, my big blue eyes."

"Oh, no, miss, but—" Hutchings halted uncertainly.

"Yes, I see," said Amanda. "The daughter of the Brass Bridge must, of course, be completely beyond the pale." She experienced an unexpected and quite unwarranted twinge of anger.

"Yes, miss," replied Hutchings simply. "There was Sir George—last year, but he was only a baronet, and your papa said that nothing less than a viscount would do for his little girl."

"Like he really gives a twig about his little girl," Amanda muttered. A thought struck her. "If the Bridges rank so low on the totem pole, how is it that we are invited to the Marchfords' ball? It sounds like a fairly posh function."

"Posh? You mean *tonnish*? Yes, it is. The Marchfords aren't in the uppity upper of the *haut ton*, but they're considered one of the nobs, even though Sir Ralph ain't—isn't—a peer. It's 'cause of your mama that you're invited. Mrs. Bridge's granddad was an earl, you see." Hutchings continued chattily. "I hear it caused quite a stir at the time, even though Mrs. B.'s pa was only a third son. Her family didn't exactly cast her off when she married Mr. B., but things was pretty stiff for a while, I apprehend. When your mama and papa moved here to Upper Brook Street, your mama began to take up with some of her old school friends, and since she's so rich now, they decided to be nice to her."

"I see," said Amanda, her eyes narrowed in comprehension. "Mr. and Mrs. Bridge hover on the fringe of society, hoping by their daughter's marriage to gain access into the inner circle."

"That's about it, miss. You've got some nice friends—some of them even the daughters of the nobility—'cause of where *you* went to school, but you've never been inside Almack's. Your mama says, though, that now you're betrothed to Lord Ashindon, you'll receive vouchers."

"Almack's," repeated Amanda thoughtfully.

Hutchings nodded. "It's a place where they hold assemblies, miss." She breathed the words as though she were describing the Ark of the Covenant to a rabbinical student. "Six of the highest ladies of the *ton* have a sort of club, and they hold dances there every Wednesday and Saturday. You can only come if you're invited, and they don't hardly invite anybody unless their umpty-great grandpas came over with William the Conqueror."

"Oh, yes, I remember reading about it. Good grief, how ridiculous."

Hutchings shot her a curious glance, but said nothing more.

With a lift of her eyebrows requesting dismissal, she bobbed a curtsy and hurried from the room.

Amanda sank down on the chair before her dressing table and stared once more into the mirror. This was the first moment she'd had alone since returning from her encounter with the flower woman, and resolutely she drew the image of the old lady before her. That her appearance in Oxford Street held some significance was indisputable, but what?

All right, let's be logical about this. First, she met an old man in an old church, and shortly thereafter fell unconscious. When she awoke, she found herself in a dreamworld, where she inhabited Regency London, where, in turn, she met an old woman who closely resembled the old man. She could only assume that her meeting with the elderly gentleman had impressed her more profoundly than she realized at the time, thus he showed up, transformed in gender and station in life, in her hallucination. Yes, that must be it. This would also account for the old woman's seeming knowledge of Amanda's situation. Although, on reflection, the flower woman's words could have been uttered innocently, merely a part of her sales patter.

Or . . . A small voice whispered in the back of Amanda's mind. Or, her own presence in Regency England was not a figment of her imagination, but was real, and the old man and the flower woman represented an outside force of some sort—a force that had purposely uprooted her from her comfortable life as a professor at a prestigious university to cast her adrift in another time.

No! Such a thing was impossible, and she was mad to so much as consider it.

On the other hand, continued the insidious voice, the concept of such a transference would explain a great deal. The verisimilitude of her surroundings, the complexity of the lives of her "family," and their intricate relationships.

No. This was absolute nonsense. And even if her maniacal suppositions were true, why her? Why should plain, unremarkable Amanda McGovern be chosen to make a journey through the centuries to be placed in the body of a young woman who had lived a hundred and eighty years ago? Why would Amanda Bridge's life be cut short in order to provide a receptacle for that of someone else?

No. The whole idea was too ludicrous to contemplate. She

leaned her head on her hands, still gazing at the girl in the mirror, and was aware of a dull throbbing behind her eyes. Not the stabbing pain of the headache she had experienced in Grosvenor Chapel, just a common, garden-variety, this-is-all-too-much-and-I-can't-think-about-it-anymore headache.

Rising swiftly, she hurried from the room.

The ladies of the family dined alone again, and once more Amanda was treated to a catechism of the persons who might be expected to appear in the Bridge drawing room that afternoon. Serena made no reference to her daughter's earlier insubordination beyond a lachrymose declaration that she might well be driven into an early grave if this sort of behavior were to be repeated.

The first visitor appeared shortly after luncheon in the form of a Mrs. Fordham, and her daughter Cordelia. Amanda recognized her instantly from Hutchings' description, and when the plump young woman settled herself with a little twitch in a settee near the fire, Amanda indeed felt herself in the presence of a very nice, pink-nosed white rat.

"How are you feeling, Amanda?" asked Mrs. Fordham in a tone of matronly concern after she had been plied with tea. "I heard you have been a little under the weather."

Amanda exchanged a quick glance at Serena and elected to let Mama field this one.

"Yes, we have been rather concerned about our little one." Serena issued a bright smile that indicated the concern had been short-lived. "She swooned yesterday—trotting too hard, as I've told her many times—and she hit her head when she fell. Her memory has been a bit vague ever since, but the doctor said we have nothing to worry about, and she'll be right as rain in no time."

"What a dreadful thing to have happen to one!" exclaimed Miss Fordham, her watery eyes wide with concern. "And how awful not to remember things. You do remember me?" she exclaimed anxiously.

"Of course," replied Amanda, laughing. "How could I forget one of my dearest friends in the world?"

This encomium seemed to please the young woman. She glanced quickly at Serena, who had engaged Mrs. Fordham in conversation, and rose to seat herself next to Amanda. She grasped her friend's arm and hissed in a sibilant whisper, "But what happened yesterday morning? I vow, I was on pins and needles all day, expecting to hear that you'd flown with Mr. Satterleigh. There was no news, though, even though I stayed at home all day, waiting, and then to hear you had taken to your bed! Well, I've been near expiring. You must Tell All! I can't stand it another minute!"

Amanda sucked in a startled breath. It appeared young Amanda had not kept her plans a secret. This was not surprising, she supposed. A girl planning an elopement would no doubt feel the need for moral support from her friends. She would rely on the age-old determination of the younger generation to keep its secrets against the older.

After a few seconds of internal debate, Amanda sighed heavily. "Oh, it was so dreadful, Cordelia! I managed to creep out of the house unobserved. With my heart in my throat, I entered Grosvenor Chapel and sat down to wait." She shivered dramatically, warming to her subject. "Unbeknownst to me, Lord Ashindon came to call here at the house, and when I was nowhere to be found, they coerced Hutchings into revealing everything. I had only been in the chapel a few moments, when he and my parents came *roaring* in."

Her audience was hanging on every word. "Ooh," breathed Cordelia. "Was Mr. Satterleigh there?"

"N-no. He had not yet arrived, I expect. At any rate, Lord Ashindon actually put his hands on me!"

Cordelia's pale eyes grew round. "No! Oh, the wretch!"

"Yes." Amanda lifted one graceful hand and pressed it to her brow. "And that's when I came all over faint. I fell, and must have hit my head on the pew. When I regained consciousness, I did not recognize Lord Ashindon—or Mama or Papa, either."

Cordelia's reaction was all that a budding thespian could hope for. She bounced in her seat, her face quite pale with excitement. "Did they beat you? Did they put you in your room on bread and water? Did they—"

Much as Amanda hated to throw cold water on her own climax, she felt matters had probably gone far enough. "No, of course not. They could hardly berate me when I did not even know who they were. Of course," she added hastily, "I have recovered mostly since then, though a lot of things are pretty fuzzy."

"But what about Lord Ashindon? He must have been absolutely furious. Is he still—that is, is he going to—?" Cordelia dropped her eyes and flushed.

An image of the rage in Ash's dark eyes as he lifted her from the chapel floor sprang before Amanda's eyes. "Yes, he was angry, but he came to the house again later that afternoon and we—we made up."

"And what about Mr. Satterleigh? Has he contacted you? Oh, my gracious, if this isn't the most romantic situation!" Cordelia said with an expressive sigh.

Or the most absurd, thought Amanda. The conversation was beginning to bore her, and when she heard Serena say to Mrs. Fordham, " . . . and his lordship will be accompanying us to Lady Marchford's ball next week," she nodded significantly at Cordelia and then turned to draw her young friend and herself into the conversation between the two older women.

A few minutes later, more guests arrived, and again, Amanda was able to guess their identity from Hutchings' trenchant descriptions. A small quiver of surprise flew around the room when a young woman whom Amanda recognized instantly as Charlotte Twining entered the drawing room. Her expression as she greeted those already in the room was a blend of offended dignity and blatant curiosity, and the smile she turned on Amanda was one of candy-coated venom.

"Dearest!" she cooed. "I heard you were ill and I had to come over immediately to assure myself that your indisposition is not serious."

Amanda pasted a welcoming smile on her lips and rose to greet the newcomer. Hutchings had been correct in her assessment of Miss Twining. She was an attractive young woman, although inordinately thin and somewhat sharp-featured. Her pale blond hair was curled and crimped so that she looked a lot like a frazzled Q-tip. Amanda put forth her hand. "Charlotte! How very nice of you to call. Yes, I have been a trifle unwell, but I am nearly recovered."

Serena opened her mouth, but before she could proffer the authorized version of Amanda's indisposition, Cordelia interrupted excitedly.

"Oh, Charlotte, it's the most dreadful thing. Amanda has lost her memory!"

Not unnaturally, this statement garnered Charlotte's complete attention as well as that of her mother, who hovered in the background. Charlotte hurried to Amanda and seated herself in a nearby chair.

"But, my dear," she breathed, leaning forward with an expression of avid curiosity on her face, "you must tell me all about it."

Once more Amanda spun her tale of the swoon and the bump on her head and her subsequent fuzzies. Charlotte seemed to accept the story and smiled slyly. "And what about Cosmo Satterleigh. Surely you have not forgotten him?"

Amanda shot a glance at Cordelia, but received no help from that damsel's blank visage. Lord, was Charlotte in on the Satterleigh elopement plot? Probably not, if she and Amanda had been on the outs for the last week or so. She took a deep breath and assayed a careless laugh.

"Of course not, although I have not seen him since—well, to be truthful, certain details of my, er, friendship with him are a little hazy, but I'm sure that when I see him again—"

"Oh, but have you not heard?" Charlotte's high-pitched titter was tinged with malice. "Mr. Satterleigh has left town!"

Charlotte clearly expected a reaction other than Amanda's casual, "Oh?" and her face fell ludicrously. "Yes," she continued, regrouping, "Mama and I encountered Mrs. Throgmorton on our way here—she is Mr. Satterleigh's aunt, you know—and she said that Mr. Satterleigh was called unexpectedly to his family home in—" She turned to Mrs. Twining. "Where is it, Mama? Shropshire, or some such place."

"Yes," replied Mrs. Twining repressively. "Although, I am sure the young man's whereabouts are of no interest to Amanda." She shot a propitiatory glance at Serena, who had swollen visibly during this exchange.

"No, indeed," snapped that lady, "we—that is, Amanda has no interest in the young man's direction, as he has been told."

Amanda dropped her gaze demurely to her lap, and in a few moments Serena had turned the talk to a more innocuous subject. More visitors arrived and left and Amanda, with Serena's support, was able to converse without committing any irretrievable blunders. Cordelia and Charlotte remained for another half hour or so and Charlotte maintained a semblance of brittle cordiality that continued until she and Mrs. Twining rose to depart.

"We really must return home now," said Charlotte prettily, "for I am obliged to change for my drive in the Park this afternoon with Lord Glendenning."

Serena sent a sharp glance to her daughter before saying hesitantly, "His lordship is becoming quite particular in his attention, is he not?"

Amanda caught the message. It was time for a little fence-mending. She smiled widely. "Oh my, yes. Why, when we danced together recently, all he could talk about was you, Charlotte. I'd say he is quite smitten."

Charlotte's surprise was unconcealed by the gratified flush that spread over her sharp features. She said nothing, but indulged in a bit of simpering, and the warmth of her farewell to Amanda indicated to those present that all was forgiven.

It was another hour before all the guests had gone, and the door knocker was silent once again.

"Well," said Amanda with a sigh of relief, "I think we brushed through that fairly well, don't you?"

Serena's relieved smile spoke volumes.

"You were wonderful, Amanda. A couple of times you were almost caught out, but I don't think anyone suspects you of—of—"

"Of having skidded round the bend?" finished Amanda. "I believe you're right. Besides, it's wonderful how much conversation can be carried on by simply smiling and nodding a lot."

"You see?" said Serena, beaming in satisfaction. "I told you you would be right as rain in a few days. By the time of the Marchford ball, I just know you'll be completely recovered, dearest."

Amanda stared blankly at her. Good God, did the woman really believe in the charade they had pulled off this afternoon? As for the ball—well, her bluff had been successful so far, and surely she had overcome her worst obstacle. If Lord Ashindon should ask her about it again, she would assure him of her intention of making an appearance. She was aware of a guilty tingle of anticipation at the thought of her next meeting with the enigmatic earl.

Chapter Seven

As it happened, Lord Ashindon did not put in an appearance in Upper Brook Street for some days.

Having returned his betrothed to the bosom of her family after the expedition to Oxford Street, Ash returned to his lodgings to find a missive awaiting him. He held the note in his hand for some moments before breaking the seal and opening it, for he recognized the flowing script adorning the elegant stationery. It was with a sense of dread, mixed with a guilty delight and the familiar ache of betrayal and defeat that always accompanied the thought of his cousin's widow that he perused the casually scrawled lines.

> Ash,
> I am come to town and would appreciate your attention, when and if it is convenient to you. You will find me at our old town house in Cavendish Square.
> Lianne

Why had she come? was his first, anguished reaction to her words. It did not surprise him that she would send for him almost immediately on her arrival, for she knew he would make it his first priority to see to her needs, just as he always had. He recalled the last time he had seen her, the bleakness of her widow's weeds serving only to accentuate the whiteness of her skin and the purity of her features.

"Do not worry about me, my love—my first and only love," she had whispered, crystal tears filling her green eyes. "I shall live out my days here in solitude and loneliness—and I shall never forget you."

With this mournful farewell, she had kissed him once on the cheek and hastened into the fastness of her parents' home. He had known she would not stay there forever, of course. A nunlike life of solitude and loneliness was not for one so vital and pleasure-loving as Lianne Wexford, née Bonner, the Countess of Ashindon.

Ash sighed heavily. He should reply with another note, informing the countess that he was unable to wait upon her but that he would remain at her service. Yours, etc. etc.

Even as this laudable intention formed itself in his mind, he called for his curricle to be brought round again, and a scant half an hour later he found himself knocking at number 3 Cavendish Square, his hat in his hand.

He was ushered into a small sitting room at the back of the house, a shadowed chamber, heavy with an atmosphere Ash could not name. Lianne was alone in the room, seated in a small, satin-striped armchair near the fire.

"Lianne." Her name sprang to his lips involuntarily, and when she turned her head at his entrance he had the oddest sensation that she had been positioned thus for hours, as much a part of the furnishings of the room as the ormolu clock that sat on the mantel, and that she had come to life only at the sound of his voice.

The impression was dispelled the next instant as Lianne jumped lightly to her feet and ran to him. She grasped his hand in both of her own, and Ash's heart lurched within his breast as he gazed down at the vibrant little face that had changed so little in the past year.

She was small-boned and delicate, with a heart-shaped face surrounded by a cloud of dark hair. High cheekbones lent an exotic slant to green eyes that smiled intimately into his.

"Ash! I am so glad you have come. If you knew how excessively weary I have become of my own company . . . "

She led him to a small settee by the window. "You must tell me all that you have been doing since you came to Town. I was shocked to hear that you have sold Ashindon House. Where are you living now?" She seated herself and with restless hands arranged the skirts of her dove gray morning gown about her and gestured to Ash to sit next to her.

He did so reluctantly. "You must know that it has been necessary to sell everything I could—rather like throwing all nonessential items from a sinking ship."

"Oh, Ash. Is it as bad as that?" Her mobile mouth turned down in distress. "I knew, of course, that Grant was wasting his substance, but I had no idea—"

"Actually, by the time Grant got around to wasting it, there wasn't much substance left. My uncle, you must know, had no head for business, but thought himself a financial wizard." Ash smiled painfully. "Grant's inheritance was greatly diminished, although—" he caught himself.

"Although," finished Lianne, her lips curving bitterly, "he could have come about had he not made matters even worse by his dissolute ways. I am so sorry, Ash," she concluded in a throbbing whisper.

In an effort to lighten the mood, Ash laughed shakily. "Yes, but I did not come here to prate about my difficulties. You are all right?" he asked. "Your jointure, at least, was preserved. You are comfortable, are you not?"

Lianne smiled sadly. "Comfortable? Oh, yes, of course." She lifted her head in a significant gesture, conveying the impression that she left much unsaid.

Ash shifted. "But what can I do for you, Lianne?"

"Do for me?" She frowned in puzzlement, but her face cleared immediately. "Oh, you mean my note. I'm sorry, my dear friend, I did not mean to sound importunate. I thought, merely, that you probably did not know I was in town, and that you might condescend to brighten the hours of a lonely widow."

Her mischievous smile belied her dramatic words, and he returned it hesitantly. "I find it hard to believe Lovely Lianne could spend more than five minutes in solitude. You do not mean to tell me that your knocker has been still since you arrived."

She made a dismissive gesture. "Oh—the dandies and bucks on the strut. Of course, just let word of a new female in town be spread about and they spring up like weeds in one's front garden. And there are the gossips, and the hangers-on. But, oh, Ash . . . " Her long, dark lashes fluttered appealingly. "I have so longed for a real person to talk to. Someone who truly knows me and with whom I can feel comfortable."

She lifted her hand, and without thinking, Ash cradled it in his.

"I realize," he replied, his voice a harsh rasp, "that under the circumstances, while friendship is the only commodity left at my disposal, I'm afraid—"

Immediately, Lianne withdrew her hand and turned her face away. "Please forgive me, Ash. I know I have no right to ask such a thing of you. I know that whatever was between us is over." A small, choked sob escaped her.

"It was over long ago, Lianne." Ash could hardly speak past the hard knot that had formed in his throat. "It ended the day you accepted my cousin's offer for your hand. You can't—"

"Oh, God, Ash." Lianne's emerald eyes glittered darkly against the pallor of her face. "You know that I could not help myself. My father would have disowned me . . . I could not go against his wishes—and those of my mother."

"I know," said Ash, his voice suddenly gentle. "I know." He patted the slender hand that lay curled in her lap. He took a deep, unsteady breath. "Of course, I will be your friend. I always have been, after all, and I suppose I always will be."

Like a child who has escaped punishment, Lianne sighed and smiled widely in relief. "Oh, my dear, I can't tell you what that means to me. Now, do let me call for some refreshment. And I must let Aunt Biddy know that you are here. You remember her, do you not?"

Ash remembered very well the formidable woman who was Squire Bonner's sister. A picture formed in his mind of a profusion of iron gray hair and a long, large-featured face that put one in mind of an affronted horse. Beatrix Bonner was a force to be reckoned with in the Bonner household, and Lianne had chosen well in persuading her to act as chaperon.

Lianne rose, and with a fluid movement crossed to the bellpull. Turning to Ash, she remarked casually, "Do you go to the Marchford ball next week? I collect all the world and his donkey will be there." At Ash's assenting nod, she continued smoothly, "I shall take you up on your declaration of friendship by being so bold as to solicit your escort. There is nothing so wretched as attending a ball with one's aunt, after all." Musical laughter flowed from her lips like silken ribbons.

Ash's insides clenched. "I—I'm afraid that will not be possible," he said slowly. He read the disbelieving surprise in her eyes and continued hastily. "I am escorting someone to the ball."

"Escorting someone?" Her expression grew rigid for a moment before she smiled and asked archly, "Is she anyone I know?"

"I rather doubt it," he replied dryly. "Her name is Amanda Bridge."

"No, her name is not familiar to me." Lianne's gaze was concealed by the silky curtain of her lashes. "Is there something I should know, dear friend?" she asked playfully.

Ash took a deep breath. "Perhaps there is. I have proposed marriage to her, Lianne."

Her eyes flew open and she stared up at him, shock apparent in every line of her body. "Marriage?" she whispered, her hand at her throat. "Oh, Ash, how could you?"

At this, Ash stood abruptly. "What do you mean, how could I?" he asked bitterly. "Did you expect me to enter a monastery?"

"No, of course not—I only meant—"

"It is my duty to marry, after all. I must produce an heir, to say nothing of repairing the Park. And there are Andrew and Dorothea. Andrew is studying for the bar and Dorothea has gone to live with my Uncle Breverton and his wife, the Park having become virtually unlivable."

Lianne exhaled a sharp, little sound that seemed to echo in the silence of the room.

"This Miss, er, Bridge is wealthy, then?" she asked in a barely audible voice.

"Her father is a mill owner, and has fingers in a hundred other pies. I daresay he could buy Golden Ball."

"I see." Lianne's lovely mouth curved in a tentative smile. "I must ask for your forgiveness once again. I, of all people, have no right to censure you for making an expedient marriage. Although, I wish—" Her hand fluttered upward to come to rest on his sleeve, and he covered it with his own. Unknowing, he moved closer to her until she was suddenly standing in the curve of his embrace.

"Oh, Ash," she said, gasping, "I cannot bear it!" She threw her head back against his shoulder, and tears glistened in the dark lashes that fanned her cheeks. "Surely, there must be some hope for us!"

Ash's arms tightened around her involuntarily, and with a

groan he bent his head to hers. Her mouth was as soft and warm as he remembered, and he felt a familiar tide of wanting sweep over him. His kiss grew hot and urgent. Lianne's supple body shuddered in response and her lips parted under his. His hands moved along her slender back, only to be stilled at the sound of footfalls in the corridor outside the parlor. Abruptly, he released her and she sprang away from him, her eyes wide and staring.

In the few seconds before the door opened to admit the butler, she had patted her hair and composed herself. "You may serve us, now, Hobbes, and please inform my aunt that we have a visitor."

Ash, his heart thundering in his ears and his breathing so ragged that he could hardly speak, lifted a hand. "No. Do not bother, please, Lianne. I cannot stay. I must be on my way." He was already backing out of the room. "I shall look forward to seeing you at the Marchford ball."

Lianne made no attempt to stay him. Instead, she put out her hand in an oddly formal gesture, and in a voice no steadier than his own replied, "Of course, my lord. I appreciate your calling so promptly. Do come again when you can stay longer, for I know Aunt Biddy will want to see you."

He nodded stiffly, and having gained the entrance hallway, gathered up hat and gloves and fairly flung himself through the door. Once outside, he grasped the iron railing of the tiny porch fronting the house and drew in great lungfuls of air as though he had just escaped from a burning building.

On legs that would barely carry him, he mounted his curricle and spent some moments driving aimlessly through streets of whose names he was unaware.

Good God, the unthinkable had happened. He had almost been caught on the verge of making love to his cousin's widow. He groaned aloud. He might have known he would be unable to keep himself from gathering her in his arms. He had told himself he was no longer in love with her, but only a few minutes in her company had dispelled that notion.

How could it have been otherwise? he thought in a burst of clarity. He had been in love with Lianne Bonner ever since he knew what the word meant. And before that, they had been inseparable playmates. He had been her protector from the time she could toddle unassisted, and when she began to fulfill the promise of beauty her early years had forecast, he had worshipped her helplessly. She had returned his love, and from the first shy wondrous kiss shared in an old apple orchard they had made plans to marry.

Then, fate took a hand in their affairs to dash their hopes. Grant had returned from Oxford on holiday. Lianne was sixteen, a budding flower of exquisite womanhood, and Grant, who had heretofore scarcely been aware of her existence, suddenly plunged into a feverish infatuation with her. Lord Ashindon had hoped for a more suitable *parti* for his heir, but if Lianne was what Grant wanted, Lianne was what he should have. Squire and Mrs. Bonner, while aware of the precarious financial situation at the Park and the tendency toward prodigality already displayed by the heir, nevertheless were quite taken with the idea of marriage to an earl for their little girl.

For months, Ash had railed against fate and the implacability of his uncle's decision. Grant expressed a good-natured regret for his suffering, but assured his young cousin that he would get over it. "Besides," he concluded with a lazy chuckle, "if I'm marrying for love, you're going to have to marry for money, old man."

It was with a great deal of difficulty that young William had refrained from beating Grant senseless. He could have done so with ease, for even at eighteen he was taller and stronger than his cousin, and lean as a whip.

An elopement seemed the only answer, but although Lianne passionately declared herself willing to fly to the border with him, she could not bear to fail her family so abysmally.

"For I do not think Mama's heart would stand up under the shock," she had sobbed against his chest, her hair a fragrant drift under his chin. "And how can I deprive my sisters of the opportunity to come to London for husbands. Just imagine the wealthy bachelors who will flock to Ashindon House when Grant and I— Oh, William! I did not mean to say such a thing, but I am only a woman, and I have been raised to honor my obligations."

William had raised his brows as Lianne began to speak, for they had agreed long ago that Mrs. Bonner's frequent spasms were merely a device to keep her husband in line, but he was struck by compunction as she continued. Of course, Lianne would always put her family's needs above her own.

Thus, little more than a year later, William had attended his cousin's wedding and had somehow survived the festivities that followed. Lianne had looked at him directly only once during that terrible day and with a small, brave smile had turned away instantly.

A career in the army had not appealed to him when the possibility had been broached earlier by his uncle, but now he welcomed the haven of a life in uniform. Almost immediately upon the purchase of his colors, he was posted to the Peninsula. He heard through his aunt's frequent letters news of Grant and his new bride, and worries of Grant's continuing profligacy were plainly evident. He was unable to return at the death of his aunt, or for that of his uncle, a few years later. It was only after Grant's death that he saw Lianne again.

He had been struck to the heart by her appearance, for she had changed so little. Her air of fragility was, perhaps, more pronounced, but her vitality remained undiminished. His visit at her family's home had been brief, for he could not bear to remain in her presence any longer than necessary, and when he bade farewell to her outside Fairwinds, the Bonner manor, he had ridden away as though pursued by devils.

He had not seen Lianne, the Countess of Ashindon, since. He had remained at Ashindon Park for many months in his futile effort to bring the estate finances about, but he had steadfastly refused to give in to the almost overwhelming temptation to avail himself of her company. He did very little socializing during that period, and was careful to attend only those functions at which he knew Lianne would be absent. On the eve of his departure for London, he had sent her a formal missive informing her of his plans to seek additional financing and his promise to render assistance to her if she should need him. He had left early the next morning, carrying a picture of her in his heart as she had appeared on the morning she had averred her intention of remaining in the fastness of her parents' home.

Now, she was in London, and what was he to do? He supposed he could continue to avoid her, although it would be difficult, harnessed as he was to his newly betrothed and her social obligations.

By the end of the day, the only conclusion to which he had come was that while he would under no circumstances visit

Lianne again, he was also wholly averse to playing the gallant to
Amanda Bridge. How could he spout pretty platitudes to golden
curls and blue eyes, when an image of raven locks and eyes of
emerald green was engraved on his heart forever? He had almost
a week before the Marchford ball to gird his loins to the performance of his duties. He would indulge himself in the luxury of
those few days' solitude. He would then emerge, if not like a butterfly from a chrysalis, at least as a reasonable facsimile of a
happy bridegroom.

   If Amanda noted the earl's absence, she said nothing to the
other members of the household. She did, indeed, wonder a little
and admitted to herself that she missed him. With him, she could
be herself—more or less. That she also missed the sardonic flash
of gray eyes and muscled shoulders contained in an elegantly tailored jacket, she forbore to discuss with herself.
   Instead, she filled her days with activity. She practiced the
piano and went for long walks through the fascinating streets of
London. That Serena insisted she be accompanied on these excur-
sions by Hutchings and a couple of footmen was a source of irritation to which she tried to accustom herself. She returned to
Grosvenor Chapel on several occasions, despite Serena's strictures, with no more felicitous results than before. She still could
not come to grips with the possibility that she had actually traveled through time. There must be some other explanation. The
only one that suggested itself, however, was that she'd gone completely bananas, and she somehow found that less than acceptable.
   In the meantime, she found it almost impossible to pass a mirror without gazing at herself in rapt admiration. She supposed that
she would eventually become inured to the dazzling beauty of
young Amanda Bridge, but right now she planned to wallow in it.
She reveled in the strength of her legs, and immersed herself even
farther in Serena's black books by walking out alone on several
occasions.
   She found that she was forced to revise her earlier, unfavorable
opinion of young Amanda's mother. Serena was an irritating flea-
brained dingbat, but she was possessed of a basic kindness, and
truly did seem to have her daughter's interest at heart. The fact

that what would be good for her daughter varied so markedly with Amanda's idea on the subject was scarcely Serena's fault.

The woman's major flaw was her absolute, mindless submission to Jeremiah. Amanda was aware that her behavior was the norm for her time, but, thought Amanda resolutely, for however long she was to remain in this time period, she would make it one of her first priorities to liberate Serena Bridge, no matter that she was only an illusion. She had already begun her campaign by purchasing for Serena a copy of Byron's *The Bride of Abydos*, which, she knew from an earlier conversation with Jeremiah, to be on the list of things forbidden to Serena. When she had told Ash of this, he had laughed and suggested she offer the book to Serena as a gift from himself.

"For surely," he said, the merest twinkle at the back of his eyes, "your estimable papa can have no objection to a gift from his soon-to-be son-in-law."

Her days were full. Social activities absorbed an astonishing amount of time, with visits during the day, rides in the park in the afternoon, and small parties at night. Despite the general inanity of the conversations obtained at these functions, Amanda found that she was enjoying herself. She was able, with Hutchings' continued help, to avoid most of the pitfalls caused by her ignorance of young Amanda's past.

She was even, after a foray into the kitchen that left the lower staff astonished and not a little discomfited, able to teach Hutchings how to make a fairly decent cup of cocoa. This was not as easy as it might have been, because, apparently, cocoa had not been created yet, and drinking chocolate was concocted by breaking chunks of solid, very bitter chocolate from a large bar, to be ground in a chocolate mill. This accomplished, Amanda instructed Hutchings to melt the resulting granules in a small quantity of hot water. She added what Hutchings declared an inordinate amount of sugar to the mix and poured in a generous dollop of milk. The finished product was, if Amanda said so herself, quite tasty, particularly when Hutchings added a pinch of crushed vanilla bean.

"Next week," promised Amanda grandly, "we'll whip up a batch of fudge."

"That will be nice, miss," replied Hutchings expressionlessly.

As the days passed, she was uncomfortably aware that the realism of her stay in Regency London seemed to increase. Some of her experiences surely came from the depths of the research she had done for various papers, but she was sure she had never considered the everyday discomforts of life in the early nineteenth century. The air pollution, from thousands of coal fires, was much worse than anything she had experienced in her own time. And when, she wondered dismally, would the invention of toilet paper come to pass?

Thus, the days slid by until one morning, Serena announced to Amanda just after breakfast, "No walks in the Park for you today, missy. You will stay home, if you please, and rest." At Amanda's blank look, she continued in some indignation, "Don't tell me you have forgotten about the Marchford ball? It is tonight, and I want you to look your best."

Amanda knew a moment of panic, for this would be her first large formal occasion. She forced herself to relax. She had managed her masquerade with relative ease, so far. Not one of young Amanda's acquaintances suspected there was anything wrong with her beyond a small disruption of memory due to a bump on the head. The ball, she assured herself, would be a piece of cake.

In this assumption, she was to be proved very much mistaken.

Chapter Eight

In preparation for the evening's festivities, Hutchings took more time than usual over her ministrations, and when the little maid had finished, Amanda gazed at herself for some moments in the mirror. She could hardly believe her eyes. Could this apparition truly be Amanda McGovern, plain of face and twisted of body? She was gowned in a robe of celestial blue satin, over which floated a tunic of silver net. About her slender throat lay a web of sapphires that exactly matched her eyes. Her golden hair was gathered in an artful knot atop her head, circled by a tiny fragile tiara of the same stones. Airy tendrils escaped to curl deliciously about her classic features. Dear God, Amanda breathed, she'd never before fully appreciated the concept of "drop dead gorgeous."

She turned to her maid. "You've really outdone yourself, tonight. Thank you, Hutchings."

"It's a pleasure to have the dressing of a beautiful lady like you, miss," replied the maid with a little grin. "You're a credit to me."

Amanda's responding smile was a little apologetic. "I hope Papa pays you well to turn me out in such style. Good God, you're at my beck and call every waking moment of your day. Don't you ever get some time for yourself?"

"Why yes, miss," replied Hutchings in surprise. "I have every Thursday afternoon off, and all the staff is allowed time to go to church on Sundays. A good Christian household, this is. And I'm almost the highest paid servant in the place," she added pertly. "Twelve pounds a year, your papa pays me, and that includes my meals and a room of my own."

"My God," breathed Amanda. "That's less than twenty dollars!"

"I don't know about that, miss, but it's more than many a lady's maid earns, and it does me fine. Plus, with the gowns you give me—the ones you don't wear anymore—I don't have to pay anything for clothes—except my working things, of course."

Amanda gazed at her in disbelief, but said nothing, and after a moment, at Hutchings' lifted brows, raised her hand in a gesture of dismissal. When the maid had whisked herself out of the room, Amanda sat for some moments with her chin in her hand. Her gaze drifted again to the image in the mirror—the flashing jewelry around her neck and in her hair. She glanced at the box on her dressing table overflowing with more hideously expensive baubles, all bought for Jeremiah Bridge's daughter for his own greater glory. All the while, how many thousands clung, like Hutchings, to the bare edge of survival? Amanda knew an urge to dash into the streets, crying out against this horrendous inequity. The twentieth century had its problems, but at least some progress had been made against such wickedness.

Amanda glanced at the little clock that stood on her bedside table. Lord Ashindon would be arriving any minute. Why had he absented himself from the Bridge household for lo, these many days? Had his meager supply of ardor cooled so soon? Was he regretting his proposal? It had surely been given grudgingly enough. Odd, she wouldn't have pegged the earl as a fortune hunter. A man who wore his pride and arrogance like a suit of ceremonial armor scarcely seemed the type to grovel at a rich man's feet for the hand of his daughter.

She shrugged. None of it really made any difference, after all. Suppressing the flutter of excitement mixed with panic that made itself felt in the pit of her stomach, she ran a hand over her blue satin skirts and stepped out into the corridor.

As it happened, she began her descent of the stairs just as Ash was admitted to the house. Handing his outer coat, hat, and gloves to Goodbody, the butler, he turned to watch her approach down the curving staircase. A guilty pleasure flooded through her as his eyes widened.

"You are looking exceptionally lovely tonight, Miss Bridge." He brushed her gloved fingertips with his lips. "I shall be the most envied man at the festivities. Perhaps," he added, drawing a small packet wrapped in tissue paper from his waistcoat pocket, "you will deign to carry this."

Carefully unwrapping the little parcel, Amanda gasped in delight as she drew out a fan. It was made of silk, stretched over slender, carved ribs of ivory and delicately embellished with medallions depicting mythological scenes.

"Thank you, my lord," she said simply. "It is lovely."

And you're looking pretty fantastic yourself, she added to herself. Lord Ashindon in coat and pantaloons was an impressive sight, but in evening dress he was nothing short of magnificent. He wore satin breeches that molded themselves admirably to his muscular thighs. A coat of dark silk afforded a glimpse of embroidered waistcoat and nestled in his intricately tied cravat, a single diamond winked in the candlelight.

"I shall ask immediately that you save me the permitted two dances. I would ask for more, but there is no point in affording speculation for the gabble-mongers until your mama makes our declaration public."

"Oh!" Amanda nearly dropped the fan. "I do not dance—that is . . . " Her laughter came faint and high-pitched. "I seem to have forgotten how."

"Indeed," said the earl imperturbably. "You have no knowledge of cotillion—or quadrille? How about the waltz?"

"Oh, yes, I can waltz."

Ash's brows shot up. "Now that is peculiar. The workings of the human mind are indeed inscrutable, are they not, for one to forget the steps to one kind of dance, but not another."

His expression held nothing but polite interest, but Amanda felt her back stiffen.

"You implied at our last meeting, my lord, that I was pretending a loss of memory, but I thought you must have discarded that ludicrous misapprehension by now." Lord, she thought, startled, she was beginning to sound like something from a Jane Austen novel. "However, if you—"

"Not at all, Miss Bridge. You are too quick to take me up. I was merely voicing a certain curiosity. You shall find me at your side when the first waltz is struck."

"My lord, you are here!" Serena Bridge bustled into the hall from the back of the house. "I did not hear you arrive. Amanda, what can you be thinking of to let his lordship stand about like this." She grasped the earl's arm and propelled him purposefully into the drawing room. "Mr. Bridge will join us in a moment. He is in his study at present—or no, here he is now."

Jeremiah Bridge, garbed in evening dress, provided a marked

contrast to Ash. In breeches and coat, the man looked as though
he were being physically restrained in a prison of cloth, and that if
he were to breathe deeply, coat, breeches, waistcoat, and cravat
would fly apart in all directions. Disregarding his wife and daughter, he advanced, smiling on the earl.

"Ah, my lord," he said with a wolfish smile of gratification.
"Good of you to join us tonight." Leading Ash into the drawing
room and followed dutifully by his wife and daughter, he gestured
expansively to a settee covered in amber satin and with his own
hands poured a glass of sherry for himself and his guest. Seating
himself in a chair opposite, he launched into a lengthy explanation of the press of business that had kept him occupied until late
in the afternoon.

"Ugly business, this advance of Napoleon," he concluded. "Got
the market stirred up as though someone had let a hive of bees
loose."

Amanda pricked up her ears. Let's see, if this was April of
1815, the Corsican Monster must have escaped from Elba only a
few weeks ago. He must be marching on Paris right about now.

"Where is Wellington?" she asked interestedly. "If I remember
rightly, he must be in Brussels."

Both men swung toward her as though she had just requested
directions to the nearest bawdy house. Jeremiah's formidable
brows beetled in astonished disapproval.

"What?" he asked in his customary bellow.

Amanda began to repeat her words, but was interrupted by Serena.

"Goodness, Amanda, dearest, this is certainly not a topic for a
well-bred young lady." She pinched her daughter's arm and shot
her a meaningful glance.

"You mean," Amanda snapped, "young English ladies aren't
supposed to know that young English men are dying in a foreign
land for their country?"

"Amanda!" Serena was close to tears. She shot an anguished
glance at Ash, who was staring intently at his betrothed. "You
must forgive her, my lord. She is still sadly discomposed by her—
her recent ordeal."

Ash said nothing, but his eyes remained on Amanda as Serena
hastily turned the conversation to a more innocuous subject.

At the table, Amanda, of course, was seated next to Ash, who

held the place of honor to Jeremiah's right. She could think of little to say to him and addressed herself vigorously to the serving
of indeterminate meat set before her.

"What is that?" she asked in some puzzlement.

"Why, it's calves' brains, dear, made up in the Florentine style,
just the way you like them."

Amanda stared dubiously at her plate. "Really? Do you—we—
have this stuff often?"

Jeremiah sent her an uneasy glance. "It's good English fare,"
he barked. "Now, let's hear no more about it." He swung to Ash
and said hastily, "By the by, did you sink any funds in the new
gas works, as I told you to do? Made a tidy profit on that today."

"Yes, I did," Ash replied easily, but Amanda noticed that his
grip tightened on his fork.

"Ah," said Jeremiah, his satisfaction apparent, "how much did
you invest?"

Ash's mouth tightened and the fingers holding his fork turned
white. His tone was casual, however, as he replied, "Surely, sir,
this subject cannot be of any interest to the ladies." He turned to
Serena. "I wonder if you have read the copy of *The Bride of Abydos* that I procured for you the other day, ma'am."

Amanda eyed him curiously. Though he frequently allowed his
contempt for Jeremiah to burst through his mask of indifference,
Ash was unfailingly courteous to Serena. Was he genuinely kind?
she wondered, or was it that his unbending pride demanded a
rigid standard of behavior toward those who had no defense
against rudeness.

Serena's gaze flew immediately to her husband, and she shifted
in her chair agitatedly. "Oh! Yes—that is, no. You see—"

"Bride? Abydos?" Jeremiah bellowed. "Isn't that some of
Byron's rubbish?" He glared down the table at his wife. "Didn't I
tell you I wouldn't have any of his stuff in the house?"

"Oh, yes, dearest." To Amanda's disgust, she observed that
Serena was very nearly in tears. "But, all the world reads his
work, and—"

"Have you read the poem—Papa?" asked Amanda innocently.

"Of course not!" Jeremiah's cheeks mottled in anger. "I
wouldn't dirty my hands with such trash let alone permit it in my
house."

"Well, it's a little silly in spots," remarked Amanda, "but I don't know as I'd go so far as to call it trash."

Jeremiah's mouth fell open, which was, perhaps, unfortunate, since he was at present masticating a large portion of calves' brains. "Don't tell me you've read the thing?"

"All right, Papa," replied Amanda demurely. "I shan't tell you anything of the sort."

"Now see here, missy—"

"It is entirely possible," said Ash coolly, his voice falling on Jeremiah's incipient diatribe like a spray of water, "that now that he is married Byron will settle down and become a loving husband and father."

Amanda laughed shortly. "I wouldn't bet on that. By this time next year, Anabella will have left him, with their baby, and not too long after that—" She stopped abruptly. "At least—that's what will probably happen," she murmured lamely, and finished in a rush. "I wonder, could I have some more of those delectable calves' brains?"

The dinner plodded on through several more courses, which included beef and lamb in various forms, covered in various sauces, and concluded with a massive assortment of pastries. Amanda could only marvel at the earl's continued sang froid, even though, to her heightened perception, distaste and a sort of sad horror radiated from him like dissonances from a badly tuned violin.

Afterwards, the Bridges and their guest gathered in the drawing room for postprandial conversation. After fifteen minutes of this, Amanda was ready to grab the earl's hand and dash out into the night for a lungful of fresh air. At last, however, Serena rose.

"It's time we were leaving, my love," she said to Jeremiah, who heaved himself to his feet with some reluctance. Outer wraps were called for and the carriage brought round. Amanda's last thought as she was handed in to sit beside her mother, was that tonight's party could not possibly be any more of an ordeal than dinner had been.

Sir Barnaby and Lady Marchford lived in Hill Street, a quiet thoroughfare that sloped down to Berkeley Square. "A fashionable address," said Serena Bridge, her lips curving in satisfaction, "but hardly of the distinction of Upper Brook Street."

Tonight, the street was anything but quiet. A multitude of carriages of every shape and description jostled for position, with the general destination being a large town house just about halfway down the hill. Flambeaux lit the exterior in a flickering radiance and footmen and link boys scurried like mice, responding to shouted orders from coachmen and other servants.

Amanda drank in the sight, for it was the embodiment of a hundred scenes she had absorbed from books. She could hardly wait to get inside.

Her wish remained unfulfilled for almost an hour, and when the Bridge party at last disembarked on the sidewalk outside the Marchford home, they found themselves immediately swept up in the procession entering the impressive edifice. Once inside, another wait lay in store for them as they joined a long line of guests that wound through the hall and up the staircase to the ballroom above. The persons just ahead and behind the Bridges were apparently unknown to them, so there was little conversation, but a good deal of nodding and genteel waving took place. Serena, her fixed smile never wavering, kept up a steady stream of instruction to Amanda under her breath.

"Look, there is Lady Bumfret in the puce satin. That is her daughter Hermione with her. You and she went to school together, although she has not deigned to take up the connection. Odious woman!" The words were accompanied with a widening of her smile and a waggling of her fingers at the lady in puce.

"And, see," continued Serena, "just coming in the door are Lord and Lady Robert Meecham. You must be particularly nice to her, for she is a friend to Lady Jersey, and when your betrothal is announced I count on getting vouchers from her. Oh!" She gave a start. "If that isn't Georgina Faversham and her mama. Wave, Amanda. Gracious, doesn't the girl look a fright in that gown? Why in the world would Maude let her wear yellow?"

The catalog continued without interruption as the group slowly ascended the stairs, and Amanda was acutely conscious of Ash's presence just behind her. Good grief, what must he think of the Bridge family? Although, by now he must be perfectly aware of the general awfulness of his soon-to-be-acquired relatives. Meanwhile, Amanda listened carefully to Serena's monologue, gleaning clues for future reference.

At last, they reached their destination, and, at the entrance to the ballroom were announced in rotund tones by a liveried servant. A plump matron with a profusion of teeth, all of which showed when she smiled, grasped Serena's gloved hand.

"Serena! How lovely to see you! Good evening, Mr. Bridge." This in slightly less cordial accents. "And, dear Amanda—in looks, as ever, I see."

Her husband, whose protuberant eyes twinkled from beneath bushy eyebrows, chuckled in agreement. "You'll have 'em all buzzin' around, m'dear, like bees to a honey pot."

"Lord Ashindon!" exclaimed Lady Marchford. "You have come, after all. Welcome." Her gaze darted between the earl and Amanda, and she bestowed a knowing congratulatory smile on Serena before turning her attention to the next guests in line.

Amanda looked around in appreciation at the scene before her as Serena steered her daughter into a large drawing room. Crowds of guests drifted in and out of the room, young women garbed in whites and pastels provided a backdrop for the older ladies, who looked very much like blossoms cast adrift on a stream in their gaily colored gowns. The gentlemen all wore sober colors, thanks, Amanda supposed, to the influence of Beau Brummell.

With a bow, Ash left the ladies to their own devices, and Amanda was surprised at how forlorn she felt at his departure. Which was, of course, absurd. The man was merely a presence in what she persevered in calling a hallucination. The fact that her fantasy was becoming ever more complex and real to her and seemed to be lasting an awfully long time was becoming of greater concern to her—but she wouldn't think about that now.

She became aware that Serena was speaking again. "Here comes Candace Macclesfield. Do you remember her?"

"Yes, Mama. She has come to visit twice since my accident."

Miss Macclesfield, a plump brunette of twenty summers, was not one of Miss Bridge's close friends, but her recent betrothal to the Viscount Ramsden had propelled her into the parlors of everyone of her acquaintance so that she could gloat in a suitably genteel fashion. Amanda had dealt with her handily, since the damsel's thoughts were so taken up by her coming good fortune that Amanda's few lapses were hardly noticed. Amanda turned to greet the young woman with a smile and was soon deep in conversation, most of which concerned bride clothes and nuptial journeys.

From across the room, Ash watched Amanda unobtrusively. He was surprised at the look of sympathy mixed with exasperation he had intercepted earlier from her, when they had still been standing on the stairway, mixed, he thought, with a tinge of embarrassment. All three, certainly, were understandable. He would make it one of his first priorities when they were married to put as much distance between himself and Papa and Mama Bridge as possible. When he was married. He experienced the most peculiar sensations as the words echoed in his mind.

The past week had not been pleasant for Lord Ashindon. For the first few days after he had left Lianne, his thoughts had been wholly occupied with his lost love. The taste of her mouth beneath his haunted him and her green eyes plagued his dreams. As he had so many years ago, he found himself railing again at the fates that conspired to rob him of his one chance for happiness. He recalled the anguish in Lianne's eyes at the news of his betrothal. For the first time, he knew a twinge of irritation at this most perfect of females. Had Lianne really expected him to remain unmarried? To deny his duty to his family? Did she begrudge him the right to make a life of his own, after she had come close to destroying it?

Ah well, Lianne was what she was and perhaps could not be blamed for being unwilling to relinquish the devotion of one who, after all, had declared himself hers, heart and soul. She was only human, after all. It was borne to him with some astonishment, that he had never before thought of the lovely Lianne in the light of mere mortality. He was even more astonished some days later, when his thoughts persisted in drifting to Amanda Bridge, and he discovered that he was looking forward to the Marchford ball with more anticipation than he would have thought possible.

Now, gazing at her, he thought back to the moment when she had descended the staircase toward him, straight and slender as a young goddess. She moved with a grace and surety she had never displayed before her "incident," as he was coming to think of her swoon in Grosvenor Chapel. What had happened to her in those few moments, to change her so completely? Where before she had simpered girlishly and giggled at every pleasantry, her smile was now all womanly mystery. He watched her as she moved through the crowd of guests, her long-legged stride at once seductive and innocently appealing. It seemed to him that she moved with an athletic grace she had not displayed before, as though, suddenly, she reveled in her youth and strength.

A thoroughly unladylike concept, he mused, and thoroughly un-Amandalike. She usually took small, kittenish steps. And speaking of thoroughly un-Amandalike, was it really she who had evinced an interest in the affairs of Napoleon and Wellington? To say nothing of her passionate sentiments on behalf of those who had spilled their blood for England. Good God, did the little Bridge actually possess a brain?

For the next hour or so, Ash performed his social obligations. He danced with his host's daughters, and those of several of his acquaintances. He conversed lightly with various matrons who had been friends of his mother's, and he chatted with gentlemen known to him from his clubs. At last, from the ballroom, the sound he had been waiting for struck his ears.

He moved to Amanda's side, and as he took her hand in his, he was conscious of a surge of anticipation rising within him.

"They are playing a waltz, my dear, and I think this is our dance."

Chapter Nine

Amanda's eyes widened as Lord Ashindon, without speaking, led her onto the floor. It was with some trepidation that she lifted her arms to him, for she had not been entirely truthful when she had told the earl that she could waltz. She was acquainted with the steps and had lurched around the floor once or twice in her father's arms at family get-togethers, but she had never in her adult life actually danced. On the few occasions when she had been asked, she had refused, unable to bear the whispers and pitying looks she was sure would follow her progress.

Thus, it was no doubt sheer panic that caused the trembling deep within her when Ash placed his arm about her waist and began to draw her into the compelling rhythm of the dance.

In 1815, Amanda knew, the waltz was considered quite daring, for the lady allowed her waist to be encircled by her partner, to whom she might not even be betrothed! In 1996, of course, the dance was almost laughable, an amusing anachronism favored by golden-agers and ballroom dance contestants.

What Amanda felt, however, as Ash swept her about the room in great, lazy circles, was not amusement. The pressure of his hand on her back caused a slow heat to rise within her that simmered and bubbled in the sheer exhilaration of movement. This was wonderful! She felt as though her feet might leave the floor, taking her to unimagined heights and delights. She was light as thistledown—she was snowflakes on the wind! She wished the music would go on forever, and when it ended, she wanted to cry.

His dark eyes hooded, Ash bowed formally. "You were right, my dear," he murmured as he returned her to the group of giggling damsels with whom she'd been conversing earlier, "You are very well acquainted with the steps of the waltz."

Amanda looked after him, the last strains of the music still fizzing in her veins like champagne, and it was some moments that she became aware that Cordelia Fordham was speaking to her.

"Goodness!" exclaimed the girl breathlessly. "I have never seen you dance so well, Amanda. Nor did I suspect that Lord Ashindon had such talent. The two of you were the cynosure of all eyes!"

Before Amanda could reply, a very young gentleman materialized at her elbow, requesting, in worshipful tones, her hand for the next dance. Since the orchestra was tuning up for what sounded like a jig, Amanda refused politely, but she watched in interest as a number of couples took to the floor for some sort of reel. The young gentleman asked Cordelia to dance, and Amanda found herself alone.

But not for long.

"My love," a voice whispered tensely in her ear, "I have been waiting in agony for a chance to get you alone!"

Amanda turned sharply to behold one of the handsomest men she had ever seen. His hair was almost the same shade as hers, molded just as artfully into a tumble of curls. His eyes, however, were not blue, but a curiously light gray. He was just above medium height and wore his evening wear with a slender elegance. He grasped her hand and squeezed it before running fingers up along the inside of her arm.

Amanda stepped back hastily, observing that he was not nearly as good-looking as she had thought on first glance. The gray eyes were flat and unrevealing, and rather close set. His full lips were petulant, just now pursed in a slight pout. The beginnings of a paunch could be glimpsed beneath his satin waistcoat.

"Sir!" she exclaimed in her best affronted-maiden manner.

The gentleman removed his hand at once. "Forgive me, my darling. I was overcome by emotion. You cannot know my anguish at not beholding your angelic countenance for over a week!"

By now, Amanda was beginning to feel slightly ill. She also

had a pretty good idea with whom she was speaking. "Cosmo?" she asked in amazement. "I thought you'd left town."

"Surely," breathed young Amanda's suitor, "you did not think I could stay away. But, come . . . " Once more, he took her hand in an attempt to lead her out of the ballroom. "Let us go somewhere where we can be private."

Amanda simply stared at him. How could young Amanda have preferred Cosmo Satterleigh to a man like the Earl of Ashindon? Next to Ash, Cosmo was shoddy merchandise, and seemed faintly ridiculous. Besides, she'd be willing to bet good money it wasn't young Amanda's *beaux yeux* that had Cosmo in such a lather. The guy had fortune hunter written all over his dissolute features. Was this the only breed she was going to meet during her sojourn in Regency England?

"I don't think so, Cosmo," she snapped. "I have to—to return to my mother." She started to move away and then paused. "By the way, what happened to you the other day? At Grosvenor Chapel?"

Cosmo pressed a shapely hand to his heart in a theatrical gesture. "Oh, my love, you cannot believe what I have suffered! An unforeseen circumstance forced me to be a few minutes late. My fool of a man could not find my walking stick! I arrived at the chapel just in time to witness the Earl of Ashindon bundling you into his curricle like some low woman of the streets. If your papa had not been on the scene, I should have called the wretch to account, believe me! I was devastated! And I have spent every moment of every day since endeavoring to see you. But you are watched constantly," he concluded bitterly.

Not a very enterprising fellow, thought Amanda. She watched as he ran slender fingers through his golden locks in a studied motion.

"When can we meet?" asked Cosmo as he availed himself once more of her hand. "Can you get away tomorrow? Perhaps we could—?"

"No," replied Amanda, firmly disengaging herself. "I don't want to meet you, Cosmo, tomorrow or any other time."

Cosmo gasped disbelievingly. "Do I hear you aright?" He groaned. "I knew it! Your mama and papa have succeeded in turning you against me!"

"It's not that." An urge to laugh rose in her throat, which made her feel guilty, which led her to be gentle with him, which, in turn, proved to be a tactical error. "I find, Cosmo, that I have, er . . . I fear I was mistaken in my affections." Surely she had read that phrase in *Pamela*, or, perhaps, *Clarissa*. She placed her hand in his, whereupon he promptly clutched it to his bosom like the last rose of summer.

"You cannot mean this!" He was gasping again. "Please, my dearest—my angel! We can still fly away together. Do but let me—"

"I believe the lady would like her hand back, Satterleigh." The voice cut through Cosmo's babble, and Amanda turned with a start. Her eyes widened in surprised gratitude and her lips curved tentatively, but Ash did not return her smile, keeping his gaze fastened on the hapless Satterleigh.

"You!" cried Cosmo in accents of loathing. The next moment, he recovered himself and stiffened to his full height, which was slightly less than that of the earl. "The lady and I," he said dismissively, "were engaged in a private conversation."

"Not all that private, actually," drawled Ash insultingly. "I expect half the room could hear you." He turned to Amanda. "Would you care for some refreshment, Miss Bridge?"

"Yes," she replied. "Yes, I believe I—" But she was interrupted as Cosmo grasped her arm roughly. "You are just going to go with him?" he asked in a choked voice, and to Amanda it seemed as though there was a hint of desperation in his tone.

Ash stepped forward, but Cosmo, at the expression in the earl's eyes, released Amanda's arm immediately.

"We shall continue our conversation later, Miss Bridge," he said loftily, and his bow as he turned to leave contained a nice blend of insolence and loverlike determination.

"Good grief, what a jerk!" exclaimed Amanda as she watched him swagger away into the crowd.

"Jerk? Mm, I believe you used the word not long ago to me, and I detected a certain censoriousness at the time. Can it be that you and Cosmo have had a falling out?"

She shot the earl a glance from beneath her lashes. "You could say that." She smiled wryly. "Somehow, a man who can't show up on time for his own elopement doesn't seem a very good bet as a lifemate. Besides, at the risk of repeating myself, I don't re-member him."

For a moment, Ash stared at her, nonplussed. From all ac-counts, Amanda's passion for Satterleigh had been genuine, if misplaced. Could she truly have forgotten a man she had pro-fessed to love?

A couple jostled them on the way to the dance floor, and Ash became aware that the orchestra had swung into another country dance. He bent his head to Amanda. "Are you sure you are unable to accomplish the steps to the quadrille?"

Amanda watched the dancers with undisguised interest. "Yes, I'm sure, but it looks like a lot of fun." She turned to face him, and once again Ash was struck by the magical quality her eyes had assumed over the last week. "Would you teach me?" she asked.

He nodded dazedly, aware in a corner of his brain that he would have complied if she had asked him to give her lessons in animal husbandry.

"On one condition," he added, his lips curving upward. "That you save the supper dance for me. If it is not a waltz, we shall spend the time promenading in stately fashion about the edge of the floor, nodding to acquaintances and exchanging scurrilous re-marks about the other guests' taste in clothing."

At this, her smile positively blinded him. "That sounds like more fun than I've had since—"

"William!"

The voice was soft and musical, but held an unmistakable note of command. Amanda watched with some interest as Ash stiff-ened and the laughter fled from those disturbing gray eyes. In the next moment, he turned to greet the newcomer.

"Lianne," he said, and Amanda thought she detected a slight tremor as he spoke the word. He bent to salute the slender hand that was lifted to him and said quietly, "Lianne, allow me to pre-sent Miss Amanda Bridge. Amanda, this is my cousin's widow, Lady Ashindon."

The widow was small, and, thought Amanda, as exquisite as an Augustin miniature. Was she imagining things, she wondered, or was there the merest hint of malice in the jeweled green eyes lifted to hers? The countess grasped Amanda's hand gently in both her small ones and exclaimed prettily. "You must call me Lianne, as well, my dear. I understand that you will soon be joining our family." She whirled to face Ash. "But you did not tell me, Will—she is quite astonishingly lovely! I am so happy for you, dearest."

Amanda glanced swiftly into Ash's white face. The tension between the earl and his cousin's widow was thick and heavy, pulsating with an emotion that she found herself reluctant to contemplate.

"Have you brought her to meet Grandmama yet?" asked Lianne, her eyes bright and interested.

"The betrothal has not yet been announced," said Ash curtly. "However, Grandmama has been made aware of my intentions, and I intend to bring Amanda to visit her within the next day or two."

"She is such a dear old lady," said Lianne to Amanda, her gaze mischievous. "I know she will love you. And now, my dears, I must leave you. I have promised the next dance to Reggie Smythe-Wolverton. You remember him, do you not, Wi—Ash? Do forgive me," she added with a sad smile. "I cannot accustom myself to calling you that." She shook her head slightly, then said to Amanda, "Do please call on me tomorrow." The roguish sparkle returned to her gaze. "We can have a lovely, comfortable coze. And do not bring W—Ashindon with you, for I mean to tell you all the family secrets." She shot Ash a wicked glance from beneath her thick fringe of lashes and with a silvery laugh moved away.

Ash stared after Lianne, his features rigid and his eyes glittering darkly in his white face.

"Family secrets?" asked Amanda at last, in a tentative tone.

For a long moment he did not answer, but when he finally turned back to her, his gaze was blank. "All families have secrets," he said with what might have been called a smile. "The Wexfords have their share, but I don't suppose they are any worse than most. I trust you were not looking forward to a juicy exposé."

"No," replied Amanda tartly, "but I'm looking forward to discovering more about the Wexfords. For example, this is the first I've heard of Grandmama."

Ash looked startled, and a little ashamed. "Grandmama is the Dowager Countess Ashindon and our matriarch. She is rather— eccentric, and, frankly, I saw no reason to burden you with the ordeal of meeting her until after I had formally asked for your hand."

Good heavens, thought Amanda a little wildly. Was she one of the family secrets? One of those hopeless loonies that used to be kept locked in a garret?

Before she could answer, a gentleman approached to whom Ash turned with a marked expression of relief. "James!" he exclaimed, fairly grasping the man by the elbow. He was tall and thin and rather bookish-looking, with brown hair that fell over his forehead and brown eyes whose depths held a mocking light.

"Miss Bridge," said Ash, "allow me to present James Wincanon, my very good friend and erstwhile comrade-in-arms. We were at Eton together, and later served in the same regiment in the Peninsula."

Mr. Wincanon declared himself extraordinarily pleased to make Miss Bridge's acquaintance. "For," he added a bit stiffly, as though unaccustomed to social conversation, "you are every bit as lovely as Will has said."

Amanda was in no danger of interpreting his words as an overture to flirtation, for they were uttered without a smile, yet with a rather unnerving glint in his gaze.

"You have not met James before," said Ash, "because he cannot usually be pried from the fastness of his place in Lincolnshire. He is something of a scholar, you see, and plods about the countryside searching for Roman antiquities."

"Really!" exclaimed Amanda in delight. "That is an interest of mine. Where are you excavating at present? Perhaps—" She stopped suddenly, aware of Ash's openmouthed gaze. Mr. Wincanon, too, was staring in amazement. "That is . . . " she continued lamely. She took a deep breath and turned in relief as another gentleman, a stranger, solicited her hand for the upcoming dance. Since it appeared to be a waltz, she accepted with alacrity and was soon spinning away from her betrothed and his friend.

"Well, well," said James sardonically. "You did not tell me the beautiful Miss Bridge is a bluestocking."

"But she's not! At least—Good God, James, I find I do not

know my intended in the slightest. She is nothing like the well-brought-up miss with whom I thought I was acquainted."

He stared after Amanda in perplexity.

Amanda had not a clue to her partner's identity, but the gentleman apparently knew Amanda Bridge well, for his conversation was sprinkled with references to persons and events of which she had no knowledge. After one or two near-disastrous responses to his inconsequential chatter she exclaimed in desperation, "But do not let us talk, sir. I wish to lose myself in the dance, for I find the waltz most exhilarating."

Which was not quite true. It must be that the novelty of her newfound strength and agility was wearing off, for this waltz fell far short of the magical experience of dancing with Lord Ashindon. It was pleasant, however, and when it was over she accepted her partner's thanks with a cordial nod.

Amanda made it her priority for the rest of the evening to stay out of trouble, thus she confined her conversation to Serena and those of young Amanda's friends who already knew of her mental fuzziness. She circulated through the Marchfords' public rooms, each more crowded than the last, chatting with what she hoped resembled a practiced ease. It was more than an hour later that Ash approached her again.

"The supper dance is upon us," he remarked lazily. "It appears that the orchestra is settling into a boulanger. Shall we take a turn about the room?"

Wordlessly, Amanda placed her hand on the arm he proffered and, scooping up the train of her gown in a careless gesture that had taken her some hours to perfect, she walked at his side.

"Just what is a supper dance?" she asked at length.

"It is the dance just before supper, of course. Usually, a lady then goes to supper with the gentleman who partners her for the supper dance." He slanted a glance at Amanda. His eyes, thought Amanda, were like a winter sea—cold, yet changeable and sometimes touched with sunlight. "You truly have no memory at all of the infinite social minutiae so critical to what we call civilization."

Amanda laughed. "That's one of those sentences that my stu"—she gulped—"that require dissecting before one can answer." Good Lord, she'd almost blurted out that she was a teacher in her "real life." But was it her real life anymore? Every rational fiber of her being screamed that she could not possibly have traveled through time to take up residence in a Mayfair town house in what was really the last gasp of the eighteenth century, but the alternative options seemed to be dwindling. She shook herself and replied calmly, "But you are right, my lord. I truly have forgotten everything that makes Amanda Bridge who she is. I seem," she added cautiously, "to be another person altogether."

Since her words coincided so precisely with the earl's reflections on the subject, he paused in their peregrinations to look directly at her, startled. She found it hard to meet his gaze and was relieved when a plump heavily jeweled matron strode up to greet the earl.

"Lady Chuffing, how are you this evening?" he responded courteously. He turned to Amanda. "Do you not remember, Miss Bridge, we spoke just a few moments ago of Lady Chuffing's delightful garden party last week. You were saying she served the most marvelous pastries."

"Oh yes!" cried Amanda, taking her cue. "I'm afraid I made a dreadful spectacle of myself, devouring so many."

"Why thank you, my dear," replied her ladyship, condescending so far as to offer her gloved hand to Amanda. "You looked lovely that afternoon, as you do this evening." She leaned forward confidentially. "I suppose I should not mention it"—her cheeks creased in a coquettish smile—"but your mama told me we may look for an interesting announcement soon." Her eyes darted questioningly from the earl to Amanda.

"Oh dear," said Amanda. "I—"

"As to that, my lady," interrupted Ash smoothly, "I'm sure Mrs. Bridge did not wish to imply something that would contribute to the rise of gossip—which I know you abhor."

Lady Chuffing pursed her small mouth in disappointment, but accepted defeat with good grace. After another few moments of chatter, she continued on her way, bestowing a significant smile on the pair as she turned away.

"My," breathed Amanda, "I'm impressed. You skewered her right through the gizzard and she never knew it."

"An acquired skill," he murmured. "Would you care to step

outside? It's very warm tonight, so I think you will not need a shawl."

Indeed, the evening was almost sultry, and several of the ladies, also promenading with their partners on the small terrace that led from the back of the house, plied their fans vigorously. The scent of spring flowers was heavy in the air, and Amanda exclaimed in delight, "One of the things I love about England are the gardens. Even here in the city, flowers can be seen around almost every home."

"It's our country roots, I expect. Many of those who dwell in Mayfair grew up on rural estates. At Ashindon House, in Bruton Street—well, it's someone else's house, now—but the garden was kept meticulously."

Amanda glanced up at him, but his face was closed. Really, she thought, he had the most unrevealing features of any man she'd ever met. He'd make a great poker player. She turned away and moved down the stairs. The gravel on the path bit through her thin slippers and she stepped onto the grass.

"Mmm." She bent to sniff at a small bush covered with tiny, fragrant blossoms. She turned to face the earl, only to find that he had been following her so closely that her nose bumped against the diamond stickpin in his neckcloth. She drew back hastily. "Tell me about your rural estate, my lord. Ashindon Park, is it?"

Ash smiled down at her. He was still rather too close for her peace of mind, she thought, but when she tried to move away, she found she was backed up against the little bush. His nearness was having a most peculiar and not altogether welcome effect on her.

"As I think you know, the Park is in Wiltshire. It was built in the time of Queen Elizabeth, by Henry, the fifth Baron Grantham, later the first earl of Ashindon. It was erected in a plain square, but over the years it has sprawled out in all directions, so that it is more or less a hodgepodge of various styles. I have always thought it beautiful, and it holds many fond memories for me. Perhaps," he concluded unencouragingly, "you would like to visit the Park—after our betrothal is announced. The place is not livable at present, but the dower house is still in reasonably good repair. I leased it to the vicar's cousin last year, but the family will be leaving within a month or two."

"I'd like that," murmured Amanda. Would she still be here in a month or two? She was surprised at the stab of disappointment that shot through her at the thought she might not be. "And Lady Ashindon?" she asked. She did not really want to talk about Lianne, but something about Ash's reaction to the presence of the lovely countess impelled her to ask the question, rather like probing at a sore tooth.

Ash shrugged. "She has recently arrived in London. In the country, she makes her home with her parents, whose estate marches with ours."

"Ah, you've known each other for a long time."

"Almost all our lives." Ash faced her abruptly, and the faint glow of candlelight from the house turned his eyes to molten silver. "She and I were to be married," he said harshly. "Is that what you wanted to know?"

She stared at him searchingly. "Are you still in love with Lianne?" she asked finally in a low voice.

For a long moment, he said nothing. Then, in a sudden movement, he grasped her to him and bent his head. "I shall let you be the judge of that," he growled just before he brought his mouth down on hers.

Chapter Ten

All in all, thought Amanda sipping her chocolate contemplatively the morning after the ball, the evening had been interesting, to say the least. Events surfaced in her mind like dolphins displaying themselves to spectators on a ship. There was the dizzying magic of the waltz with the Earl of Ashindon, the confrontation with her supposed lover, Cosmo Satterleigh, the rather peculiar meeting with the beautiful Lady Ashindon, supper with Ash—and later that shattering kiss.

There had been nothing tender about it. His lips had ground into hers with a brutal ferocity, and his arms had enveloped her so tightly that she struggled for breath. She had been outraged at his tactics, but she had recognized almost immediately the anguish that surged within him. Instinctively, she realized that he was lashing out in pain like a wounded animal. And, if truth be told, something in her responded to the feel of his mouth on hers and the hardness of the body pressed so unrelentingly against hers.

After only a few seconds he had pulled back, an expression of appalled astonishment on his face.

"I—I'm sorry," he rasped. "My God, Amanda, I'm sorry. I don't know—" He had grasped her arm once more and without another word he propelled her back to the house. She had seen almost nothing of him until the end of the evening, and the ride back to Upper Brook Street with Serena and Jeremiah had been silent except for her mother's steady stream of self-congratulatory chatter on Amanda's success. He had left the Bridges at the door with a strained promise to visit later in the week. As he turned to go, he looked at Amanda again as though he would have said more, but he simply bowed and wheeled out into the night.

Amanda took another sip of her chocolate. It was not as though she'd never been kissed before, although Derek had been her last lover. Since then, she had been the recipient of friendly busses from time to time, plus the occasional consolation-seeking embrace from friends who had just broken up with other friends. Even before Derek, her carnal encounters had been few and far between. It took a special sort of man to go beyond deformities of the body to reach the spirit beneath, and that kind, like they said, was hard to find.

Now, she reflected ruefully, even with her new Miss America makeover, she was still being kissed by men who loved somebody else.

For there could be no doubt that Ash was in love with the lovely Lianne. She experienced a forlorn flutter in the pit of her stomach at the thought. What had happened? she wondered. He said they had been betrothed. What had driven them apart? Surely she must have known—what was his name? Grant?—during all her growing-up time. Why had she waited until Ash had declared himself to decide she preferred the cousin? And why, for God's sake, now that Lianne was free, was Ash mooching around Amanda Bridge?

Well, that was a pretty stupid question, wasn't it? Obviously the widow of his impoverished cousin wouldn't have two pennies to rub together, and Ash wanted money very badly. Wanted it more than he did his lost love, apparently.

Amanda found she was gripping the handle on her cup so tightly her knuckles had whitened. She was unwilling to contemplate whether her distress was caused by the thought of Ash's greed or the fact that he was in love with someone besides her own gorgeous self. At the very least, she found the latter thought startling. She had always assumed that it was her flawed face and figure that had driven men away. Perhaps the flaws went deeper. Perhaps it was simply the woman beneath that was unlovable.

My God, there's a cheerful concept to start out the day, she thought grimly. She set her cup and saucer down on the bedside table with great precision and tossed back the coverlet. She had more important things to think of right now. Like how she was to end this whole ludicrous charade. Who knew how much time was elapsing in her own life while she flitted about the social scene in Regency London? Her vacation was slipping away, and in a few days she was due back at work. Her desk would be piled high with reports to grade, her schedule filled with meetings, phone calls, and the other assorted impedimenta of academic life.

Where was Amanda McGovern right now? Lying comatose in a hospital ward somewhere? Dear God! She cried the words silently. She had to do something! She began scrambling frantically into one of the few gowns she possessed that she could don by herself. Having accomplished this, she sank dejectedly onto the little chair before her dressing table. Do what? Listlessly she drew on stockings and shoes, then rose to stare unseeingly out the window at the vendors on the street. She'd spent hours in Grosvenor Chapel, meditating furiously, with no result. She'd kept a constant eye out for the apple-cheeked little old person who was apparently her only connection with her real life, but she—and/or he—had made no more appearances. She'd tried everything but prayer and fasting, and she still awoke every morning in this fussy little bedroom with a cup of grainy hot chocolate set before her. She could have screamed with frustration—and a growing, unnamed fear.

For some moments, she continued her fruitless deliberations until, despite herself, her attention was caught by a youngster juggling apples from his mother's cart. The boy's back was to her, and, though he could not have been more than eight or ten years old, his skill was remarkable. He turned toward her suddenly, revealing diminutive features and a pair of tiny spectacles and—wait a minute. Spectacles on a street urchin? Yes—and cheeks like little pomegranates!

Amanda whirled and ran from the room.

Reaching the street, she expelled a sigh of relief. The kid was still there, bobbing and weaving around the cart as he tossed more and more apples into the air. Flinging herself forward, she grabbed his arm with a breathless, "You! I've got to talk to you!"

"Now looka whatcher done!" exclaimed the boy, scrabbling after the fruit that fell to the ground around them. He turned to Amanda with a cheery smile. "Buy an apple, lady?"

"I don't want any apples," Amanda fairly shrieked. "I have to talk to you!" She grasped his arm once more and shook him. His mother, absorbed in dealing with a customers paid no attention. "You have to tell me," breathed Amanda, quivering in her intensity, "what am I doing here?"

"Doin' 'ere?" The boy looked about. "Why," he answered in a curiously gentle voice, "you lives 'ere, miss."

"That's just the point! I don't live here, as you very well know. Please," she cried. "I must go home. You must tell me how to get back!"

"Oh no," replied the boy, still in that kindly tone, so at variance with his gamin features. "You lives 'ere, miss. There's no 'back' t'go to, doncher see."

"No, I don't see. Don't *you* understand? This is making me crazy!"

The boy broke into a gusty laugh. "You ain't crazy, miss. You're too pretty to be crazy. Ye just gotter take things as they comes, is all. You jist remember where you lives now and ye'll be right as rain."

The boy made to scamper off, but Amanda's grip was still firm on his arm. "Oh, no you don't, you little devil—"

The boy's cheerful laughter rang out again. "Nah—I ain't no devil, miss. Ye got the wrong end of the stick, there."

The next moment, despite her best efforts, the boy had slipped away from her and her last glimpse was of his slight figure nipping around a corner and out of sight. Amanda whirled to the apple woman, who was staring at her in stolid disapproval.

"Please," gasped Amanda. "Your son—I must speak to him. Where do you live?"

"Son?" The woman snorted. "He ain't none o'mine. He's jist one o' them street arabs that pesters the life out o' honest folk like me. Didjer want ter buy an apple, then?"

Wordlessly, Amanda shook her head and, turning, stumbled back to the Bridge house. She was intercepted on the front steps by a worried Hutchings.

"Miss! Goodness, what are you doing out here? Are you all right?"

Amanda's knees were trembling so badly she could hardly stand, but she brushed past the little maid. "I—I'm fine, Hutchings. No," she added as the maid scurried after her up the stairs inside the house. "I need to be alone. I'll be—down presently."

Having gained her room once more, she fell on the bed and lay there motionless for several minutes. Had what just happened really happened? Had she just been instructed by a prepubescent

Munchkin to more or less go with the flow? She felt as though the universe were disintegrating around her.

She sat up slowly. She had asked for guidance, and she had received it. She supposed. Sentence by sentence, she reviewed the conversation with the apple boy. Was she actually to believe that she had really and truly been transferred in time? That she was no longer Amanda McGovern, successful, approaching-middle-age academic, but was now Amanda Bridge, beautiful, pampered, young, and rich? And under the thumb of a tyrannical father, she added, to say nothing of being engaged to a man who was in love with somebody else. How could such a thing be possible?

The obvious answer, of course, was that it was not possible. Yet, here she was. For the past two weeks she had watched events unfold precisely as they would have if she really were a traveler in time, a dweller in someone else's body.

And who, for God's sake, was the person or persons who kept showing up in her life? She moved to the little writing desk near the window, and taking paper and quill in hand, began a systematic catalog of all that had happened to her since she sat down in that shadowed pew in Grosvenor Chapel.

All right, despite her confident pronouncements, her life as Amanda McGovern had not been altogether happy. Deprived of a whole body, she had grown bitter and resentful. She was jealous of friends who loved and were loved in return, yet she was incapable of truly giving of herself. Her success at the university was the one bright spot in her life, and lately even that small happiness seemed to have dimmed. She wanted more.

"Life in 20th c. not great," she wrote.

The old man in the chapel had seemed to understand her unhappiness. He and the old flower woman and the boy at the apple cart were either very closely related or were one and the same person in various guises. Was it—he—she—some sort of supernatural being? Had she been searched out for a purpose?

"Old man in church—agent for change?"

She had been having headaches, and the one that had struck her in the chapel was a real killer.

Wait a minute. Killer?

Amanda Bridge had also been having headaches. Was it possible the two Amandas had been suffering from some sort of terminal awfulness? She had heard of aneurysms striking down people without warning.

Oh, God. Oh, dear God.

Was Amanda McGovern dead? Or, at least, the body in which Amanda McGovern had dwelled for twenty-eight years? Had her mind and spirit been transported to the body of Amanda Bridge, just as that young woman was about to die from the same ailment?

It all made sense.

It made no sense at all. Such a thing was impossible.

Which brought her back to square one.

For the rest of the morning, she pondered her situation, coming to the conclusion at last that her best option would be to carry on as though she, Amanda McGovern, really had been siphoned into the body of a Regency miss. The whole concept seemed ghoulish in the extreme, but she supposed she could get used to the idea eventually.

She had no idea what she was going to do about the Earl of Ashindon. She had nothing against the idea of marriage, but she was not, by God, going to let somebody else select her husband for her, thank you very much. At the earliest opportunity she would turn the impoverished peer loose to find another honey fall. She resolutely squelched the quiver that raced through her insides at the thought. Good grief, at her age she certainly was not about to go all melty over a lean, hard body and a pair of sea-colored eyes that made her toes curl.

Determinedly, she rang for Hutchings and accepted the maid's assistance in turning her out in the most fashionable ensemble in her wardrobe.

At his lodgings in Jermyn Street, Ash was expounding unhappily to James.

"I could not believe it when Lianne launched into a pretty little welcome-to-the-family speech. She actually invited Amanda to tea."

"I'd like to be a fly on the wall during that tête-à-tête." James grinned, his lean body draped across a comfortable chair as he thumbed idly through the latest edition of *Gentleman's Quarterly*.

"She said she planned to tell Amanda all the family secrets," Ash added gloomily.

"Ah, and what secrets might those be?"

"Well, that's just it—we don't have any. Not really, at least."
Ash rose and began a restless perusal of several cards of invitation to various balls and soirees tucked into the mirror above the mantelpiece. A fire burned in the grate, for the day was cloudy and cool. The rooms were comfortable and spacious, furnished with items kept aside at the time of the sale of Ashindon House. Ash turned abruptly to face his friend. "Amanda asked me if I was in love with Lianne."

James lifted one shapely brow. "And are you?"

"Good God, you know I got over her years ago. I've scarcely seen her since she and Grant were married."

"It looks as though you will be seeing a great deal of her now, though," James said meditatively.

"I suppose—but purely in a social context. I do not plan to visit her again."

"I'm pleased to hear you say that, old man, for it would be the devil of a trick to serve on Miss Bridge."

"Of course it would," snapped Ash. "What do you take me for?"

A sardonic gleam flashed in James's expressive eyes. "A man with a problem."

"What problem?" Ash growled. "It's all very simple, really. Lianne is free, but I cannot marry her. I am going to marry, instead, the Brass Bridge's daughter, thus fulfilling my familial duties."

"And Lianne is going to be content with that arrangement?"

"There is no arrangement—at least as far as Lianne is concerned, as I have told her."

"And yet, Lianne usually gets what she wants."

Ash advanced on his friend. "What do you mean by that?"

"At the time she married Grant, your family was still reasonably solvent, wasn't it?"

"Yes."

"And it was Grant, not you, who was to inherit the title."

"By God, James, if you're implying . . . Lianne had no choice, any more than I do now!" Ash's face was white, his fingers clenched into fists.

"No need to cut up stiff, old fellow. I only meant that Lianne may have something more in mind for the two of you than a brother/sister relationship. Particularly if her love for you was as strong as you say. No, no," he concluded with a slow smile at the protest almost visibly forming itself on Ash's lips. "I don't mean to come to cuffs with you." He unfolded his length from the comfortable wing chair in which he had been ensconced. "I must bustle off. I have an appointment with a fellow at the British Museum. Says they've just acquired some Roman artifacts unearthed near Gloucester."

After James had departed, Ash remained standing, pacing the floor abstractedly. He was forced to admit at length that, yes, he did have a problem. Despite the aching joy he had felt at the sight of Lianne, he wished wholeheartedly that she had not elected to return to London. He was determined that he would not allow himself to succumb to the feelings for her that still tore at him, but her proximity would be like living in a garden of poppies for an opium eater.

She had mentioned something about hope for them. Surely, she did not mean . . . The idea slid into his mind, sly as a thief at midnight. Almost every married man of his acquaintance kept a mistress, and many of those women had not been raised to be harlots. Some of them were gently bred, and not a few of them were ostensibly respectable widows. A vision flashed into his mind of Lianne greeting him at the door of a discreet house in, say, Chelsea. She would be dressed only in a filmy peignoir, beneath the folds of which her piquant little body would be almost wholly revealed, her full breasts thrusting toward his touch.

He shook himself suddenly, almost gasping in revulsion. What kind of swine was he, indulging himself in lascivious fantasies? Particularly since the fulfillment of those fantasies would be paid for by the father of the woman he planned to take to his bosom in matrimony. God, how could he even think such a thing? And surely, Lianne would never be a partner to such a despicable liaison.

In addition, even if Lianne's nearness were to drive him into the frenzied madness of passion, he had been truthful with James at least in saying that he would not serve Amanda such a trick. Dammit, he *liked* her. He had not expected to—he was not sure he had even wanted to like her, but he did. She was not the pretty little widgeon he had first thought her. She was a per-

son—a lady, and deserved his regard, even if he could not give
her his love.

He shrugged. Many successful marriages of the *ton* were
launched with less chance of staying afloat. All he had to do was
steer clear of Lianne and continue to treat his betrothed with the
respect due her. That sounded simple enough, didn't it?

With a sigh, he flung himself into a chair and stared at the dry-
ing dregs of wine in the glass from which he had drunk in fellow-
ship with James.

"Miss Bridge! You did come. How delightful!"

Lady Ashindon rose to greet her visitor, and as she moved forward, Amanda felt large and awkward next to her petite loveli-
ness.

"And you have come alone," continued Lianne.

Amanda became aware that she had committed a slight sole-
cism in paying a call without her mother. "You did say you
wished to be private," said Amanda, smiling. "And I am not, after
all, a schoolroom miss." (Really, she was getting quite good at
tossing off these little Regencyisms.)

Lianne uttered a charming tinkle of laughter and settled her
guest in a comfortable chair by the fire. Having ordered tea, she
sank gracefully into a chair nearby.

"I am sorry my aunt is not here to greet you, but she should be
home shortly. I know she will love you—she is the dearest old
thing. Now"—an impish smile curled her lips—"you must Tell
All. How did you and Will—no, Ash—how did you and Ash
meet? Was it love at first sight? Did he spy you from across the
room and lose his heart instantly?"

Amanda's returning smile was less than wholehearted. Despite
Lianne's insouciant manner, Amanda sensed a hint of mockery
behind her words.

"Oh, it was nothing so romantic, I'm afraid," she said, silently
cursing her inane stiffness. She spoke carefully. "Lord Ashindon
was looking for a wife, and a mutual friend introduced him to my
father." Amanda saw no reason to mention that the "friend" was
Ash's solicitor. "When we became acquainted, we decided that
we would suit. Nothing has been announced yet," she added
hastily. "My mother wishes to wait until next week, when we are
giving a ball."

Lianne's green eyes twinkled. "Yes, but that is not what is going to make your betrothal official. Did you not receive an invitation from Grandmama Ashindon to her dinner party, to be held Tuesday next? No? Ah, well, mine came only this afternoon. Yours will no doubt be awaiting you when you arrive home."

"Perhaps," said Amanda carefully, "you should tell me a little about Grandmama Ashindon."

Lianne laughed aloud. "She's three-and-eighty years old. She is small and feeble and frail and the entire family goes in terror of her."

"Why?" asked Amanda, drawing in a startled breath.

"Because there's nothing at all feeble about her mind, and she has a tongue like a whip thong."

"Oh."

"She loathes almost everyone in the family, with the possible exception of Ash, which is something of a mystery, because he is sometimes insufferably rude to her. I'm sure she will like you—if only for Ash's sake."

"Oh."

Amanda cast about in her mind for a subject with which to change the conversation. "Ash tells me you are recently returned to London from your home in Wiltshire."

"Yes, this is my first visit since Grant—passed away."

"I—I'm sorry," said Amanda faintly, wondering how genuinely the widow grieved.

"Don't be," said Lianne with a brave smile. As though she had read Amanda's mind she added, "I am done with grief. I have put off my blacks, and although I shall be in half-mourning for a few more months, I plan to get on with my life."

And the pursuit of the Earl of Ashindon? wondered Amanda uncharitably. "I understand," she said after a moment, "that you and your husband knew each other as children."

"Oh, yes. Grant and Ash and I grew up together. That is, for a while. Grant was two years older than Ash and I—I was much younger than Ash, so Grant seemed quite the sophisticated young man to me."

I don't think so. Amanda's worse side continued to hold sway over her thoughts. From what Ash had said, Lianne was only slightly his junior. The little widow must be inching up on thirty.

"You and Ash were—much attached to each other as children."

Amanda hated herself for the little game she was playing, but she seemed driven to discover how much Lianne and Ash meant to each other.

Lianne sobered. "Has Ash told you nothing of our—relationship?"

"He said that you and he intended to marry. I'm sorry—" Amanda began again, but Lianne lifted her hand as though she could not bear to hear more.

"Yes, it's true." Tears bedewed her thick lashes in crystalline drops. "Even as children we knew we were destined for each other, and when our families conspired to destroy our happiness, it broke my heart." She dropped her gaze to her lap. "I had no choice but to marry Grant. I had a great affection for him, but it was nothing to the love I bore Ash. Ash, too, was devastated." Her voice caught. "We saw each other only a few times after I married Grant, but he came to see me last week—almost immediately after my arrival here. Even after all this time"—she sighed—"our hearts still beat as one. When he k—that is, it took but one look from him to tell me he still—" Lianne looked up suddenly, an expression of alarm in her eyes. "Oh, dear God, I cannot imagine what came over me to speak so. I should not be saying these things, but I feel you have a sympathetic heart."

Despite her tendency toward the purple in her speech, Lianne's anguish seemed genuine. "No," replied Amanda gently. "I appreciate your confidence, for I wish to hear the truth—if it is not too painful for you."

Lianne sighed. "My family is of the gentry, so to speak, my father being the third son of a lord, but he thought the marriage of his daughter to an earl would be of great advantage. He knew Grant's inheritance would be relatively meager, however the title is old and prestigious, as was the estate that went with it. The Park at that time was one of the largest estates in the country, though it had not been well managed. Father thought that, under his guidance, Grant would bring the place back to its former prosperity. Things did not work out that way," she concluded dryly.

"Ash told me," said Amanda hesitantly, "that Grant was something of a . . . spendthrift."

"He was—and not 'something of.' He was an out and out wastrel, and even if he had been inclined to listen to Father, he was never home long enough to do so. He spent most of his time in London."

"But he—he died at home?"

"Not exactly at home," replied Lianne bitterly. "He peltered down to Wiltshire on one of his periodic repairing leases and on his first night back rode over to The Barking Dog, a disreputable ale house in the village. He drank and gambled there, and fell into a dispute with John Binter, a local farmer. Grant was so drunk he could hardly stand when he and Binter went outside to settle their differences. Binter felled him with one blow. Grant hit his head on the edge of a watering trough and died instantly."

"Dear God," breathed Amanda.

An awkward silence fell in the small salon at the back of Lady Ashindon's house, and Amanda was vastly relieved when Lianne rose to greet an older woman who entered the room.

"Aunt Biddy! You have finished your errands? Excellent, for you are just in time to meet Ash's betrothed—or, at least, almost betrothed." She shot an apologetic glance at Amanda. "Miss Bridge, this is Miss Beatrix Bonner, my father's sister. She was good enough to leave her pursuits in the country to act as my companion."

Amanda dropped an uncertain curtsy and Miss Bonner nodded regally. The nickname bestowed upon her by her niece was, thought Amanda, singularly appropriate, for she was the very personification of a Regency "ape leader," and looked like a well-bred, but cantankerous horse. She seated herself in a satin-covered chair near her niece and accepted a cup of tea from her.

"Miss Bridge," said Lianne with a slight tremor in her voice, "was just going to tell me about her family."

"Er," said Amanda. "Yes. My father—"

"Yes," interposed Miss Bonner. "I have heard of him. Jeremiah Bridge." She sniffed. "He is a wool merchant, is he not?"

Amanda knew a spurt of irritation at such blatant snobbery, but she answered calmly. "Yes, among other things. My mother—"

"Yes, I remember Serena Blythe. Such a to-do when she married your father."

"So I understand," replied Amanda through clenched teeth. Good grief, if Lianne considered her aunt to be "the dearest old thing," what must Grandmama Ashindon be like?

After another fifteen minutes or so of conversation, during which Miss Bonner oozed genteel venom all over Lianne's parlor, Amanda made her escape. With expressions of pleasure at the opportunity to converse with the countess and to meet her delightful aunt, and a declaration that she would be counting the days until the dinner party at the home of the dowager countess, Amanda fled the house and flung herself into the haven of the Bridge town carriage.

On the way home, she contemplated all that she had learned in her conversation with the widowed countess. It was obvious that Lianne and Ash were still deeply in love. Silently, she renewed her determination not to continue in her empty betrothal to Ash. She still could not understand how Ash could deny his love for Lianne merely to seek an advantageous marriage for himself. He simply did not seem the type. Ah well, she thought wisely, if a bit dispiritedly, the call of the almighty dollar—or in this case, pound—was often loud enough to drown out the sound of a man's conscience.

She looked out the carriage window and saw, to her relief, that she had arrived home. Odd, she was having less and less difficulty in referring thus to the house in Upper Brook Street. She could never think of Jeremiah and Serena Bridge as her parents, but she felt, somewhat to her dismay, that she was beginning to put down roots here among the alien corn.

Chapter Eleven

Amanda entered the house to discover Ash standing in the entrance hall. Jeremiah had evidently come out of his study to greet him. "Ah, Amanda, we have a visitor." He rubbed his hands briskly. "What can I do for you, my lord? Have you come to discuss the marriage settlements?"

Ash's face stiffened for a moment before his lips curved into a pleasant smile. "Actually," he said, "I have come to instruct your daughter in the performance of one or two country dances."

Jeremiah's jaw dropped open unbecomingly.

"I have quite forgotten how to do them, Papa," said Amanda hastily. "My—unfortunate accident, you know."

Jeremiah glowered suspiciously but was seemingly unable either to find a reason for Amanda's lying about such a thing, or to fault her proposal to spend an unexceptional hour with her betrothed in a genteel pastime under her papa's roof. Throwing his hands over his head, he stamped out of the room.

"Perhaps we ought to start with a reel," said Ash a few minutes later as they entered the music room. "This is going to be somewhat difficult," he continued, "without the presence of several more dancers, but we will make do. Can you hum?"

Amanda searched his face, but there was nothing there that spoke of a kiss shared in a scented garden. She suppressed a stab of disappointment. "Hmmmmmmm—mm-mmm—hmmm," she thrummed uncertainly, phasing after a moment into the only reel song she could think of, *The Irish Washerwoman*.

"Ah," said Ash. "Very good. Now, take your place opposite me at the head of these two lines of dancers." Raising his arm, he swept an arc toward an imaginary grouping. "We are now the first couple. Now, come toward me—no, don't stop humming—move in a hop, and we change places, thus." He advanced on her in a step that she remembered from elementary school gym classes. "And move past me, and—change places. All the other couples in the lines will have done the same thing. Now, we repeat the process, only instead of changing places we will meet in the middle, cross hands, and promenade down the line of dancers. We will separate and circle around the last couple in each line and promenade back to our original places. Ready? Don't forget to step in time."

Amanda almost giggled aloud, for the words struck her as bizarrely humorous. That's what she had been doing for the past two weeks—stepping in a time that was not her own, to a rhythm that was unfamiliar and frightening. She hadn't done too badly, though, and if she could only remember to keep stepping in time, she might eventually adjust to this new rhythm. She laughed inwardly at her absurd philosophizing.

Amanda found she was able to complete the steps indicated with little difficulty, and again she reveled in the sureness and facility of her legs. As she had in the waltz at the ball, she became exhilarated with the sense of motion and her joy in her own body. She hummed faster and fairly threw herself into the rhythm of the dance until Ash called a laughing halt.

"How was that?" asked Amanda breathlessly. "Did I do well enough to dance in public, should anyone ask me to join in a reel?"

"My dear young woman," he said with mock severity, "if you persist in tossing your skirts up in such a disgraceful manner, you will certainly not lack for partners."

She giggled, and an unexpected wave of tenderness swept over Ash. With her golden hair tumbling about her face, her cheeks flushed and her eyes sparkling like sunlight on the sea, he felt that the very spirit of the music was smiling up at him.

He took her hand, wanting very badly to pull her toward him so that he could bury his face in that scented tangle of curls. He shook himself. Lord, had he learned nothing from that scene in the Marchford garden? What had possessed him to kiss Amanda Bridge in that fashion—or in any fashion at all? He had been, he realized, intent on punishing her for her impudence in prying into his affairs. And punishing himself, if he was to be truthful, for his continuing illicit feelings for Lianne. The moment his lips tasted

Amanda's, however, all coherent thought had fled, and he found himself lost in her warmth and softness. Her pliant body seemed made to fit against him and in that instant he wanted so much more from her than a kiss. It had taken everything in him to draw away from her and to lead her back to the house.

Dazedly, he returned to the present, and with a conscious act of will detailed in a cool voice the instructions for the quadrille.

"Yes, that's it," he said finally, after a half an hour of intensive instruction. "Just remember to point your toe, thus, on the *jeté* and keep in mind that you must lift your arms, so, when you *chasse*."

"Good grief!" exclaimed Amanda, sinking down on the piano bench. "I always wondered how Regency heroines managed to keep their shapes with the amount of food they were confronted with every day. Now I know. Country dancing beats aerobics all hollow."

"Aerobics? Is that yet another new dance craze? One can hardly keep up with them. Last week, I was severely chastised by a young woman because I could not perform the figures of something called the mazurka, which seems to me to be nothing more than a glorified quadrille."

Amanda smiled but did not respond, turning instead to face the keyboard. She lifted her hands and began the slow strains of the Brahms Waltz in A major. Ash seated himself next to her and Amanda was immediately conscious of the slight pressure of his thigh and hip against her. Good grief! she thought irritably, she was being absolutely ridiculous. She came from a time when men and women found themselves in close proximity in even the most innocent of social situations—sports, riding in elevators and crowded trains, cocktail parties. Yet she had never experienced the jolt of sensation that swept over her every time this cold, saturnine aristocrat so much as bowed over her hand. Even Derek's touch had brought no more than a lovely warmth and a sense of belonging.

"That's beautiful," said Ash, his voice husky. "What is it?"

"It—it's by Brahms." Oh, no, Amanda thought, dismayed. Johannes Brahms had not even been born. "He's not very well known as yet."

"Ah. Well, I predict an illustrious future for him. I had no idea," he continued, lightly brushing her fingers with his own, "that you were so accomplished on the piano."

Amanda shivered. "Not as much as I'd like to be. You'd think I'd be a regular virtuoso after—" She stopped abruptly. She had almost said "after fifteen years of lessons." She took a deep breath. "After practicing so industriously as a child," she finished, instead.

"Play something else," commanded Ash. "Something with a little more élan."

Without giving herself a chance to think, Amanda launched into "The Entertainer" and continued with excerpts from a few more Scott Joplin rags. She noticed that the earl's foot tapped vigorously in time to the rollicking music.

"That was—extraordinary," he said when she had finished.

"Did you like it?"

"I—I don't know. I've never heard anything like it."

Nor will you ever again, thought Amanda, at least, not in this life.

"Where did you learn it?" continued Ash.

"I—I must have heard the tune from a street musician," Amanda replied hastily. Ash bent a strange look on her, but said nothing.

Amanda let her hands drift over the keys in a nameless melody, and for a while a comfortable silence fell in the music room. Coming to a decision, she dropped her hands suddenly and turned to face Ash. This movement brought her face into such close proximity with the earl's that she rose quickly.

"My lord," she began. "That is, Ash . . . "

"Yes?" he said encouragingly.

"Ash, I have come to the conclusion that our betrothal is a colossal mistake."

"What?" Ash's brows snapped together and the warmth that had been in his expression was replaced by an arctic fury.

"You're a very nice man, I suppose—No," Amanda said hastily. "What I mean is, you don't love me and I don't love you."

He stood to tower over her. "Please correct me if I'm wrong, Miss Bridge, but I believe that love formed no part of our agreement. Are you reneging?"

"No, of course not. Well, yes I am—in a manner of speaking. The thing is, when I entered into our bargain, I did not realize you were in love with someone else."

A dark flush stained the earl's carved cheeks. "I don't know what you're talking about." He spoke the words in such a low growl that she could barely distinguish them.

"Please, Ash, if nothing else, let us be honest with one another. It is obvious to me that you are in love with Lianne—that you and she have loved each other for years. Please, believe me," said Amanda, lifting her hand as Ash's mouth opened in protest, "I find your situation touching and very sad, and I am certainly not going to come between two people who belong with each other."

Ash rose from the piano bench and faced her directly. She had never seen a human being look so angry. His black eyes fairly spat venom and the power controlled in his rigid stance was almost frightening. Almost, hell. She was quaking in the absurd silk creations that passed for her shoes.

His voice, when he spoke, was quiet and menacing.

"My personal life is of no concern to you, Miss Bridge. My offer for your hand did not include permission to delve into the most intimate details of my existence. My feelings for the Countess of Ashindon are not for your intrusive scrutiny."

His gaze pierced her until she felt like a moth pinned to a board. "Please," she gasped. "I did not mean—I didn't think—"

"Of course, you did not think," he said contemptuously. "You were merely amusing yourself with a tale of love lost and hearts sundered. When, in your short, pampered life, have you ever truly considered the distress of another? If you had, you would not make a mockery of it in your mindless efforts to insert yourself into a situation that has nothing to do with you. Now, listen to me carefully. I have offered for you, and I have shaken hands with your father. The arrangements have been agreed upon. I am going to marry you and you are going to marry me, no matter what our feelings are on the subject. I am marrying you for your money, Miss Bridge," he said cruelly, "or, had you forgotten that you gave your girlish promise to a fortune hunter?"

Amanda stared at him, wide-eyed. A number of scathing retorts sprang to her lips, but the anguish that had prompted his outburst was too genuine and too near the surface for her to dispute just now the injustice of his words. Instead, she drew a deep breath and said coolly, "Well, I seem to have hit a nerve, haven't I?"

"What!" he said again in a voice like thunder, and Amanda watched as surprise, outrage, and indignation battled across his features.

"Please, just hear me out, Ash. I truly do not wish to pry into your private affairs, but you must admit that your being in love with another woman sort of impinges on my private affairs, too. I am merely saying that perhaps, if we mull things over, we might come up with another solution."

All the while she was talking, she was uncomfortably aware of the twinge skittering through her at the thought of Ash's devotion to someone else, and with some annoyance she thrust the idea to the back of her mind.

Ash was still visibly simmering. "Do you think," he asked, his tone bristling with sarcasm, "that I did not spare a thought or two to other options before I offered for you?"

"Yes, but as you pointed out, I am rich and you are not. If I could somehow provide you with funds on my own, perhaps—"

"Oh, my God! Spare me your simpering expressions of charity. Do you think I can repair the Park on your pin money? Do you plan to give my sister her Season and my brother his law education on your winnings at silver loo?"

Amanda simply gaped at him. "Is *that* what you want the money for?" she asked in stupefaction.

Caught off stride, Ash returned her stare. "Of course it is. What did you think I was planning to do with it?"

"Uh—I guess I thought you wanted some ready cash for all the usual Regency rake stuff—gambling, wining and dining, women . . . "

To her surprise, Ash's answering laughter was genuine. "You really are the most extraordinary female," he said at last. "Have you no idea of the requirements of my position?"

Dumbly, Amanda shook her head.

"To begin with, there are approximately four hundred souls living at the Park who depend on me for their livelihood—field laborers and their families, the house staff, etcetera. Even the vicar and his wife and children, for I am responsible for the upkeep of the church. I own several other estates, as well, all of which are in worse shape than the Park. There used to be more, but everything that was not entailed was sold off years ago.

"The house at the Park is heavily mortgaged and, but for your father's largesse, I should have lost it to the Crown by now. Oh yes, he has already started on the payments he agreed to in the marriage settlements. A very generous fellow, your papa, not to wait until the thing was signed, sealed, and delivered."

"And your brother and sister?" whispered Amanda, horrified.

"As I think I told you, they were raised at the Park with me, but recently I have had to move Dorothea to the home of our Aunt and Uncle Breverton in Gloucester. They are an older couple and not well circumstanced. They have been all that is kind to Dorothea, but her presence presents a financial burden to them. Andrew is in the City, studying Law. He has a small inheritance of his own from a distant uncle that is barely keeping a roof over his head, and meals. He augments this income by working in the office of one of the barristers in Lincoln's Inn Fields."

"Dear Lord," said Amanda, once more sinking onto the piano bench. "I had no idea."

"It is probable, then," Ash replied austerely, "that you also have no concept of what I owe to the family name."

She stared at him uncomprehendingly.

"Quite. The Ashindon title dates back to the time of the Tudors, and this means a great deal to my family—all the uncles, aunts, and cousins. My Grandmama Ashindon has been at me to marry since I acceded to the title, because my primary function in her eyes is to beget an heir. She repeats 'The line must continue' to me like a litany every time we are together. So, you see, Miss Bridge, it is not simply all your lovely money that I'm after."

"Oh. Oh-hh," Amanda said again as the implications of this statement sank in. A mental image of the earl's lean body above hers, naked in a candlelit bedroom, flashed through her mind and she could feel herself blushing. She shook herself. She was not an ignorant virgin, after all. Well, yes, she supposed she was a virgin, for surely the young Amanda was unsullied, (She uttered a silent, hysterical giggle. Who says you can't get it back?) but since she had no intention of marrying this man, her maidenly trepidation was absurd. Besides, she knew very well his lordship would much rather be doing his begetting with his cousin's beautiful widow.

"Well, all right, then," she said after a thoughtful pause. "You say my father has agreed to hand over a lot of money to you. How much will he be giving you before the actual ceremony?"

"What—?" Ash drew a long breath. "This is not a matter that concerns you, but he has agreed to pay off the mortgage immediately. He will also provide the wherewithal to begin repairs on the

Park so that by the time I bring my new bride through its portals it will be fit to live in."

"I see. Well, that sounds as though it will bring in quite a chunk of change right there. I should think all we have to do—"

"You really have acquired the most peculiar phraseology," interrupted Ash irritably. "Yes, I know," he finished in unison with Amanda. "Your bump on the head. What was it you were saying? Not that any of it makes sense."

Amanda breathed a small sigh of relief. At least he was speaking to her in tones of reasonable civility. "I should think," she continued patiently, "that all we need to do is milk Papa to the max over the next few months. From what Serena has said, I can get thousands of pounds just for clothes—and there's the wedding trip."

"What the devil—?" began Ash in angry puzzlement.

"A few weeks before the wedding date," Amanda continued as though he hadn't spoken, "we can just call the whole thing off. By then you should have enough to solve your immediate cash flow problems, don't you think?" She smiled brightly, anticipating his ready agreement to such an eminently sensible plan.

Instead, Ash's glare increased in intensity so that she felt she was in danger of melting around the edges.

"I think," he rasped, "that knock on your head permanently damaged your powers of reason. Even if such a course of action were not despicable—which it is—and even if it were to solve my problems—which it would not—your papa would be within his rights to sue me for breach of promise—which he undoubtedly would."

"Oh," said Amanda, undaunted. "But how about if I call it off instead of you?"

Ash, who had been pacing the carpet, whirled to face her.

"Have you any idea what the repercussions would be of such a move?"

"Mm, I suppose Papa would not be happy, but—"

"That is the understatement of the century. Your father wants this union very badly, and when men of his stamp are thwarted in what they want very badly, they tend to get very ugly. I expect at the very least you would be sent to the country to live on bread and water for an extended length of time."

"If that's all—"

"In addition, it would be years before you could show your face in London again. The tabbies would have a field day with you, and I would be made to look ridiculous. Not that that matters to me, but—"

"Oh, dear, I hadn't thought of that."

"Of course, you had not." He grasped both her shoulders and shook her ungently. "You may as well resign yourself to the fact of this betrothal, Miss Bridge. Whether you—or I—like it or not, we will marry, and you will have to make the best of it—as I intend to do."

He released her so suddenly she almost toppled backward and, turning, he left the room without another word. In a few moments, she heard the slamming of the front door.

Well hell, that had not gone at all as she planned. She shrugged. She would just have to confront him once more, the next time he came to the house. She was not about to allow herself to be trapped in a loveless marriage, particularly with a man who was besotted with somebody else, and so she would tell him. Sooner or later, he would realize that she was not going to marry him, and this being the case, the earl might as well reap the benefit of her refusal.

Amanda reflected in some dismay on Ash's words pertaining to her own money. She had not considered the matter before, but it was apparent that she was totally dependent on Jeremiah Bridge for every facet of her existence. Women in these days, as a general rule, had nothing of their own. Every move they made was at the discretion of the men in their lives. Dear God, what was to become of her? How could she bear to be "cabin'd crib'd and confin'd," as Shakespeare put it, for the rest of her life? Her years in the twentieth century had conditioned her to a freedom of movement that was unheard of here. She simply could not sit in her father's or her husband's drawing room and occupy herself with embroidery, while outside a fascinating world was going about its business.

Jeremiah seemed determined that his offspring bring him the social acceptance he craved so badly. Would he cut his recalcitrant daughter off without a penny when she ultimately refused to marry the impoverished earl? How would she earn her own way in this alien environment? She smiled sourly. If only she had known she was about to find herself in this situation, she would have boned up on her Regency minutia. It would be a very handy thing to know right now who would be the winners of upcoming prizefights, or parliamentary elections. She could make a small fortune at the track—provided she could find a way to circumvent the absurd restrictions on female activity currently in vogue.

Her academic skills would certainly be of no use to her here—unless, perhaps she could hire on in one of the ladies' seminaries that seemed to dot the Regency landscape. But no, a knowledge of literature was not required of young ladies of the *ton*. Perhaps she could teach music, although except for the piano, her expertise in that field was limited.

Well, she was a raving beauty. Perhaps a career on the stage. Mmm. Her experience in "the theatah" was limited to a performance as Tiny Tim in the fourth grade, but with a little luck and a lot of chutzpah, maybe—

She brought her hands down on the keys with a discordant jangle. This was getting her nowhere. What she really needed to do was find a way to get back to her own time. Despite the advantages of a whole beautiful body and the bloom of youth, she did not belong here. Her former life had not been wholly satisfactory, but she had carved a niche for herself there. She had acquired the security of a good career, and she enjoyed her work. There would be no Lord Ashindon in 1996. The thought flashed, unwanted, in her mind, and she was obliged to suppress very firmly the pang she experienced as a result. Good grief, dark-haired earls with eyes like a winter sea had no place in her life. No, there was no question in her mind that she wished to live out her life in her own time.

Now then, if her earlier calculations were correct, her former self was six feet under by now, but if who or whatever was responsible for bringing her here had such a facility with time, surely she could be brought back to her own century in time to fix her aneurysm or whatever it was that had done her in.

She shook her head. This was really confusing. If only she could connect up again with the person in the spectacles. If she did encounter him/her, she would grab hold and not let go until she got some answers.

Why in the world, she wondered, had Ash been so upset at the idea of getting as much money as possible out of Jeremiah before the big breakup. The old foof had plenty and it might as well be put to some use besides gratifying his own selfish wishes.

With this laudable thought in mind, she went up to her bedchamber for a thorough perusal of her jewel box.

Chapter Twelve

In the days following her instructive self-confrontation, Amanda endeavored to confine her activities to those befitting a proper Regency miss. She paid morning visits with Serena, she practiced her stitchery, for which she discovered she had absolutely no aptitude, and, under her mother's tutorial eye, poured over volumes of *The Lady's Magazine* and *La Belle Assemblée*, choosing bride clothes. She found herself in Serena's black books only once when she went jogging early one morning in Hyde Park. It was her lack of anything resembling proper footwear, however, rather than her mama's strictures that prevented a repetition of this activity.

Lord Ashindon did not come near the house in Upper Brook Street, and by the end of the week Amanda was in a state of boredom bordering on the frantic. When the day arrived of the dinner party at Grandmama Ashindon's, she welcomed it almost with relief.

The earl was to collect his betrothed and his future in-laws shortly before the whole party was expected at Lady Ashindon's, and in her bedchamber Amanda fretted and jittered as Hutchings performed her tasks.

"Now, miss," said the maid, "if you do not hold still, you're going to look as though you were pulled into this gown backward. And it is so lovely, you will not wish to ruin the effect."

Indeed, thought Amanda gazing once more in bewildered awe at her reflection in the mirror, Serena had outdone herself, for the gown was her mama's choice. It was gold satin, of a shade that almost exactly matched her hair, and it fell in heavy folds to her feet. Atop drifted a tunic of palest gauze, embroidered with gold acorns, and with it she wore a topaz necklace that gleamed richly

against the creamy smoothness of her skin. Hutchings had
foresworn the usual curls this evening, instead sweeping
Amanda's hair into an old-fashioned polished coil that lay smooth
as taffy on her neck. A few tendrils escaped to frame her face in a
tantalizing filigree. Amanda longed for a camera to capture this
fleeting moment of beauty that would vanish like the golden glory
of a dawn sky should she ever manage to assume her own shape
in her own time.

She was alone in the drawing room when Ash made his appearance, and his gray eyes darkened to the shade of embers shot
through with lingering traces of fire.

He said nothing, but bowed over her hand, his lips brushing her
fingertips with a sensuous warmth that she felt down to her toes.
She was breathless, suddenly, and welcomed the bustling entrance of Serena a moment later, followed by Jeremiah.

Her father immediately instituted a machine gun burst of conversation, and Amanda realized with some surprise that he was
nervous.

"Evening, Ashindon. Fine evening, eh? Well, don't you look
pretty as paint, Amanda? I reckon her ladyship will welcome you
with open arms tonight. Don't you think, my lord?" He plowed
ahead without waiting for an answer. "Of course, my Serena is
well acquainted with many of the nobs who will be at your grandmama's house tonight. Her grandfather was the Earl of Brashing,
you know. Will you take a glass of Bordeaux, Ashindon? It's a
LaFitte, and prime stuff, I assure you."

This, however, the earl declined with suitable expressions of
regret, remarking that Lady Ashindon was expecting them
shortly.

"And if there's anything that sets Grandmama's back up it's
tardiness," he concluded.

Amanda glanced at her father, but the expected heightening of
color and belligerent stance did not appear. Instead, Jeremiah
ceased all conversation, bellowed for Serena, who appeared at his
side just as he opened his mouth, and bustled his family anxiously
into the hall, calling for outer garments and the carriage, which
was already waiting at the curb.

The Dowager Countess of Ashindon resided in one of the
smaller domiciles of Grosvenor Square. "The old girl may have
been forced to economy," Ash whispered to his betrothed, "but

she says she's damned if she will live in some shabby-genteel neighborhood in the wilds of Knightsbridge or Kensington."

The little party was greeted at the door by a butler of such supercilious mien that Amanda could be forgiven her initial assumption that he must be a visiting duke who happened at the moment to be passing through the entrance hall. A liveried footman escorted them up the elegant, curved staircase to the drawing room above. The servant announced their presence in stentorian tones and Amanda found herself almost flinching as a phalanx of quizzing glasses and lorgnettes were raised to catch the glitter of candlelight.

"Come in, come in," called a clear voice from the center of the group. "Don't just stand there gawping." Amanda focused on a small figure swathed in black and seated in a large wing chair. Her snow white hair was swept into an imposing coiffure and topped with a feathered turban, and round her thin neck twined several feet of jewel-encrusted gold chains. Her feet, which would not have reached the ground, rested on a tapestry footstool and a glimpse of frivolous satin slippers peeked from beneath her heavy bombazine skirts.

Slipping a hand beneath Amanda's elbow, Ash drew her toward this absurdly august presence and Serena and Jeremiah followed in meek procession.

"Grandmama," Ash said easily, "may I present Mr. and Mrs. Jeremiah Bridge and their daughter, Miss Bridge."

"Yes, yes." The dowager waved her hand impatiently. "I know who they are." She fixed Serena with a glittering stare. "I remember you. Polly Marshfield's gel, ain't you? Married to disoblige your family, didn'tcher?" She swung her glare to Jeremiah. "And look how it all turned out." Her grimace erased any doubt as to the inference that might be drawn from this statement, and Serena wilted perceptibly.

Once more, Amanda waited for the explosion that should have resulted. Jeremiah's heavy jowls reddened, but he said jovially, "Pleased to make your acquaintance, your ladyship." In the awkward silence that followed, he looked about him and rubbed his hands. "Nice place you have here—everything bang up to the echo."

Amanda cringed inwardly and Lady Ashindon sniffed. "How would you know?" she asked baldly, and before Jeremiah could respond, turned her attention to Amanda. "Come forward, gel," she ordered. "Let me look at you."

Amanda felt she should extend her arms and turn slowly about, but she stood motionless, her gaze calm as the dowager's snapping black eyes surveyed her from head to toe.

"Mmf." The countess sniffed again. "Never did care for simpering misses with yaller curls."

"That's unfortunate," replied Amanda, smiling. "For there's not much I can do about the yellow hair. However, I try to keep my simpering to a minimum."

A collective gasp rose from those gathered around the dowager, whose eyes gleamed with the light of battle. Once more her gaze traveled the length of Amanda's form. "You need more meat on your bones. I greatly deplore the tendency of our modern misses to starve themselves for fashion. Look at those hips. Too narrow by half for breeding."

An explosive, embarrassed giggle escaped from a tall woman who stood at the dowager's side.

"Do you think so?" asked Amanda reflectively, her gaze surveying the old lady in turn. "You seem a bit on the scant side yourself, my lady, but I understand you presented your husband with—what was it?—eight children?"

The group shuddered as one and all eyes turned toward the dowager, who uttered a sharp bark of what might have been laughter. She leveled her jeweled lorgnette at Amanda's décolletage. "At least, you'll be able to suckle your young 'uns by the looks of those bubbies."

At this, a gurgle of vocal embarrassment rippled through those gathered behind the dowager, and Amanda felt Ash's fingers tighten on her arm. She had earlier, in the privacy of her bedchamber, protested at the expanse of bosom displayed by the gold satin gown, and knew she was blushing at the old woman's outrageous remark. Nevertheless, she straightened—thereby emphasizing her mammary capabilities even further—and looked the dowager in the eye.

"Why, thank you, my lady. It is always reassuring to be told that one is well fitted for what must surely be a woman's primary purpose in life."

She heard Ash's indrawn breath and felt the amusement that shook him silently. The dowager bent a sharp look on her guest and expelled another gust of laughter. "Well," she wheezed, "at least you ain't one of those niminy-piminy milk-and-water misses." She turned and glared at her nearest and dearest, still assembled behind her. "Come forward and introduce yourselves instead of herding together like a pack of sheep. Emmie, stop that insane giggling and introduce yourself."

The tall woman, who was by now crimson-cheeked, stepped forward, her hand outstretched. "I am Emily Wexford." She smiled hesitantly. "I am Ash's aunt. I live with Grandmama as her companion." She ignored the audible snort that issued from the old lady. "And this," said the woman, turning to the person on her right, "is Ash's cousin, James Brinkeley, who is married to my niece, Hortense."

The rest came forward then, and the next few minutes became a blur of assorted aunts, uncles, cousins, and a few friends, who all expressed themselves delighted to welcome dear Miss Bridge, and of course, her mama and papa into the family.

Their delight, thought Amanda, seemed more than easily restrained, for their greetings to the Bridges were blatantly condescending. Next to her, she felt Ash stiffen, and she smiled her most brilliant smile at the gentleman bowing over her hand.

"Lord Meecham, so nice to meet you. And Lady Meecham, you are the daughter of whom? Ah, I see, another cousin. Yes, indeed, I had no idea that Ash's family was so large."

In the background, Serena twittered determinedly and Jeremiah, for once at a loss for words, loomed at her side, silent and distressed.

"Bravo, Amanda!" said a familiar voice in her ear, and Amanda turned to behold the younger of the two countesses of Ashindon. Her gown of soft gray silk embroidered in silver brought out the emerald splendor of her eyes. "I don't believe Grandmama has absorbed such a set-down since she tried to out-insult the Tsar's sister last summer at the Peace celebrations."

"Oh," said Amanda, startled. "I did not mean—"

"Of course not," interposed Ash easily. "Grandmama was merely testing your mettle. She will ride roughshod over anyone who allows it, but she loathes those she can bully. I believe you can consider yourself vetted, my dear," he said to Amanda, and on hearing the laughter in his voice she looked at him quickly to see it reflected in his cloud-colored eyes.

Lianne's glance flickered between them and she said rather pettishly, "Well, we all know you can twist Grandmama about your little finger, Ash. How nice that your bride will be able to do the same thing. Oh, there is Melissa waving at me. Melissa Wexford," she said to Amanda. "Cousin George's wife. I have not spoken with her for this age."

Her smile, as she hurried away with a waggle of her fingers, seemed a little strained to Amanda and she turned to Ash.

"I think talk of twisting about fingers is a little premature. Your grandmama did not actually bite me, but I hardly think she considers me granddaughter-in-law material."

Amanda thought she saw a hint of admiration in Ash's returning smile. "You spoke up to her and lived to tell about it. Believe me, the fact that she did not bite you bodes extremely well for your future relationship with her."

After that, there was little chance for private conversation with her betrothed, for they found themselves virtually surrounded by curious relatives until the butler entered to announce majestically that dinner was served.

Jeremiah had been placed on the dowager's right, and it became immediately obvious that he and her ladyship had not hit it off. She flayed him with stilettolike barbs and slashing insults until Amanda fully expected him to start dripping blood all over the pristine table cover. She had no love for the bully who was her father, but she watched, sickened, as he simply clamped his jaws shut and bowed his massive head under the onslaught. Next to him, Serena sat silently, her face screwed into an expression of pained helplessness.

Ash sat on the matriarch's left and joined with Amanda in an effort to divert his grandmother from her malicious pleasures.

"I have spent a pleasant week, Grandmama, in instructing Amanda in country dancing."

"Instructing!" exclaimed the countess. "Good God, gel, don't you know how to dance?"

"Of course, she does," said Ash hastily, looking as though he wished he had chosen another subject. "I told you of her recent, ah, accident and her subsequent loss of memory. She recalls the waltz, but—"

"Is that what they're calling it?" asked the old lady with a great show of indignation. "In my day we had another name for it. If

you ask me, carrying on in such a manner in plain view of everyone else in the room is nothing short of—well, enough said. I
don't know what's happened to old-fashioned decency these days.
I hear they're even doing it at Almack's."

"I would not know about that," said Amanda, serenely cutting
her fricando of veal. "I have never been inside Almack's."

"Eh?" The dowager's voice cracked in surprise. "Do you mean
to—"

"The thing is," interposed Serena nervously. "We—Amanda
has not—as yet—received vouchers."

"Ump," growled the old lady. "Patronesses snubbing you, are
they? Spiteful cats." She glared at Jeremiah, placing the blame for
this circumstance clearly where it belonged. "Well," she continued at length, "we shall see what we shall see. I have chosen to
retire from the social scene, but I believe I am not quite without
influence."

Amanda thought privately that the dowager could probably
topple governments if she were so inclined. Serena perked up
considerably at her words and beamed impartially upon the countess, her husband, her daughter, and her future son-in-law.

By the end of the meal, it had become apparent to all those
present that the dowager countess of Ashindon had decided to ap-
prove of Amanda, and the atmosphere warmed noticeably.

After dinner, when the gentlemen had joined the ladies in the
drawing room, the assembly was treated to musical performances
by various of the attendant females. Cousin Susan Wellbeloved
played two selections on the pianoforte, and Aunt Jane Wexford
produced a lengthy étude on the harp. Aunt Melissa Gentry sang
several country ballads in a sweet soprano.

"Grandmama," said Ash at length, "perhaps you could prevail
upon Miss Bridge to play for us. She is truly a gifted pianist."

To her surprise, neither Serena nor Jeremiah demurred, her
mother only lifting her brows a little. "Have you anything prepared, dearest?" she whispered across Ash. Amanda experienced
a small start at this evidence that young Amanda must have possessed a musical talent, and she nodded uncertainly.

"Let's hear you, gel," said the dowager autocratically, and
smiling with a confidence that was belied by the trembling of her
fingers, Amanda rose to take a seat at the rosewood piano.

She began with a short series of Hayden variations, and having accomplished this without mishap, followed it with Mozart's Turkish Rondo. She was greeted by such an enthusiastic burst of applause that she launched into the passionate third movement of Beethoven's "Moonlight Sonata." She was not sure if this particular piece of music had been written yet, but at least Ludwig was alive now and had been composing for some years. She concluded with Bach's "Sheep May Safely Graze."

A woman of many talents, his betrothed, mused Ash, watching from the back of the room as Amanda left the piano to seat herself next to her mother. Most men, he reflected sadly, would consider themselves fortunate to take her to wife. A wave of bitterness swept over him. If only he had never known Lianne, perhaps there might have been a chance that he would come to love his wife. But Lianne had always been a barrier between him and every other woman he had subsequently come to know. She was as much a part of him as his breath, and he would never be free of her memory. Even now, he had but to close his eyes and her image rose before him as clearly as though he held her in his arms. He could almost feel her soft, dark hair tickling his chin, and the magic of her green eyes stirred him to his depths. Oh, God, if only . . .

His thoughts trailed into oblivion as he became aware of a familiar scent assailing his senses. He turned, and his heart lurched as he observed the object of his reverie seating herself beside him.

"She plays beautifully," said Lianne a trifle wistfully.

"Yes." *Please, my love, do not sit so close. For God's sake, I cannot bear it. Please just go away.*

Instead, she placed a small hand on his sleeve. "Ash, I must speak to you. Now, while everyone is occupied—see? Cousin Arabella is going to sing, and she will go on forever. Please, let us slip away for a moment."

"Lianne—" But at the expression in her eyes Ash was unable to complete his protest. Reluctantly, he rose to follow her as she left the room and slipped into a chamber a few feet down the corridor. When she turned to face him, her face was wet with tears.

"Oh, Ash," she sobbed, "I am so unhappy!" Without waiting for a reply, she hurled herself into his arms and buried her face in the folds of his cravat.

"Lianne," he began again, "my love, do not torture yourself." Gently he removed her arms from about his neck and bent to kiss her gently on the lips. When she would have pressed against him for more, he pulled away. "We must not," he concluded, his breath harsh in his throat.

She stepped back, her gaze stricken. "Dear God, Ash, it is as I feared. You do not love me. She has won you over." She averted her face. "I suppose it was to be expected. She is so very beautiful—and charming—and rich." She spoke the last word with loathing.

"You are wrong," Ash growled. "You know how I feel about you—but there is no future for us, my darling. I have chosen duty over love—as you were forced to do once before. I must get on with my life now, and so must you, for there is nothing left for us."

"Oh, but, Ash, there might be." Once more Lianne lifted her arms, this time to place her hands on his lapels in a supplicating gesture. She took a deep, shuddering breath. "I have thought and thought about us, my love."

"And . . . ?" whispered Ash softly.

"I don't think I can bear to say good-bye to you. When I married Grant, you left right away and for years we did not even see each other. I was not forced to—to look at you all the time and know that what we felt for each other could never be. But, now—I am part of your family, and we shall constantly be forced into each other's company."

"Yes," groaned Ash, "I know, and that's why—"

"Can you tell me, dearest, that you will be content with, 'Good day, Lianne. Is your mother well? Have you been to the Opera lately?' Will you be able to greet me day after day, month after month, year after year without—this?" She stood on tiptoe and brushed his lips with hers, lingering until his breathing deepened and became rough. Unthinking, his arms went about her, tightening into an embrace that left him shaken with guilt and longing.

"My God, Lianne!" Ash pulled away and stared at her, horror-stricken. Deep in the green depths of her gaze, he thought he detected the ghost of a smile, but the next moment, all he could see was the mirror of his own passion.

"It isn't fair, my darling, that we should have to give up the only happiness each of us will ever know." Once more, tears glittered like rain in a forest. "Will you at least visit me once in a while?"

"Lianne, I do not think—"

"If I can share just a small portion of your life, perhaps I could—manage to live my own." Once more, a shuddering sigh escaped her full, red lips. "But I will understand if you feel you cannot." She glanced at him from beneath the thick forest of her lashes.

"My dearest . . . " Ash's voice was almost metallic in his intensity. "You cannot have considered—You know what it might lead to."

"I am so tired of considering, and I can see no other way for us to be together." Another sob escaped her as she spoke. She ran her fingers lightly over Ash's cheek, and he shivered.

"My dearest love," he whispered, sweeping her hand away to clasp it in his. "We will see each other frequently, and every moment will give me pain. If we were to be alone together, I don't see how I could not—"

Lianne smiled sadly. "I understand, Ash. Truly, I do." She shook herself a little. "We must return before we are missed. Perhaps you are right. I must have been mad to importune you in such a manner. Please try to forget that I so lost myself. I wish I could say that I shall be brave, but I'm not sure I can do that. I shall just—" Her breath caught, and as though she could not bear to speak further, she turned and whirled from the room.

Slowly, every movement seeming to require more effort than he was capable of, Ash followed her.

Amanda watched him as he entered the room again. She had noticed his departure, as well as that of the young countess, and now her eyes widened a little. Lord, Ash looked as though someone had just kicked him in the stomach. She did not attempt to speak to him, however, and they did not come together again until much later, when Ash brought his betrothed before the dowager to say farewell.

"You play very well, gel," said the old lady. "Come see me again, Amanda. Perhaps later this week. There is a matter I would discuss with you."

The ride home was enlivened by Serena's glowing predictions of Amanda's future as the wife of the Earl of Ashindon.

"For the dowager likes you, my dear," she said blissfully. "Mark my words, by next week you shall have your vouchers to

Almack's." Her cup obviously running over, Serena continued in this vein at some length.

"And then," interposed Jeremiah with sour satisfaction, "mayhap we'll see the inside of some of the grand places in Grosvenor Square—and Berkeley, as well. I've always wanted to visit Devonshire House," he finished with relish.

Amanda glanced at Ash, but he was a chill silhouette against the carriage window. What had happened, she wondered, between him and Lianne during their brief absence from the drawing room? Right now, she could feel distaste and a sense of despair radiating from him, and she immediately clamped down on the desire to reach out her gloved hand to touch him. It was uncanny, she reflected, how attuned to his moods she seemed to be, and she wasn't sure she cared for that one whit. She had no desire to increase the intimacy between herself and this man, for there could be no future for her with him.

Watching his face, her heart skidded in her breast. Dear God, what *was* her future to be? And why did the thought that whatever that future might hold, it would not contain William, Lord Ashindon, cause a knife-edged pang to shoot through her?

Chapter Thirteen

Later that evening, Ash sat alone in the sitting room of his chambers in Jermyn Street. Sipping meditatively at the brandy placed at his side by his valet, he reviewed the events of the evening. It was done, then. Amanda had been accepted by his family—most particularly by its matriarch, which somehow, despite the signings and handshakes earlier with Jeremiah Bridge and his attorneys, made the betrothal truly official. All that remained now was Serena Bridge's announcement ball and the notice in *The Morning Post*. He sighed heavily, waiting for the familiar sense of despair to descend on him. Instead, his lips curved in a smile as a picture rose before him of the confrontation between his fiancée and his grandmother. There was no question Amanda had routed the old dragon, foot, horse, and artillery. "Bubbies," indeed. He laughed aloud. Most women he knew would have simply dissolved in a paroxysm of embarrassment, but Amanda had remained cool and possessed. He drew a rather unsteady breath as he thought of the splendor of her bosom, displayed to such advantage in the low-cut gold gown that swept on to cling tantalizingly to hip and thigh.

Good Lord, he thought, startled. He was not in the habit of harboring such thoughts about a woman other than Lianne. Well, no, that was ridiculous. He had not lived like a monk, after all, in the years since her marriage to his cousin, but his liaisons were generally with a different sort of woman, carried out as a giving and taking of transitory pleasure. He was not used to assessing the charms of unmarried ladies of breeding, with whom, in the normal course of things, he had little social contact. Of course, few ladies of his acquaintance possessed the blinding attributes of Amanda Bridge.

He paused in thought, his glass halfway to his lips. But it wasn't merely Amanda's beauty that drew him to her, was it? No, he found the inner woman equally compelling. Her artless, frank conversation was fascinating, and even when she was at her most infuriatingly unconventional he had to admire her wit and her intelligence.

The smile died. Amanda had declared her intention of ending their betrothal. Coming from any other woman he would have seen her offer as some sort of ploy—an indication that she had set her sights on a richer prize. A duke, possibly—one that was not impoverished? Or perhaps she was still harboring a tender sentiment or two for that hedge-bird Cosmo Satterleigh. But—no, he was convinced her only thought was to free him so that he could marry the woman he truly loved. A charming, if somewhat impractical aspiration.

Not that he wasn't tempted, of course. To marry Lianne was the summit of his dreams, was it not? He allowed himself to slip into the familiar daydream of life with Lianne. He thought of the two of them, living in the quietude of Ashindon Park, working together to bring the place back to its old glory.

He frowned as he recalled her words earlier that evening. Visits from the Earl of Ashindon to his cousin's widow in the presence of the widow's very proper maiden aunt would surely be considered unexceptionable. Yet somehow he felt this was not what Lianne had in mind. Her demeanor had suggested clandestine assignations without benefit of chaperon. Good God, such a situation would be only slightly less forbidden than if she were his mistress. He could not believe Lianne had made such a suggestion. It warmed him, naturally, that she would turn her back on the standards of a lifetime, but the prospect appalled him, nonetheless.

He had thought Lianne unchanged from the lissome girl she had been when she married Grant, but he was mistaken. She certainly had not aged noticeably—she was still achingly beautiful—but her voice seemed a trifle more shrill, her expression just a little harder than he remembered. He chastised himself immediately. Of course she had changed. Six years of marriage to Grant was bound to change anyone for the worse, but she was still his love, the woman he would give his soul to possess.

It was not to be, however, and he may as well face that fact. He would have to persuade Amanda to face it, as well. Amanda Bridge was shortly to become the Countess of Ashindon, his wife, the mother of his heir. A guilty surge of pleasure shot through him at the thought of getting a son on that golden beauty, and his throat tightened as he wondered how the silken sweep of her hair would feel splayed across his chest.

He shook himself. My God, this had to stop. How could he love one woman and think so lasciviously of another? His jaw tightened. He would do well to remember that it was not just Amanda he was marrying. He could talk of separating himself and his bride from the Bridges, but he would be inextricably wed to her family, all the same. It was a prospect almost too dreadful to contemplate. Serena could be borne, but the thought of being bound to Jeremiah Bridge socially and emotionally for an interminable stretch of years weighed down on him like death itself.

Ash rose from his chair, and stiffening his shoulders, he set his glass down on the table beside him. It would be all he could do to maintain his fortitude for the immediate future, for Serena Bridge's confounded ball loomed before him, and that was enough to cut up any man's peace.

Cursing softly, he took himself off to bed.

Amanda woke early the next morning, though the events of the previous evening had kept her staring wide-eyed at the canopy above her bed for some time the night before. She was rather surprised to discover that, for the most part, she had enjoyed herself. She had found the confrontation with the dowager countess exhilarating and rather thought she and the old lady might become friends. Since she had been asked to return, it might be assumed the dowager felt the same.

It was too bad the meeting between the old countess and Jeremiah had not been so felicitous. Couldn't the man see that groveling was not the way to the dowager's esteem? How could he have brought himself to behave so? It was perfectly obvious by now that groveling was as foreign to his nature as it was to hers. How sad that he so desperately wanted the approbation of the *ton*. Particularly since, even with his daughter married to an earl, he was so unlikely to achieve anything close to social acceptance by "the nobs."

Amanda shrugged. Jeremiah Bridge was what he was, and as such was not deserving, in her opinion, of much sympathy. She addressed herself to the chocolate and biscuits brought a few minutes earlier by Hutchings. She smiled wryly. It had not taken her long to become accustomed to being waited on hand and foot. If and when she ever made it back to the twentieth century, she'd have a hard time combing her own hair.

Later, over breakfast, Serena detailed plans for a shopping expedition that morning, adding with the air of one proffering a special treat, that Charlotte and Cordelia would be welcome as well. Amanda, always willing to add a new experience to her sojourn in Regency London, agreed.

It was not long, however, before Amanda regretted her impulse. She had always found shopping tedious in the extreme, and changing time periods had not rendered it any more pleasurable.

"Dearest, do you not agree that this would be perfect?"

"I beg your pardon?" asked Amanda wearily. She was vaguely aware that they were standing in perhaps the sixth draper's shop they had visited during the course of the morning. As soon as they had collected Charlotte and Cordelia, Serena had ordered the coachman to Leicester Square, and during the short drive had volubly consulted the list she carried. Now, Amanda became aware that the footman trailing behind them staggered under a mountain of parcels to which not only Serena had contributed, but Charlotte and Cordelia as well. For the two damsels, each accompanied by excruciatingly proper companions, were also in the throes of choice for what Amanda was coming to think of as The Home Stretch Ball.

"This blue satin," replied Serena. "It is just what we have been looking for. It almost exactly matches the color of your eyes—and it is the dearest merchandise in the store," she concluded with satisfaction.

When Amanda made no response beyond an abstracted nod of her head, Serena shook her own sadly. "I don't know what's come over you, my dear. I suppose you are still suffering the effects of the blow to your head, but you are sorely cutting up my peace. You used to be in alt over the prospect of a shopping trip, particularly for a ball gown. Now—"

Amanda was swept by a wave of compunction. She bent to examine the material under discussion. "Oh, Mama, this is lovely.

I'm sorry if I have been somewhat distracted, but it's not every day a girl becomes engaged. Please say you forgive my fidgets." She hugged her mother briefly. "I agree, it's absolutely perfect. Do we need a tunic, do you think? It seems a shame to cover even so much as an inch of this magnificent fabric."

"Mm," said Serena judiciously, "I believe you are right, dearest. The gown we selected from *La Belle Assemblée* calls for an overdress of net, but the design . . . Yes, it will do much better alone." She turned to consult Charlotte and Cordelia and their two minions, all of whom after due consideration agreed that the blue satin should stand on its own merits.

"I do envy you," remarked Charlotte. Was there a touch of spite in her tone? "Mama still will not allow me to dress in any other color beyond a proper pastel. I'm afraid that even next year, when I turn twenty, I shan't be allowed anything more dashing— that is, something more colorful."

"Yes, of course," replied Amanda sweetly, "but pale colors suit you so much better than they do me, don't you agree, Cordelia?"

Cordelia, apparently unaware of the pit that was being dug at her feet, agreed vehemently, and was rewarded by a flash from Charlotte's watery blue eyes that promised future retribution.

Before open warfare could break out, Serena hastily pointed out that all three damsels required material for scarves to complement the stuff chosen for their gowns. She drew Amanda to a display of gauzes.

"I'm not sure what shade would be best . . . " But, Amanda's interest had failed once again. Instead, her thoughts turned again to her predicament. If she was going to break officially with Ash, it seemed logical that she should do so before their engagement was announced. On the other hand, her original plan—that of squeezing as much juice from Jeremiah as possible before releasing Ash from the betrothal—held a great deal of appeal. On yet another hand, however, Ash seemed to consider that idea untenable. Men, from no matter what century, it seemed, had such ridiculous concepts of honor. The fact that Jeremiah Bridge was all but forcing his daughter into marriage with a man she did not love could scarcely bind said daughter into a perfectly medieval arrangement.

She came to with a start, realizing that a clerk stood at her elbow. "No, there is nothing just yet," she replied mechanically to his offer of assistance. "My mother will shortly—" She turned to face him and gasped in shock. There was nothing remarkable about the young man, whose brown hair was combed neatly, his suit pressed impeccably, and his shoes shined to a blinding gloss. Nothing, that is, except for the glittering spectacles that perched on the end of his short nose, and hard, round cheeks that glowed like little lollipops.

"You!" Amanda cried, grasping the young man's arm.

"I beg your pardon, miss?" asked the young man in bewildered accents.

"Never mind my pardon," said Amanda through clenched teeth. "I want to talk to you. Now. Where can we go?"

An apprehensive expression crept over the clerk's features. "I don't understand, miss. I merely wished to give assistance."

"Well, that's what I want above everything. Assistance." Bodily, Amanda hauled the young man to a quiet corner of the shop. "Now, I want you to tell me how I got here and how I can get back to my own time."

"P-please, miss," stammered the clerk. "I don't know—that is, if you will just let me get the manager . . ." Vainly, he attempted to pry Amanda's fingers from their steely grip on his sleeve.

"Oh, no you don't. Not a step will you stir until I get some answers."

For a long moment, the young man stared into her face, and when he spoke, finally, it seemed to Amanda that the very timbre of his voice had changed to a tone of depth and reassurance. "How can I help you?" he asked quietly.

"I just told you—"

"You are right in the conclusions you have reached so far. Amanda Bridge is dead, and Amanda McGovern was chosen to fill out the span of years that would have been hers."

"Oh, God." Amanda was forced to grasp the edge of a display table for support.

"You seem to be experiencing an inordinate difficulty in adjusting," the clerk continued with some severity. "It will not do, you know, to try to live as you did in that other time. You must learn to abide by the conventions of the time in which you are living. Your early morning jog in the park, for example, was reprehensible." He stared disapprovingly through spectacles that threatened to slide completely off his face.

"Well, what was I supposed—?" began Amanda indignantly.

The man's tone softened suddenly. "You live here now, Amanda. You must make adjustments."

"That's just it," said Amanda miserably. "I don't think I can. Is there no way I can return to my own time?"

"This is your own time, now." The man's tone was gentle, but inexorable. "If you but try, you will come to appreciate the gift that has been given to you. You are whole and strong now, and you have a whole new life to live."

Amanda's jaw jutted stubbornly. "But I want the life I had. I want *my* life back."

The man sighed. "You are only making things difficult for yourself. You must give yourself more time here."

Amanda's heart lifted. "You mean, there is a chance I can return if I cannot work things out here?"

The man pushed his spectacles into their original position. "I did not say that. But"—he paused, as though listening to another voice—"I can speak with you no longer now." He turned as though to move away, but Amanda tightened her grasp on his sleeve.

"No! You must help me."

"I am trying to help you, my dear, if you will but listen. Ah." He sighed. "We will talk again, if you insist. From now on, you must make a sincere effort to fit into your new life, but if you find yourself in real difficulty and need to speak to us again, we will come."

Once more he turned to go and once more Amanda clutched at his arm. "No!" she cried again. "You must—"

"What on earth are you doing way over here, dearest?" Amanda whirled to find Serena at her elbow. "Are you looking at laces? We shan't need any for the ball gown, but perhaps your new carriage dress—the one of Cheshire brown, could stand some trimming."

Brushing impatiently at her mother's hand, Amanda turned again, but the young clerk was nowhere to be seen. Her frantic gaze swept the little shop, but the clerk had vanished as though he had escaped from the face of the earth. Which, thought Amanda in despair, he probably had.

Chapter Fourteen

"Isn't this just splendid, my dears?"

It was just a week after Amanda's confrontation with the jinni with the spectacles, or whoever he, she, or it might be, and Serena was bubbling over with gratification as she stood at the head of the stairs with her husband and daughter. "All the world is here tonight, and I shouldn't wonder if tomorrow everyone is saying our little party was the worst squeeze of the Season!"

For once, Jeremiah seemed satisfied with Serena's arrangements, and he stood at his wife's side, beaming impartially on his guests, the servants bustling to and fro with delicacy-laden trays, and on his family, whom, he had declared earlier in the evening, had "done him up proud, and that's a fact."

Amanda felt very much on display in the costly blue satin gown. The deep sapphire did indeed almost exactly match her eyes and the candlelight turned the delicate gold threads woven through it into streaks of liquid fire. Her shoulders rose, white and shapely, from a cunningly designed décolletage that discreetly emphasized the swell of her bosom. About her neck lay a diamond necklace, a gift from Jeremiah just before the family had taken their stations in the line. It featured clusters of small diamonds arranged about a central jewel nearly the size of a grape. It was crude and vulgar and positively blinding, and Amanda felt she had just been given her own personal albatross. At any rate, it weighed damned near as much. Nestled in the golden sweep of curls that made up her coiffure, a small intricately fashioned diamond tiara lay winking in the candlelight.

Serena and Jeremiah had good reason for their satisfaction, for Grandmama Ashindon had evidently been at work. So far, the guests processing through the Bridge receiving line had included

Lady Jersey and two other patronesses of Almack's, as well as three dukes and their ladies, several earls, and an assortment of viscounts and lords. She had fallen into a dazed reverie when she came to, startled, as the butler intoned, "Mr. George Brummell." Her eyes flew open. She was actually going to meet the Beau!

To her startled amusement, a rather plump gentleman somewhat past the first blush of youth bent to kiss her hand. He was a little above medium height, with dark hair and eyes, and an expression of pained boredom screwed his Cupid's bow mouth into a tight little bud of discontent. His words were courteous, however, and his glance was mild as he surveyed her discreetly.

"Pleased to make your acquaintance, Miss Bridge. One sees why Ashindon has forsaken the beauties of the *ton*. Have you met my friend Alvanley?" He gestured to the gentleman just now disengaging himself from Serena's voluble welcome.

Alvanley. Had she not read about him? thought Amanda. Yes, he'd been featured in many of the reference books she'd read on the period. William Arden, second Baron Alvanley, was, by all accounts the personification of the Regency dandy in all the glory of his studied eccentricities, and perusing the figure before her, she could well believe it. The signs of dissipation were clear on his amiable features, and he was, if she was not mistaken, rather the worse for drink.

He swayed, quizzing glass at the ready, before bowing over her hand in a chaste salute. "Ah, Miss Bridge. You're right, Brummell, she's exquisite! Will you save a dance for me, my dear?"

Without waiting for an answer, he and the Beau drifted off after a murmured consultation on the direction of the nearest liquid sustenance.

Well, thought Amanda, disgruntled. So much for the scintillating repartee for which the Regency era was famed. She turned to observe that Ash had entered the receiving line. Earlier, Serena had bemoaned the fact that the earl could not be expected to join them in welcoming the guests, "But," she said, with a contented sigh, "if the betrothal is not to be announced until well after the ball is under way, it would spoil the surprise if his lordship were to take his place with us beforehand." She beamed now at the elegantly garbed peer and passed him to Jeremiah after permitting herself a quick peck on his cheek.

Amanda smiled. Ash had visited the Bridge ménage several

times since the dowager countess's dinner party. They had continued Amanda's dance lessons. Serena had joined them once or twice, and to Amanda's astonishment, Jeremiah had put his head in the door one day and decided to take part, displaying a surprising lightness of foot and an enjoyment of the music provided for them by Serena on the great piano in the music room.

Ash had also taken her for walks and drives in the Park. He told her more of himself—his time in the army and his aspirations for Ashindon Park and his family. It occurred to Amanda that she was taking altogether too much pleasure in his company. It was one thing to be physically attracted to a man, but to find so much enjoyment in simple conversation with him was dangerous in the extreme. She laughed at herself. A fine thing it would be to fall for the man she was supposed to marry. Or at least, she thought, sobering, it might be if there was any possibility of her actually marrying him—even if the gentleman returned her feelings—of which there was also no possibility.

What nonsense, she thought, shaking herself out of this somewhat muddled reverie. She was not about to fall in love with a man who had lived almost two hundred years before her own time. If she had read the little man with the spectacles right, she had every reason to believe she would be departing this scene in the near future. She was well aware that this circumstance would more than likely leave Amanda Bridge dead, but that would solve all the earl's problems, wouldn't it? By that time, Jeremiah Bridge would have coughed up a considerable sum of money to his supposed future son-in-law.

Of course, Amanda's death would be a blow to her family, but the girl would have died anyway these three weeks past. She shivered. She really did not want to think about that aspect of her impending escape.

Amanda noted with some interest that Lianne was at the earl's side as he passed through the line. Her brows lifted disdainfully. Could it not be considered a shade tacky for a gentleman to escort his beloved to a celebration of his betrothal to someone else?

A moment later she observed that the dowager countess clung to his other arm, with Cousin Emily Wexford, the countess's companion, in tow. The unpleasant churning in her stomach subsided a little. Perhaps the earl had been suborned into accompanying the matriarch and her court. The expression of long-suffering on his lordship's face gave credence to this assumption. At any rate, when his gaze fell upon her, his expression underwent a gratifying transformation to one of undisguised admiration. She fluttered her eyelashes as he bent over her hand.

"You look," Ash said huskily, "very attractive this evening, my dear."

The earl cursed himself. "Very attractive!" for God's sake. She was love's dream come to life, her azure eyes sparkling with the promise of unspoken delights, the curves of her lithe body outlined by sensuous folds of sapphire satin. On anyone else, that necklace would have been the height of poor taste, but Amanda carried it off with serenity and grace.

"Good evening, Miss Bridge."

Lianne's voice next to him was like a dash of cold water on his heated sensibilities, and with a murmured promise to seek her out for a dance later, Ash released Amanda's hand and moved into the ballroom. Lianne moved with him, clinging to his arm as they paced the perimeter of the dance floor, nodding to acquaintances.

"Oh, this is lovely, isn't it?" asked Lianne, her green eyes glinting with pleasure. As Ash's brows lifted in surprise, she added hastily, "This is a terrible night, of course, for it will set the seal on your betrothal, but"—she drew in a brave, quivering breath—"I have determined that I shall not think about that." Evidently she had little difficulty in accomplishing this feat, for she smiled sunnily. "I don't know why it took me so long to come to London. At any rate"—she turned a laughing face to Ash—"it will be a cold day before I ever return to stuffy old Wiltshire."

"Stuffy?" Ash remarked lightly. "Wiltshire? I thought you liked it there," he said, remembering Lianne's past declarations of devotion to the countryside.

"Oh, I do," replied Lianne hastily. "At least, I did, but that was before I had to spend so many months in virtual seclusion." She glanced about. "I have so longed for parties and people to talk to."

"But there are plenty of people to—"

Her laughter chimed in his ear. "Oh, but I mean interesting people, people of wit and elegance. I want to gossip of the Regent's latest scandal and who has taken up a liaison with whose wife."

"My God," was Ash's only comment, and Lianne pouted adorably.

"Do I shock you?" she asked archly. "You did not used to be such a stick-in-the-mud. Oh, look there is the Beau!" She indicated the erstwhile reigning dandy some yards distant. "I did not think to see him tonight. I hear he does not attend many *ton* affairs lately."

"No, he doesn't, but he is an old friend, and a great favorite of Grandmama's. Mrs. Bridge was only too happy to invite him."

"I do not wonder at it," Lianne commented dryly. "She must have been beside herself at the thought of the famous Beau Brummell attending her little function."

Ash stiffened, but she continued, oblivious. "Oh, my poor Ash, it breaks my heart to think of you fettered to those people for the rest of your life."

Ash murmured something noncommittal, but he seethed with inward resentment. That he had expressed these same sentiments himself did not lessen his anger that Lianne Bonner, an outsider, should take it upon herself to—

He drew in a sharp breath. Lianne, an outsider? What kind of profanation had he just committed? Lianne had every right to comment on his future. Hadn't she? He bent his head to her once more as she turned her attention to others in their immediate vicinity. Lord, Ash thought, listening to her comments lightly tinged with malice, he had not realized she could be so spiteful. It was with some relief that he beheld his friend James Wincanon approaching.

"What ho, yer lordship," said that gentleman, folding his length into an exaggerated bow. His gaze contained a sardonic glint as he kissed Lianne's hand. "Lady Ashindon—ravishing as ever."

Lianne twinkled up at him. "Why, James, I think that's the first time you have ever complimented me."

"I cannot think how I came to be so remiss," James replied smoothly, "and it certainly will not be the last."

Lianne's laughter chimed. "I have just been telling Ash how glad I am to be here tonight. It has been such an age since I have been out and about."

"You chose well," James answered. He turned to Ash. "Mrs. Bridge has netted the jewels of society for her festivities."

Lianne laughed again, this time not so musically. "You can

thank Grandmama Ashindon for that. She's been busy all week writing notes and paying visits. I don't think any other force under heaven could have dragged Mrs. Drummond-Burrell to a home that smells of the shop." She wrinkled her dainty nose and tittered behind her fan. Ash knew a moment of stunned anger. This could not be Lianne, the woman of his dreams, speaking so. He noted that James was observing the young countess, an odd smile quirking his lips.

James bowed once more. "May I have this dance, my lady? Along with the company, the music seems to be first rate." He extended his hand and Lianne, with a flirtatious smile, placed her fingertips on his arm and allowed herself to be escorted onto the floor. She sent a sparkling glance over her shoulder to Ash as she moved away. "I shall speak with you later—my lord," she called softly. A moment later she was all flying curls and pink cheeks as she whirled through the figures of a vigorous reel.

Ash stared after her in consternation. How could she have changed so dramatically? Surely it was not he who had altered during their separation. He chided himself. It was, perhaps, to be expected that a vital creature like Lianne would become overexcited at one of her first forays into society after so many years, thus leading her to speak as she would not ordinarily have done. Or perhaps her distress over his impending betrothal and marriage had led her to vent a hurt that she would otherwise have kept to herself.

"Pretty little filly, ain't she?"

Startled, Ash turned to observe Jeremiah Bridge at his elbow, following his gaze to Lianne and James. He opened his mouth to protest, but Jeremiah waved his hand expansively.

"Never mind, young fella, I know all about your interest in that quarter. I told you I'd made it my business to find out everything about you, and your previous connection to your cousin's widow was one of the first things brought to my attention. Can't say as I blame you," he added meditatively, still watching the dancers.

"You are to be commended on your thoroughness, sir." Ash's voice was chill as midnight in winter. "However, it is not necessary for you—"

Jeremiah laughed. "Oh, I know—man of honor and all that. I'm well aware I can count on your discretion, my lord. I just want to emphasize the point"—the jovial smile dropped from his lips—

"that if word of any hanky-panky were to reach my daughter's ears, I would be very, very displeased. And"—his voice sank to a whisper—"I don't think you want to displease me—my lord."

Ash was filled with such fury that he could hardly speak, but his voice was controlled as he spoke. "Mr. Bridge, are you suggesting that I would so much as consider betraying my vows to Amanda? No, of course not—for her father to voice such an idea would be beneath contempt."

Jeremiah reddened and his massive jaw thrust forward belligerently. After a moment, however, he said with a burst of forced laughter, "You're proud as be-damned, ain'tcher, my lord? No need to take me up, though. I was just setting matters straight."

"Is that what you were doing?" asked Ash coolly. "If you will excuse me, sir, it is time to claim a dance from my betrothed." He turned on his heel and strode away, teeth clenched and fists balled.

He could not believe the conversation that had just taken place. If he had understood Jeremiah Bridge right, the man had all but informed him that an outside liaison was perfectly acceptable to him as long as the matter did not reach Amanda's ears. Slowly, he relaxed his fingers and took a deep breath. Well, he had known what he was getting into—how had Lianne put it?—fettered—to a vulgar, overbearing, evil-minded pig of a man.

He paused for a moment and swore prayerfully that once he and Amanda were married he would whisk her away with all possible speed to the Park and bar the door behind them. Oh yes, he would accept Bridge's largesse, but he would work from sunrise to moonset every day of his life, and the moment the Park began to show a profit, he would repay every cent. With interest.

How would Amanda react to such strictures? he wondered uneasily. She seemed to enjoy life in London. Would she see living in rural solitude as a prison sentence? And how might she feel when told her father would be unwelcome in her own home? She displayed no fondness for the old bandit, but he was her father, after all.

His glance surveyed the throng milling about the edge of the dance floor, but Amanda was nowhere to be seen. Had she decided to try her wings in a country dance? He was about to turn toward the refreshment room when his breath caught in his throat. There, behind a pillar in a secluded corner of the room stood his fiancée in earnest conversation with none other than Cosmo Satterleigh.

His hands once more curling into fists, he started toward the couple, but he was halted by Lianne's breathless voice in his ear. "Gracious! I have not danced in such ages that I fear I am quite out of practice. Would you procure a glass of—oh!" Ash turned to observe that she had followed the direction of his glance. "My," she purred, "I wonder what Mr. Satterleigh is doing here. I understood he has been forbidden the house."

"You seem to have absorbed an inordinate amount of gossip for being in town such a short time." He almost snarled the words, and Lianne's emerald eyes widened in dismay.

"Oh, Ash. I did not mean—that is, I must admit to being incensed that Miss Bridge would so far forget herself as to indulge in dalliance with a man so disliked by her parents, when she is betrothed to you." Tears glittered on the lashes she cast down over her cheeks. "I know you do not care for her—at least, in the way you and I care for each other, but such behavior must surely cause you embarrassment and discomfort."

Ash endeavored to produce the compunction he should have felt for discommoding the woman he loved. He was still itchy with resentment, however, when he patted her hand and drew her away. "I appreciate your sentiments," he said somewhat dryly, "but you really must leave the behavior of my fiancée to me."

Lianne stared at him, startled. "Of course, Ash. I never meant to interfere. I was just—"

"Come," said Ash brusquely, "the orchestra is beginning a quadrille. Will you dance with me?"

Once again, Ash experienced a vague sense of relief that the figures of the dance permitted very little conversation between himself and his beloved. When the last strains of the music died away, however, the two were positioned opposite a door that led to a small salon.

"Come, Ash," said Lianne, smiling winsomely, "do let us talk for a moment."

Ash drew away slightly, but her hand on his coat sleeve was insistent. With a sense of foreboding, Ash followed her from the ballroom.

The moment they were well into the shadowed confines of the little chamber, Lianne turned and pressed herself against Ash, her mouth seeking his. The kiss, though deep and passionate, did not, to Ash's guilty surprise, stir him as he might have expected. His only clear thought was that he would rather not have to deal with Lianne right now. Scarcely a loverlike sentiment, he realized with a start, but he was feeling more than somewhat harassed at the moment.

Lianne ended the kiss with a sigh and leaned back against Ash's shoulder to gaze at him from beneath her lashes.

"Oh, Ash," she whispered, drawing her fingers across Ash's cheek, "I do love you so."

Ash covered her hand with his own, and squeezing it gently, brought it away from him and released her from the circle of his arms. "I know," he said softly. "But, we must resign ourselves. We must, Lianne."

"Must we?" she asked, her voice husky. She moved away a little, but kept his hand in hers. When she spoke again, a certain purposefulness was evident in her tone. "Ash, I have been thinking about our situation. I understand why we cannot marry, though it has taken me many months to accept the fact of your duty to your family and your position. But, oh, my love, it is so unfair that a love such as ours should be so doomed. It will never die, of course, for it is too strong, and I have come to the conclusion that there is only one path for us."

She drew a deep, shuddering breath and lifted her great, jeweled eyes to his. "I have decided, Ash, my dearest and only love, that I will agree to become your mistress."

Ash felt as though something very large and very sharp had exploded in his midsection. His first confused thought was that he did not remember asking Lianne to be his mistress. His second was that he could not have heard aright, and his third, contributing even further to his emotional upheaval, was the unexpected certainty that he did not want to enter into a liaison, illicit or otherwise, with Lianne, the Countess of Ashindon.

"My dear," he said swiftly, "you cannot have thought—"

"Yes, I have. I've thought and thought, and—" Lianne's voice rose. "There is simply no other way, Ash." She stepped back. "Dear God," she continued, choking, "you think me sunk below reproach for suggesting such a thing, but—"

"No, of course not. I am moved beyond words that you would turn your back on the standards of a lifetime—that you would risk ruin and disgrace for me. I cannot let you do it, Lianne. And," he said heavily, "I cannot betray the vows I am about to make. You must see that. Much as I—"

Lianne turned away suddenly. "It is as I thought," she whispered tragically. "I have lost your love—and now"—her voice broke—"I have lost your esteem as well."

"No—do not talk that way." Ash was appalled at the insincerity he heard in his voice. "You know how I feel about you." He was guiltily aware of an urgent desire to be away from her. "Lianne, I must not stay here with you. Amanda—"

Lianne stamped her small foot. "It is always Amanda, now, isn't it? Very soon, Ash, I shall begin to believe that you have given your heart to her as well as the promise of your name." She pouted adorably, and it was not until Ash began to mouth the protest that she so obviously expected that he realized his expressions of eternal devotion sounded empty, even to his own ears. The pout turned to a rather ominous frown.

"You say you love me, but you will not make the slightest push to keep our love alive."

"I wish you will believe," said Ash wearily, "that I have no choice, and neither do you, if you will but think." He extended his hand in an effort to remove the sting of his words, but with what in anyone not quite so exquisite might have been called a snort of impatience, she whirled and left the room, her silken skirts hissing her displeasure.

Ash started after her, but observing that her progress was followed with undisguised interest by those in the ballroom, he halted. Lianne was already giving the tabbies a field day; there was no sense in fueling the scandal further. He sank down on a small settee. Dear God, what had just happened here? He did not know whether he was more shocked by Lianne's suggestion or by the stunning realization that the thought of bedding her left him unmoved.

It was some minutes before he finally dragged himself to his feet and left the little salon to find his betrothed.

Chapter Fifteen

Amanda, however, was nowhere to be found. Serena was chatting to a group of matrons near a potted palm in one corner of the room, and Amanda was not with her. Cordelia and Charlotte were each on the dance floor, pointing graceful toes in the cotillion. Amanda was not. She was not in the refreshment room, nor in the card room.

Ash drifted toward the ladies' withdrawing room, but when she did not emerge after several moments, he took his search elsewhere. The terrace, the small salons bordering the ballroom, and the drawing room, where supper was to be served later, also proved unproductive. As a last resort, he made his way to the music room, and here he was successful. There, at the far end of the room, backed up against a pier table, was his betrothed—in the arms of Cosmo Satterleigh.

For an instant, Ash stood frozen in a rage that he thought might choke him. One corner of his mind observed that Amanda stood in Satterleigh's embrace, still and uncooperative. This fact notwithstanding, Ash's first instinct was to stride to the couple, wrench them apart, and beat Satterleigh into the carpet. At the sound of his step, however, the gentleman whirled about.

"Ashindon!" he cried in a throbbing tone. Observing Ash's clenched fists, his face paled, but he remained where he stood. Ostentatiously, he put Amanda behind him. "I do not apologize, my lord, for claiming what is mine by right. If you wish to call me out, you may name your seconds." He tossed his head, sending his carefully curled ringlets quivering.

"I do not require an apology, you smarmy little hedge-bird," snarled Ash, advancing menacingly. "Nor am I going to call you out. I merely intend to give you the thrashing you deserve."

Mr. Satterleigh, apparently thinking better of his bravado,

stepped backward, thereby bumping into Amanda, who moved out from him.

"Don't be absurd, Ash," she said crossly. "The silly little twit thinks I'm in love with him. He, of course, is in love with my money—which you ought to understand. I don't know how he got in here tonight, but he will be leaving shortly, as soon as I can summon a couple of footmen."

She moved toward the bellpull, but Ash stayed her with a gesture. To Satterleigh, he said coldly, "I advise you to leave on your own. Otherwise, I shall be happy to throw you out bodily—from that window over there, a story above the ground."

For a moment, it looked as though the hapless swain would hold his ground, but with a groan he lurched toward the door. "I see how it is!" he flung over his shoulder to Amanda, "You have spurned a heart that loves you with all the sincerity of my being for a noble title. I wish you joy of your choice—Countess!"

He scuttled through the door. Ash turned to face Amanda, fury rising in him once more. "Just what the devil did you think you were doing?" he demanded.

"I wasn't doing anything!"

"Nothing! What do you call kissing that oily snake?"

"I wasn't kissing him. I was merely waiting for him to get through kissing me. I thought of struggling, but nonparticipation is just as effective in dampening a man's ardor, and it doesn't ruin your hairdo."

She appeared so calm and self-possessed that Ash wanted to shake her.

"And what were you doing in this little tête-à-tête to begin with? A little far afield from the ballroom, isn't it?"

"He threatened to make a scene if I didn't talk to him, so I took him where I thought there would be people, but not too many. When we came into the room, there were several couples here, but, unfortunately, they left."

"How obliging of them," said Ash nastily.

Amanda moved toward him. "Now, see here, my lord, I hope you are not implying . . . Good grief, do you actually think I have some feeling for that ludicrous jerk?"

"No—you see here, Miss Bridge. All the world knows you planned to elope with him. Don't tell me you were going to accomplish that without feeling anything toward him."

"Oh, that." Amanda shrugged. "As I told you, I have no memory of all that, but it must have been a—a momentary lapse on my part." She hesitated a moment before lifting her hand in a propitiatory gesture. "Ash, if I were truly in love with someone else, I would not have agreed to marry you. Furthermore, please believe me when I tell you that, since I did make such an agreement, I plan to keep it. I shall not indulge in flirtations with other men. I will not kiss them in secluded nooks, and I won't encourage them to believe that I am open to extracurricular behavior when we are married."

She took a long breath and gazed at him steadily, her eyes still and deep and clear as mountain pools. Shaken, Ash took refuge in a tone of light irony. "What laudable sentiments, Miss Bridge. Are you saying that you plan to make a real marriage of our business arrangement?"

Amanda stepped back, and Ash knew a moment of compunction. "I'm sorry. I should not have said that, I merely meant—"

"I never said anything about marriage, my lord. I am speaking of the betrothal. If you will recall, it is my intention that the marriage not take place at all."

Ash swore under his breath.

"Are you still on that tack? How many times do I have to tell you that the betrothal—*and* the marriage are signed, sealed, and all but delivered. You *will* be my wife, Amanda." He stepped forward and grasped her lightly by the shoulders. "Is that so very distasteful to you?"

Amanda, staring up at him, said nothing. Ash found that he was drowning in those magical pools, and he was having a great deal of trouble with his breathing. Slowly, unable to help himself, he bent his head and pressed his mouth to hers. Her lips were warm and soft and tasted of wine. She shivered in his arms for a moment, and Ash tightened them so that she would not draw away. Instead, she shifted slightly to accommodate his body against hers, and Ash thought that nothing he had ever experienced in his life felt so good. She seemed made to fit against him, her curves filling his hollows, and her scent filling his senses. She made a small sound in the back of her throat that nearly shattered what composure he had left. His mouth moved urgently on hers, and he shuddered when her hands came up to curl in the hair at the nape of his neck. Pulling her closer, as though he would absorb her into his very bones, he ran his hands over the delicate curve of her back, then up to the swell of her breasts.

Amanda drew in a sharp breath, and at the sound of voices in the corridor outside the music room pulled away from him. Her eyes, Ash noted somewhere in a corner of his mind, had darkened to the color of a summer midnight. She stared at him, and in her gaze Ash saw the reflection of his own confusion. But all she said was, "We had best return to the ballroom, my lord."

Passing two laughing couples in the corridor, they made their way wordlessly back to the throng of dancers. They did not speak until Ash claimed her hand for the supper dance, which was a quadrille.

"You have attained a commendable skill in country dancing, Miss Bridge," Ash said with a composure that pleased him vastly. "I think you will not need any more lessons."

Her voice was somewhat breathless as she replied, "I had an excellent instructor." She laughed. "I have twice danced to music other than the waltz this evening, and I must tell you I am quite flown by the compliments on my skill."

It seemed to Ash that they communicated on two levels. Below the commonplaces during the brief contact afforded by the figures of the dance, there was a current between them that spoke of a new, unsettling turn in their relationship. Was it a turn he wished to pursue? he wondered. He had no desire to lead Amanda Bridge to the inalterably false conclusion that he wanted more from her than an amicable association. Yet the kiss had stirred him to a depth he would not have thought possible.

He had exchanged kisses with many women, of course, and, aside from those shared with Lianne, he had found them to be sexually stimulating, but nothing more. The contact with Amanda had gone beyond the physical, however. He felt they had shared a communion of spirit—a joining of essence such as he had never experienced even in Lianne's exhilarating embrace. And, frankly, it scared the hell out of him.

They were joined during supper by Serena and Jeremiah, and as the meal concluded, Jeremiah rose and cleared his throat ostentatiously. The clatter of glasses and silver silenced as Jeremiah launched into the speech that, though brief, represented the culmination of his dreams.

"My dear friends," he began, placing a slight emphasis on the last word, "I am so pleased you could be with us tonight, for we have invited you here for a special purpose beyond music and dancing. It is my very great pleasure to announce at this time the betrothal of my beloved daughter Amanda to William Wexford, the Earl of Ashindon."

If the assembled company thought it odd that Serena was given no recognition as coproducer of the beloved daughter, there was no indication in the polite round of applause that greeted the pronouncement. A toast was proposed and the guests rose to offer their felicitations to the happy couple.

Through it all, Amanda smiled and nodded and mouthed appropriate expressions of gratification, all the while feeling both numb and terrified at the same time, as though she stood in the center of a whirling maelstrom.

She felt that part of her was still in the music room, lost in Ash's embrace. She had never known a kiss could be so stirring—so eminently satisfying yet creating such a storm of wanting. When Ash's mouth had come down on hers, she had known she should protest. The man was in love with another woman, after all. But at the feel of his lips on hers, and the touch of his hands, all rational thought had fled. Her body, traitor to her will, responded with every atom of her being to the wonderful, almost unbearably right feel of his touch, and she had curled into him like an animal seeking haven.

Had he been trying to seduce her? she wondered uncomfortably. If so, he'd certainly made splendid progress in a very few moments. That first kiss a couple of weeks earlier in the Marchford garden, had been shockingly provocative, but it had not produced the spreading heat that even now, as she thought about it, caused her pulse to throb. He did not seem the sort of man who could love one woman and seek to conquer another. Yet why else would he use her so? He had apparently determined to shake off his initial antipathy toward her in order to make the best of their bargain, but nothing in his behavior toward her so far indicated anything beyond a mild liking for her.

Her thoughts continued in this muddled vein throughout the rest of the evening, and she maintained a flow of meaningless conversation with the patronesses, the dukes and their wives, and the rest. At the end of the evening, exhausted and wrung dry of coherent thought, Amanda stood with her parents at the Bridge

front door to bid good night to the earl. His lips, brushing her fingertips seemed to burn through the fragile fabric of her glove, and
she murmured an incomprehensible assent to his offer to take her
driving the next morning.

"Or—no," she said immediately. "I am promised to your
grandmother. She asked that I come alone," she added, puzzled.

"En garde, then, my dear. Perhaps I shall see you later in the
day." He hesitated. "By the by, perhaps you—all of you"—he
gestured to Serena and Jeremiah—"would like to come up to the
Park for a brief visit next week. I cannot ask you to stay in the
main house, but the Dower House has been maintained in reasonably good condition, and I think you would be comfortable."

Serena beamed her delighted assent, and Jeremiah, shooting his
prospective son-in-law a shrewd glance, chuckled. "Time to put
the dibs in tune, eh? Well, boy, I'm game. Truth to tell, I've been
looking forward to seeing the grand place where my little girl will
be mistress."

Ash nodded curtly. "Very well, then. I shall make the arrangements." He kissed Amanda's cheek lightly and, bowing to Serena
and Jeremiah, mounted his waiting curricle and clattered off into
the night.

Before the door had closed behind him, Serena, her expression
beatific, launched into an exhilarated monologue on the altitudes
into which the Bridge family had soared that evening. Jeremiah,
for once, seemed content to let his wife ramble, and stood aside,
rubbing his hands, a wide smile creasing his blunt features.

Suddenly, Amanda felt suffocated. Unable to listen to more,
she pled a headache and fled to the haven of her bedchamber. She
endured Hutchings' excited chatter as she removed the diamonds,
drew off the blue satin gown, and brushed out her mistress's hair,
but abruptly dismissed the maid afterward, declaring her intention
of donning her own nightwear.

Some minutes later, she crawled wearily under the comforter
and blew out her bedside candle. She closed her eyes, but was
distressingly aware that she could still feel the imprint of a hard,
muscular body against her own. She touched her lips. Surely they
were still swollen from that dizzying kiss.

Lord, what was she going to do about her growing feelings for
the man to whom she was betrothed but with whom her involve-
ment would shortly be over? She tried to dwell on the fact that if

all progressed according to plan she would soon leave Regency England and the compelling nobleman who lived here. Ash might mourn her departure—a little, and he would see it as a financial disaster, but, again if she could work things out, he would be possessed of what he needed to get back on his feet. He would be free to marry the woman of his dreams.

And herself? She had learned something about relationships during her sojourn in another time, and she had learned something about herself. Returned to her own place and secure in her career, she was sure she would also feel more secure in her own person, even if that person was maimed and ugly.

Given the certainty that everything was going to work out well for all concerned, why did she feel like crying? Exasperated, she turned her face into her pillow, determined to think about something else until sleep overtook her.

Grandmama Ashindon, for example. The old lady had been insistent that Amanda visit her on the morrow. What in the world could she want? Please God, not a lecture on wifely duties.

At last, her eyes closed and her breathing deepened, but her dreams that night were disturbed by an arrogant figure who strode through them, whose touch produced rivers of excitement in her veins.

The dowager countess awaited her visitor in the morning room of her home in Grosvenor Square. Today, she wore a gown of stiff, wine-colored silk, panniered in an old-fashioned style. Again, she wore an absurd pair of slippers, this time of pink satin, trimmed with swansdown. A few moments were spent in dissecting the events of the previous evening.

"I fancy," said the old lady with a grunt of satisfaction, "that you will receive your vouchers by week's end. I could see that Mrs. Drummond-Burrell had a great deal of difficulty in overcoming her distaste of the whole affair, but she will come around. I am in possession of some rather uncomfortable facts concerning her behavior when she was much younger."

Amanda chuckled. "You are nothing short of wicked, my lady. Is there anyone in London who does not fear you?"

"I certainly hope not," retorted the countess with relish. "And please call me Grandmama. I used to loathe the appellation, but now that I am finally reconciled to my years, I rather like it."

A wizened old man in butler's panoply entered, staggering
under a full complement of plate, which he set down with a flourish before the dowager. She waved him away and instructed
Amanda to pour. "Now tell me, gel, are you entering into this betrothal of your own will?"

Amanda looked up in surprise. "Why—I agreed to it, if that's
what you mean." She passed a steaming cup fashioned of paper-
thin Sevres to the old lady and filled one for herself.

"Of course, that's not what I mean," snorted the dowager. "I
mean, how do you feel about Ashindon?"

An unwelcome heat rose to Amanda's cheeks. "He—he seems
a fine man. A little on the prideful side, but married to the right
woman, I should imagine he would be a most satisfactory husband."

The countess frowned. "You sound as though you are not to be
that woman. Surely, everything is in place now. You will marry
Ashindon, will you not?"

"Um—well, yes, of course. It is just that—"

"Just that—what?" snapped the old lady. "Out with it, gel. If
you're getting cold feet, now's the time to lay your cards on the
table."

Amanda took a deep breath. "My la—Grandmama, Ash does
not love me. Yes, I know," she added hastily, "love is not supposed to enter into a marriage like ours, but the fact that he's in
love with someone else cannot help but—color our relationship."

The dowager's mouth turned down. "I collect you are referring
to Lianne."

"Yes."

"Good God, gel, you cannot seriously believe that Ashindon
truly loves that brainless little vixen."

"What?" asked Amanda, astonished. "Of course! He has loved
her all his life, and why do you call her a vixen?"

"Because I'm too much of a lady to call her a bitch, of course."

Amanda gasped. "I don't understand."

The countess looked at her for a long moment. "I'm not saying
Ash does not *think* he is in love with Lianne, and I'm not even
saying that Lianne does not harbor some tender sentiment for
Ashindon, but—oh well, actually," said the dowager grudgingly,
"I suppose she's not all that bad. She made a dreadful bargain in
Grant, but once she wed him, even after she realized the mistake

she'd made, she took it in good part and remained faithful to him. Although," she added dryly, "if Ashindon had remained on the scene, I'm not so sure she would have maintained her virtue."

"But wasn't she virtually forced to marry Grant?"

"Pho! Lianne was never forced into anything she did not wish to do. She said she loved Ash, and she would have married him, I suppose, but when she had the opportunity to attach Grant, the title holder and heir to Ashindon Park, wild horses could not have kept her from him. She made a big to-do about family obligations, but it's my opinion that it was her own self-interest that prompted her to abandon Ashindon and accept Grant's suit."

"I cannot believe this," murmured Amanda. Surely, she thought, the old lady was speaking from her own antipathy toward Lianne.

"My advice to you," concluded the dowager, "is to try very hard to believe it. Lianne Bonner, given half a chance, will snatch Ashindon from beneath your nose—whether you're married to him or not."

Amanda stared disbelievingly at the dowager. "Are you saying—"

"All I'm saying is that if you're not careful, your papa will be paying for Lianne's upkeep. Perhaps you wouldn't mind that— God knows how young people disport themselves these days, but I believe I am not wrong in assuming such a connection would displease you."

Grudgingly, Amanda nodded. She opened her mouth to speak again, but was forestalled by the entrance of Miss Emily Wexford, Lady Ashindon's companion. Amanda rose to greet her, but the spinster gestured that she should not arise.

"I hope you and Grandmama have been having a nice chat," she said a little breathlessly.

"Oh, yes," said the dowager dryly, "it quite brightened up my dull life."

Amanda bit back a laugh as Miss Wexford attempted an embarrassed dispute. After a few moments of light chatter, she rose to leave, with the promise that she would visit the dowager again. "For," she said, smiling rather painfully, "our conversation has been most instructive."

Chapter Sixteen

At about this time, Ash had just come to the same conclusion regarding a visit he made that morning to James's lodgings in Duke Street. It was not his habit to discuss his personal crises with others, but after his discourse with Lianne the previous evening and the shattering kiss with Amanda a few moments later, he felt in need of his friend's good sense and clear-sightedness.

"Mm, yes," said James as Ash began his tale. "I thought I saw you sneaking into that little salon, and—"

"I was not sneaking," interposed Ash with great dignity. "I merely—"

"Sneaking," continued James as though Ash had not spoken, "in company with the lovely Lianne, who subsequently exited the room looking as though she'd just bitten into a green persimmon. A rift in the lute, Will?" His words were spoken lightly, but his gaze was sharp as he surveyed his friend.

Ash stiffened. "I've told you repeatedly, Jamie, that there is no lute. Not anymore, that is. Oh, the devil," he concluded. "All right, you were correct, just as you usually are, damn you. Lianne told me that she still loves me. She—she demonstrated the depth of her feeling for me in a manner that was profoundly touching. I—"

"Offered to become your mistress, did she?" asked James coolly, and Ash felt his jaw drop in response.

"How the devil did you know that?" he demanded.

"Because it was the next logical step in her campaign."

"Campaign! What are you talking about?"

James shifted in his chair. "Look, Ash. You were a boy when you fell in love with Lianne. Then you went away and did not see her again for years. It's my opinion that sometime between your boyhood and the time you became a man you dropped your torch, but you were so used to carrying it you just never noticed."

"That's preposterous! My love for her has—"

"Your love for her was based, as love usually is, on an illusion." James leaned forward. "It was an illusion carefully fostered by the lady herself, if you ask me." He continued hurriedly before Ash could voice the protest that welled in him. "You thought of Lianne as loving and giving, and as dedicated to her family and her sense of duty as you were yourself."

"Well, of course—"

"Did it ever occur to you that Lianne is simply a normal female, concerned primarily with her own interests?"

"James, I don't think I care to listen any further." Ash made as though to rise, but James reached out to stay him.

"You're the one who initiated this conversation, my lad. For some time, now, I've wanted to have this chat with you, but Lianne had you wrapped so firmly around her finger, I knew I couldn't get through to you. Now, just listen for a moment. Did it ever occur to you that it was Lianne's desire to make as good a match for herself as possible, rather than her concern for her papa's feelings and her mama's nonexistent heart condition that prompted her to accept Grant's offer? No, of course it didn't.

"Nor did you consider that Lianne is living on a shoestring right now, a situation extremely displeasing to her. It cannot have taken her long to realize that her erstwhile lover would become a very wealthy man on his marriage to Amanda Bridge, and being the mistress of a wealthy man would be much better than becoming the bride of an impoverished peer."

"My God, James. I cannot believe what you are suggesting. Lianne loves me, and—"

"I'm sure she does—in her fashion. I'm not saying she's a bad person—she's merely a realist, as most women must be. They are totally dependent for their survival on men, and it behooves them to make the best bargains of which they are capable."

Ash knew a moment of disgust, both at his friend for his cold-blooded appraisal of what was the grand passion of his life, and at himself for the burgeoning, albeit unwilling acknowledgement of the truth of James's assessment.

Was it true, wondered Ash. Had Lianne simply been using him? Had his own feelings for her changed without his knowledge? Despite himself, he was aware that what James had said made good sense. Whether he would be able to accept his friend's cynical pronouncements was another matter.

Feeling oddly empty, he sighed heavily. "I cannot accept what you're saying, Jamie. Lianne would never—"

"Did you take her up on her offer?" interrupted James.

"Her—Oh. No, of course not. It took just about everything in me to refuse," said Ash, somewhat less than truthfully. "I know what it must have cost her to make it, but, my God, I'm betrothed. I know I'm unfashionable, but I plan to be faithful to my wife."

James grinned crookedly. "What laudable sentiments. Are you sure they do not spring from disinterest in the lovely Lianne rather than your exalted sense of duty? And what of your bride? Surely you do not expect her to keep her vows. The notion of fidelity is quite alien to the female nature, particularly when the female in question is as beautiful as Miss Bridge and is entered in a marriage of convenience."

Ash felt his stomach tighten. "We will not discuss Amanda, James. While I value your advice, I think I do not wish to hear just now your jaundiced view of the female character."

James smiled. "A view formed over a lifetime of experience, my boy. Very well, then." He rose lazily. "Shall we toddle over to Gentleman Jackson's? Young Fisham has been issuing challenges to all comers, and needs taking down a peg, I believe."

Ash had no desire at the moment to try the mettle of young striplings, but feeling that a bout with the ex-champion Jackson might be just what was needed to relieve his scrambled sensibilities, he agreed willingly, and in a moment the two left the house in amity, walking sticks swinging.

A few days later, an impressive party made its way through the green vales of Wiltshire. The Bridges rode in their own coach, and in another, the dowager countess made a stately progression in company with Emily Wexford, Amanda, and Lianne, whom the dowager, for reasons of her own, had insisted be included in the party. Amanda could tell nothing from Ash's shuttered expression, but she assumed he must have seconded the dowager's wishes. Lianne was obviously pleased to have been invited. Two more vehicles containing luggage and a retinue of servants lumbered behind. Ash rode his own mount.

In consideration for the dowager's advanced age, the journey had been a leisurely one. Today, conversation had been sporadic among the ladies, Emily being the quiet sort and Lianne perhaps weary of the dowager's acid responses to her comments. Amanda, too, after three days of travel, found herself disinclined to chatter. She gazed, fascinated, at her first sight of the English countryside. Lord, it was beautiful, dotted with spinneys and villages. Why did anyone live in London? At her side, the dowager dozed fitfully.

Suddenly, Lianne straightened. "Oh, look!" she cried, pointing. "There is the turnoff to Fairwinds. Oh, how I long to see Papa and Mama again, even though it has only been a few weeks since I left home."

"Then we must be nearing Ashindon Park." Amanda glanced out the carriage window to where Ash rode beside them. Even after a long, tiring journey, observed Amanda, Ash sat tall and straight in the saddle, and he looked, as always, the complete aristocrat, exuding a male assurance that called to something elemental within her. As she watched, he gestured and pointed ahead with his riding crop. "We're nearly there!" he called.

A few minutes later, the procession turned from the highway and passed through a gate guarded by stone pillars. A lodge house stood uninhabited, its windows staring emptily at them as they passed. Amanda noted missing roof tiles and areas of crumbling brickwork. They drove for some time through unkempt parkland, and glancing surreptitiously at Ash, she saw his distress in the clench of his jaw and the stiffening of his shoulders.

"There!" cried Lianne as they rounded a long curve. "There is Ashindon Park."

Amanda looked, and felt something stir within her, a deep welling of helpless yearning that nearly overcame her. The house was not large, compared to the pictures of places such as Blenheim and Woburn she had seen, but it was surely older than either of those. Constructed of some sort of golden stone, it lay against a broad, green hill in a jumble of wings and courtyards. It looked as though it had grown there, nourished by the rain and sunlight of centuries, and Amanda felt as though the place reached out to cast a spell on her. It said "home" to her as had no other dwelling she had ever lived in. She ached to explore it, to know its nooks and crannies, to sleep within its walls and to raise children in its shelter.

Amanda stared, enthralled, as they approached the manor

house, and nearly gasped with pain as the evidence of neglect became apparent. Turrets crumbled and chimneys leaned drunkenly. A tangle of overgrown ivy covered windows and cornices, reminding Amanda of a tattered shawl worn to hide the blemishes of an aging Beauty.

When the carriage halted before a stained, weather-beaten entrance, Amanda nearly fell out of the vehicle in her haste. She ran toward the stairs as to a waiting lover, but was halted by Ash's hand on her arm.

"We won't be going in just yet. We will go straight on to the dower house. I merely wanted you to see the place." He nodded briefly to Jeremiah, who was clambering down from the Bridge carriage.

"Looks as though you should pull the whole place down before it falls about our ears," he grumbled.

"No!" cried Amanda, and as the others swung to her in surprise she mumbled, "that is, I'm sure it's not as bad as it looks."

"You are quite right," responded Ash. "The repairs needed are extensive, but there is life in the old place yet. It will see many more generations of Ashindons."

As they reentered their carriages and began moving once again, Amanda cast a last glance at the house through the rear window. She suppressed a surge of anguish at the knowledge that it would not be she who would be assisting in producing those generations.

"Well," said Jeremiah a week or so later over breakfast, "I begin to think you were right, missy. It will cost a fortune, but I believe the old place can be made liveable again."

"What a magnificent edifice!" exclaimed Serena. "You will be able to entertain the entire county, I daresay, and all your London friends when they come to visit. Oh, my dear," she said ecstatically to Amanda, "you will be the reigning hostess for miles around."

"What's that to say to anything?" snorted the dowager countess, who presided over one end of the table in the dower house dining room. "There ain't nothing for miles around except shabby-genteel squires and pig farmers."

"Oh, no, surely not!" replied Serena, scandalized. "Why, just next door are the Bonners. Not perhaps the first style of elegance, but perfectly respectable, and Lord and Lady Binstaff live not five miles away. In addition," she continued defensively, "as I said,

I'm sure Lord Ashindon will wish to entertain members of the *ton* residing in London."

The dowager cackled. "Does that include you and your husband?"

Jeremiah, who had immersed himself in *The Times*, betrayed by only a slight quiver of his paper that he had attended this remark, but Amanda, who had a partial view of her father, noted the telltale crimson that flooded his heavy cheeks.

Serena twittered distressfully, but made no response.

Amanda sank back in her chair, sipping from the cup of coffee she had been nursing for some minutes. Ash was not staying at the dower house, but occupied one of the few remaining bedchambers in the manor house to provide any degree of comfort. Over the last several days, she had explored the house with him from scullery to attics, usually accompanied by one or both of her parents. Wandering through the empty, shadowed rooms in the wake of a silent and rigid Ash, she had fallen completely under the spell of the place. She should have been depressed as she traversed through the empty, shadowed rooms. Holland covers shrouded the furniture, and what could be seen of the interior was hardly promising. The deterioration was still relatively unperceptible. but one had to walk carefully to avoid the rotten places in the ancient wooden flooring. Rain pouring through holes in the roof had caused extensive staining of walls, carpeting, and furnishings. The linenfold paneling in the state dining room almost crumbled to the touch. Filthy crystal chandeliers, missing lustres clanked disconsolately in the breezes that drifted unimpeded through sagging doors and windows. Over all lay a pall of dust and grime that seemed to have been accumulating for centuries. Through it all, Amanda had fallen even more deeply in love with the house.

Her imagination peopled the drawing rooms, salons, reception rooms, and halls with generations of Wexfords. In the ballroom, visions of dancers dressed in ruffs and doublets and hose, or hoops and satin breeches rose before her eyes, and the images of chubby little lordlings playing games and pouring over books in the nursery rose clear and poignant in her mind's eye. Reception rooms and halls were peopled in her imagination by ladies of the manor playing host to the county gentry of bygone years.

Amanda shook herself and returned to the breakfast table conversation.

"The kitchen!" Jeremiah was bellowing in astonishment. "With all that needs to be done to the place, you want to start in the kitchen?"

"Well, it does need a great deal of work if Amanda and Lord Ashindon plan to entertain. We must start with the installation of a closed stove. Those huge old hearths are positively medieval, and—"

"Will you strive for some sense, woman?" barked Jeremiah. "What good is a modern kitchen if the roof falls in while they're asleep in their beds some night?"

To Amanda's astonishment, instead of subsiding into her chair Serena sat up straighter, and replied calmly. "Of course, I am not suggesting that the kitchen is more important than the roof. I was merely looking ahead to the improvements that will have to be made once the house is put into repair, and I say we must begin with the kitchen."

Amanda almost laughed aloud at Jeremiah's expression of astonishment mixed with bewilderment, as though one of his coach horses had just wandered into the room asking if he might borrow a copy of *The Times. Way to go, Serena!* she chortled inwardly.

"I've been saying the same thing for years," interposed the dowager, gazing at Serena with a startled respect. "When I lived here, I had the whole service area brought up to modern standards—at least what was up to date for that time. They've brought out so many improvements recently. In those days we had money to spend on whatever we chose, of course, and did not have to rely on funding from outsiders." Once again, *The Times* rattled ominously.

"What are your plans for the day, Amanda?" asked Serena in a pathetically transparent attempt to infuse the atmosphere with a semblance of normalcy.

"Since this will be our last full day here, Ash is taking me fishing, and," she said, laughing, "I think I'd better start searching my wardrobe for something sufficiently grubby."

"Well, you do not forget you must return in plenty of time this afternoon to change. Do not forget that we are promised to the Bonners for dinner."

Right, thought Amanda gloomily. Lianne had declined to stay at the dower house, but chose instead to sojourn with her parents at nearby Fairwinds. Still, she had spent an inordinate amount of time at the Park, following along on the house tours, her light laughter echoing incongruously through the cavernous chambers. As Ash looked on in an attitude of tender amusement, she reminisced wistfully on the days when she and Ash and Grant had laughed and played in the corridors. She choked back tears at the signs of depredation in the house and expressed in tremulous accents her joy that the manor was to be brought back to its former glory. All the while, with a wisp of handkerchief delicately lifted to her great green eyes, she assured Amanda and Ash of her happiness for them.

Amanda, frankly, was ready to throw up, and the thought of spending an evening with Lianne and her family, *chez* Bonner, cast her into a profound depression. Determinedly, however, she thrust herself into her plainest gown and donned a pair of boots, dredged from a kitchen cupboard, that were two sizes too large for her. A big floppy bonnet completed her ensemble.

An hour and a half later, Ash and Amanda set out into the sunshine. Amanda was astonished at the change in Ash. Where before he had been rigidly restrained, his anguish fairly radiating from his silent, closed figure as he listened to Jeremiah appraising his family's treasures to pound, pence, and shillings, he seemed relaxed now, and he was smiling. Garbed in old breeches, coat, and shabby brogans, he carried an assortment of fishing poles, several small boxes of what Amanda supposed contained lures, and a frowsty woven basket to serve as a creel.

Ash turned to Amanda. A smile had spread over his face on first catching sight of her, and it returned now. "My dear, I don't know what they'd say at Almack's, but you are looking perfectly splendid today."

Amanda grunted. "Well you may laugh. I almost decided to steal a pair of breeches from the knives and boots boy. I may look comfortable, but this is not what I consider walking gear."

That was another egregious disadvantage of this time period, thought Amanda resentfully. At home—in Chicago—she practically lived in jeans when she wasn't teaching. She had had just about enough of long, encumbering skirts and tight puffed sleeves. When she returned to her own time, the first thing on her agenda would be a long, hot shower and a pair of worn, comfy jeans.

At Ash's chuckle, she said nothing, however, and hooking her arm through his, set off whistling.

A longish walk through fragrant meadows and leafy lanes brought them to the stream, gurgling merrily to itself as it made its way through a small wood that lay on the north edge of the Park. Amanda breathed in the fresh country air with relish, wondering again why anyone with any sense would choose to live in smelly, sooty London when he or she could live in this idyllic paradise. She supposed, on second thought, that knowing one was about to lose the paradise to creditors would cast a pall on enjoyment of same.

Lazily, she watched Ash setting out the fishing apparatus.

"Now, Miss Bridge, have you ever fished before?"

"Once or twice—a very long time ago. My father used to take me."

"Jeremiah?" asked Ash in surprise.

She had not meant Jeremiah, but she nodded her head.

"Huh," said Ash, "I would not have thought—but never mind. Do you wish to try some casting?"

Amanda smiled. "What I wish to do, I'm afraid, is simply sit here and soak up this delightful day, but, yes, I shall do my part in massacring the poor fishy denizens of your creek. Lead me to them."

In a few moments, Amanda stood on the bank, rod in hand. Ash stood beside her, having discarded coat and hat. His black hair, tossed in windblown disarray caught the sun in ebony glints, and his arms, exposed by rolled shirtsleeves, were as muscular as Amanda had suspected they would be. Firmly turning her attention from the fascinating sight of the Earl of Ashindon in dishabille, she cast with great enthusiasm and little skill. As a result, she nearly fell into the water.

Sweeping an arm around her, Ash laughed. "Here, let me show you." He did not release her, but keeping one arm about her shoulders and with the other guiding her arm, he sent the line floating lazily into the creek, the lure landing with a plop almost halfway across.

"Now," he said, his head very close to hers, "just let it float along."

And that's just what Amanda wished to do more than anything else right then—just float along in his arms with the bees humming beside them and the glorious English sunshine warming them. She fancied she could feel his heart beating, and her own pulse thrummed in response. Oddly, she felt none of the throbbing heat she had experienced during that kiss in the music room. She merely wanted to lean into his strength, to rest her head on his shoulder, and stay right there in the warmth of his embrace for the next year or two.

The next moment, Amanda felt a jerk on her hook. "I've got something!" she cried, her tone indicating the catch must be nothing less than leviathan in scale, and, indeed, it proved to be a wriggling trout of respectable length and tonnage. Ash declared himself suitably impressed.

The morning progressed in this leisurely fashion, and after lunch they lounged, replete, on the stream's grassy banks. Conversation was desultory, and not what could be called stimulating.

"Yes," Ash said in response to Amanda's sleepy remark, "the cloud is shaped rather like a horse's head. Look over a little to the left. I rather fancy that bank is going to be a castle in a few minutes, do not you? See the turrets are already forming."

"I see it," she said with a chuckle. "Do you suppose it will have a moat and a drawbridge?"

"Of course," declared Ash solemnly. "And a dragon prowling about."

"Oh, good," Amanda replied sleepily. "I do like dragons."

Ash bent a glance on her and she returned it, a sad tenderness twisting within her. After she was gone—returned to her proper place in space and time—would he bring Lianne here? Perhaps they would bring their children with them. She hoped he and Lianne would have a big family. Yes, of course, she hoped that.

She scrambled to her feet. "I suppose we should be starting back," she said casually.

Ash rose to his feet reluctantly. "You are right. The Bonners will expect us to arrive on time."

Amanda was startled to observe a look of resignation on his face. Surely, he must be eagerly anticipating an evening spent with Lianne. Of course, she reminded herself, the prospect was no doubt painful, as well, since he believed her lost to him.

In companionable silence, they packed up the remains of the picnic lunch.

"There is one raspberry tart left," remarked Ash. "Would you care for it?"

He turned to face her, the tart proffered in one hand, and it seemed to Amanda that all the silver laughter of the stream lay in the eyes that hovered so close to hers. She put out a hand for the pastry—and suddenly stilled. For an instant, time seemed suspended as a moment of breathless clarity descended on her.

Dear God, she thought dazedly, *I'm in love with him.*

Chapter Seventeen

Some hours later, Amanda stood motionless under the ministering hands of Hutchings, staring sightlessly into the mirror as the little maid swept her hair into a nest of spun gold.

What an absurd thing to happen, she thought for the hundredth time since that blinding moment of revelation earlier in the day on the sunny riverbank. She could not possibly have fallen in love with a man whose acquaintance she had made a bare month and a half ago.

But she had.

This changed everything, she reflected wildly. On the other hand, it changed nothing. Ash was still in love with someone other than her own gorgeous self. His courtesy, his seeming enjoyment of her company—those head-spinning kisses, were all an effort on his part to create a sense of commitment to the betrothal, and she must not let them lure her into thinking he felt anything beyond a mild affection for her.

No, her duty lay clear. She must redouble her efforts to set him on his feet financially. Then she would bow gracefully out of his life so that he could marry the woman he had loved since childhood. The fact that carrying out her plan would now be so much harder than she had dreamed possible must have no bearing on her actions.

She had plenty of time, at least. Serena had decided that the wedding would take place in May of the following year, just as the Season would be moving into high gear. The even was to be held in that most fashionable of churches, St. George's in Hanover Square.

She had already begun mining Jeremiah, asking for one gown after another, until she thought he would surely balk. He was ever the indulgent father, however, and usually topped her requests by suggestions for even more finery. Unfortunately, most of her wearables were ordered from modistes and the bills sent directly to Jeremiah, thus eliminating the chance for Amanda to get her itchy fingers on any actual cash beyond that to be spent ostensibly on such minor items as shawls and ribbons and laces.

Of course, there was the Gibraltar-sized diamond that Papa had given her on the evening of the announcement ball. She could probably sell that for several thousand pounds, and there was all the other expensive jewelry in the box that was brought from Papa's safe to her dressing table when she went out of an evening. She felt no compunction about taking advantage of Jeremiah's largess, for she was certain it did not spring from generosity, but merely a desire on her father's part to impress the world to which he so desperately desired admittance. And he could afford to buy expensive baubles by the gross. Besides, Ash had stated his intention of paying back every farthing of Jeremiah's largess. If only she could come upon a really big surefire investment opportunity that would reap almost immediate results.

At least, work would be starting soon on the Park. Tomorrow, Ash's land agent, one George Creevey, would arrive for a consultation, and Ash and Jeremiah would sit down with him to decide where to start. Ash had already stated that he wished to begin with the tenants' cottages, but to Jeremiah's mind this was money wasted. It was the manor house where his daughter would live, and where she would throw lavish parties for the *ton,* thus it was the manor house that should receive immediate attention. She rather thought Ash would win out, but—

"There you are, miss, and you look a fair treat."

Amanda came to with a start, realizing that Hutchings was addressing her.

"If that Lady Ashindon thinks she can outshine you, with her black hair and her green eyes, she has another think coming." The maid spoke with smug satisfaction, and Amanda gazed at her with surprise. The interest taken by the servants in their employers' lives and the instinctive sniffing out of their primary concerns never failed to amaze her.

"Really, Hutchings," she said with a light laugh. "I am not competing with Lady Ashindon." Her heart sank as she realized the truth of this statement. She was no competition for the Lovely

Lianne, for the emerald-eyed beauty was already in possession of the prize. Amanda was not looking forward to dinner this evening at the Bonner manse.

Horatio Bonner was a tall, thin gentleman, brusque of manner and fastidious in appearance. His wife, Charity, was slender, as well, given to floating draperies and an air of fragility.

The Bonners received Ash with expressions of pleasure and greeted his guests courteously enough, though with an almost undisguised curiosity. The dowager countess was viewed with awe. Jeremiah, they obviously regarded as some sort of exotic specimen, like one of the animals in the Tower menagerie.

Lianne hovered over Ash with a proprietary air that grated on Amanda's already raw sensibilities. To her annoyance, Ash did not dissuade the young countess when she regaled the company with tales of childhood escapades with Ash and his cousin, nor did he see fit to remove her hands from his lapel when she reached, seemingly unaware of her actions, to brush away a piece of lint or to straighten his neckcloth.

The meal consisted of sturdy country fare, and Amanda—who had never considered herself a junk food addict but who now dreamed nightly of cheeseburgers and fries and would have killed for a pizza, dutifully devoured steak and kidney pie, along with sweetbreads in sauce and other items she would formerly have considered inedible.

The conversation was propelled by Lianne, who imparted to her parents and the rest of the company tales of her recent stay in London.

"Really, Papa, Lord Mumblethorpe has grown so prodigiously fat you would not recognize him, is that not so, Grandmama? And, Mama, do you remember how we used to laugh at Lady Wilburforce's unfortunate habit of wearing every piece of jewelry she owned? Well, Lord W. must be very openhanded, for now she positively clanks when she walks, and one wonders how she can make her way across the room under all that weight." Her musical laughter floated around the room.

The dowager leveled a basilisk stare at her granddaughter-in-law. "In my day," she snapped, "it was considered ill-mannered in silly young chits to pass rude remarks on their elders. Not that you're all that young anymore."

Lianne flushed and Ash spoke quickly. "But, Grandmama," he remonstrated with a laugh, "you've been passing rude remarks about everybody ever since I can remember."

Unfazed, the old lady glared back. "Young idiot! I don't have any elders. The whole world is younger than I and has been for donkeys' years. Besides, I'm not rude, I'm merely honest. Eh?" She swung toward Jeremiah, who had uttered an explosive sound. The dowager stiffened in her chair. "Sirrah? Are you presuming to comment on my manners?"

Amanda turned to watch Jeremiah, and as expected his face immediately flamed in rage. Instead of swallowing his spleen, however, he took a deep breath before smiling genially. "No," said the Brass Bridge, "I wouldn't presume to any such thing, because you haven't any. Manners, that is. I expect that's why you've borrowed those of a fishwife." Turning, he waved offhandedly to a hovering footman. "I wonder if I could have another portion of that excellent tripe. You are to be congratulated, Mrs. Bonner; your cook has a way with sauces." So saying, he bent his head to address his dinner.

The rest of the company swung toward the dowager, who spluttered in outraged astonishment for some moments before attending to her plate, completely silenced. Amanda could have sworn she detected a twinkle in the old lady's eye as she took up her fork.

Amanda applauded inwardly, but the incident proved the evening's only bright spot. Lianne continued to monopolize Ash's attention under the fond gaze of her parents, who made it evident they considered the earl very much a part of their family. Amanda found herself growing angrier as Ash responded with laughter to Lianne's sallies, until she felt that if he did not wipe that loopy grin from his face she would be forced to do so with the back of her hand.

Jaw clenched and fingers curled into talons, Amanda smiled and chatted inconsequentially through the rest of the meal—and conversation with ladies afterward—and more conversation when they were joined by the gentlemen later. Then there was tea and more conversation, until Amanda's tongue fairly clove to the roof of her mouth.

At last, it was time for the earl's party to make their departure. They rose and drifted out into the hall to don outer garments, and

with a tightening of her stomach, Amanda noticed Lianne and
Ash disappearing unobtrusively into a small corridor. As the
group stood chattering for some minutes and the two did not reap-
pear, Amanda followed them. Hearing a small, choked sound emanating from a small room just off the corridor, she peered into
the chamber. There, in a shaft of moonlight, stood Ash, his arms
tightly enfolded about Lianne, his mouth on hers in a deep kiss.

At Amanda's gasp, the couple whirled, and with an embarrassed titter Lianne rushed to the door. Pushing past Amanda
without a word, she ran from the room. Amanda, almost choking
on the hurt and humiliation that rose in her like a bitter tide,
turned to leave as well, but Ash reached her as she stumbled in
her blind exit.

"Amanda! Please—what you saw—"

Amanda swung to face him. "What I saw was the man to whom
I am betrothed—Mr. Commitment, no less—kissing another
woman."

"It wasn't like that. I was not actually—well, yes, I was, but—"

If Amanda had not been in such a painful fury, she could almost have laughed at Ash's ludicrous and unwonted loss of composure. He reached to clasp her shoulders in a convulsive grip.

"Amanda, I swear it was only a kiss for—for old times' sake—
a kiss of friendship. Believe me—"

"I don't care if it was a kiss of astral harmony!" Amanda was
horrified at the piercing screech she heard in her voice. "You are
betrothed to me, and while that engagement stands, I do not expect you to go around mauling other women."

"I was not mauling her. And Lianne is not 'other women,' for
God's sake. She—"

"Yes, I know. She is the great love of your life, your great
tragedy, your lost passion. Well, you'll have her back, I promise
you—all in good time, but in the meanwhile, I do not think it's
too much to expect you to honor our betrothal—just as if it were
the real thing."

"Of course, it is—the real thing. You must know—"

But Amanda, realizing that the torrent of tears rising behind her
eyes was about to burst from her in a noisy storm, wrenched herself from his grip and stumbled blindly from the room.

"Amanda!" he called after her, but he was answered only by
the sound of her slippers running along the corridor.

Ash stood for a moment in the silence of the empty room. Of all the people in the world to witness his farewell kiss to Lianne—Oh, God.

When, he wondered dully, had Lianne's presence become a burden to him rather than a pleasure? How was it that he had never noticed the vacuity of her artless chatter? How could he be in love with a woman and wish to be elsewhere every time she was with him? The hardness of her features that he had noticed earlier seemed more pronounced lately. She bored him when she did not irritate him to snapping point, and her voice had taken on an unpleasant whine every time she spoke to him. The evening he had just spent in her company was one of the most trying he had experienced in his life. Because she was Lianne, he had been attentive and responded with tender smiles to her absurdities. He had been almost overcome with an urge to fling her hands from him when she took persistent liberties with him. When she had drawn him into this secluded chamber, he had followed, and his appalled sense of guilt at the distaste he felt had led him to kiss her. That, he admitted, and the need to prove to himself of his feeling for her—one way or another.

He had felt nothing.

Was it possible he really had fallen out of love? He was not a callow youth, after all, drifting from one infatuation to another. Lianne had been the only star in his firmament for all his adult life. That the star had inexplicably faded was surely a reflection on his own inadequacy, and not on Lianne.

She had offered him the ultimate gift, her promise to become his mistress. He should feel honored—and humbled. Instead, he was aware only of the growing conviction that James had been right. Lianne's professed love for him now seemed superficial at best, and her offer based almost solely on opportunism.

And what of himself? He had loved her for as long as he could remember. What kind of monster was he that he could simply turn his passion off as he would a spigot. Well, no, he hadn't consciously decided not to love Lianne, but that apparently was what had happened.

"I do not love Lianne." He whispered the words aloud and was aware of a strange lightening of spirit, as though he had been released from an old, powerful spell. He tried to feel suitably depressed at the metamorphosis he had just undergone. After all, the death of love must be a profoundly moving experience, but his heart persisted in thrumming lightheartedly and his thoughts kept drifting to Amanda. He enjoyed Amanda's company more than he would have thought possible. She was intelligent, independent, and altogether fascinating. He found her sapphire gaze compelling, and even the scent of her seemed to stay with him long after they parted.

He had, of course, made it perfectly clear, as she had to him, that their marriage was to be one of convenience and that was the way he intended to conduct their union. She had given not the slightest indication that her affection was engaged. He laughed shortly. He would be fortunate now if he could persuade Amanda to speak to him again.

He certainly did not want Amanda's love, for he did not love her. Right now, he felt that he had expended his entire fund of that emotion and it had left him disinclined to enter into it again. Love, he decided, was an illusion.

On the other hand, now that he was free of his feelings for Lianne, he vowed he would do his best to make his marriage a success. Amanda deserved, if not his love, at least his total commitment to their arrangement.

His thoughts drifted back to the fishing expedition earlier in the day. For a few hours he had been relaxed and happy, able to pretend that all was well at Ashindon Park—that his home stood whole and prosperous, basking in the sun of an English summer. The morning had taken on an idyllic quality, and when he had encircled Amanda in his arms he had wanted to press his lips against the place where her golden curls met the fragile perfection of her neck. It was as though the two of them had been enclosed in a magic bubble, floating lazily under the warmth of an enchanted sky, safe and happy and protected from reality.

He shook himself. Amanda kept saying that she was not going to marry him at all. She intended, she said, to make it possible for him to marry his true love! Did this avowal disguise a basic antipathy toward him? When he had kissed her on the night of their betrothal ball, he had felt the response that shuddered through her. She did not seem the type to feign a passion she did not feel, but events had proven that his knowledge of the female psyche was not to be trusted. At any rate, he was sure he would soon bring Amanda to the realization that their marriage was inevitable.

Feeling profoundly weary, he left the darkened little salon to make his way to the voluble throng still congregated in the hall.

The next day, the group departed for London. Amanda did not see Ash until he appeared at the dower house just as the carriages pulled up. In the general confusion attendant to getting baggage and passengers stowed in the vehicles, he drew Amanda aside.

"I do not wish to speak to you right now, my lord," she said, white and rigid.

"No, I suppose you do not. Nor do I have any desire to stand here brangling with you in full view of your parents." Ash, too, was pale, but had regained his usual composure. He spoke now in tones as cool as though he were requesting her hand for a dance. "I merely wish to apologize for what occurred last night, and to assure you that it will never happen again."

Amanda did not respond, but with a curt nod turned away from him to ascend to the dowager countess's ancient traveling coach.

During the first part of the journey, she gazed studiously out of the window, unable to take part in Lianne's inane chatter or the dowager's irascible mutterings. Her stomach still roiled in help-less rage. How dare he sneak away from a family party to steal kisses from his little tart? Could he have not waited a day or two, when he would have her all to himself in the young countess's house in Portman Square? She drew in her breath sharply. She had not considered before that Ash might be keeping Lianne as his mistress. How could she not have thought of this? What did a Regency gentleman do when faced with the prospect of a loveless marriage? Why, set up a cozy armful for himself with all possible speed. And if the armful was a lover of long standing, why so much the better.

She knew she was being unfair. She did not believe Ash was a common garden-variety womanizer, and if he had availed himself of an opportunity to have his cake and eat it, too, was he wholly to blame? Amanda knew she had not acquitted herself well the previous night. She had howled like a nor'easter at his perceived perfidy, giving him no opportunity to explain. On the other hand, what could he say? The point was, Ash had stolen a moment to be alone with the woman he loved, and surely he could not be faulted for that. He had, after all, made no declarations of love to her, and if she'd had the misfortune to fall in love with him, he was scarcely to blame.

But, dammit, she didn't want him kissing Lianne, or anybody else. She'd leave him to it soon enough, but until then, she was by God not going to stand by and watch him make love to another woman.

She ardently wished she could depart the year 1815 tomorrow, but even if she knew how to accomplish this she could not in all conscience flee. She must remain here at least until Ashindon Park was put into repair, and until she had somehow enabled Ash to accrue enough money to get the rest of the estate back into working order. Then she could leave with a clear conscience. She had almost a year. Surely, that would be time enough and then some.

But how was she to live that year in Ash's constant company, watching him pine for Lianne? For that matter, she thought, twitching her skirts in annoyance, how was she to exist in the stultifying environment of Regency London for a year? She was sick to the screaming point of the constraints applied to "a gently bred female." She couldn't even vote, for God's sake, let alone help to remedy the injustice of England's swollen monarchial system with its attendant land-rich nobility.

"What?" she asked blankly, aware that the dowager had reached over to jab her knee.

"I said, what the devil are you maundering about over there in your corner? Do you mean to leave me with no one else to talk to except this flibbertigibbet?" She gestured autocratically to Lianne.

Amanda sighed. It was going to be a very long twelve months.

Chapter Eighteen

Neither Ash nor Amanda referred to the incident in the little salon again. Upon returning to the city, they plunged into what was left of the social season, though London in the middle of June was growing thin of company. In addition, Ash capitulated, not without protest, to Amanda's requests to be taken sight-seeing in the city and its environs.

Of Lianne, little was seen. She seemed to have retired from the haunts of the *ton*, at least temporarily, for she did not attend Lady Danton's musicale, or the soiree given by Lord and Lady Hammerford, or any of the other functions still dotting the social landscape.

The threat of Napoleon's plans for the reconquest of Europe scarcely caused a ripple in the lives of the *beau monde*, but from time to time word of his activities drifted in from the Continent to cloud the horizon. The news, apparently, was not good. Jeremiah spent an increasing amount of time closeted in his study with various men of business. When not thus occupied, he made hasty trips into the City, returning tight-lipped and grim.

Amanda, of course, received the scraps of information that filtered down to her female ears with complete equanimity.

One afternoon, Ash arrived at the Bridge home for a proposed visit to Gloucester House to visit the Grecian marbles brought recently to England by Lord Elgin. As Ash handed his fiancée into his curricle, Jeremiah pulled up in his small, closed carriage and, disembarking hastily, he called out, "My lord! Ashindon! I must speak with you!" Ignoring his daughter, he grasped Ash's arm. Amanda caught the words, "Boney," and "Quatre Bras" as Jeremiah pulled Ash bodily into the house. More than an hour passed before they emerged from Jeremiah's study, at which time Ash apologized to Amanda before once more assisting her into the curricle.

"What on earth was that all about?" asked Amanda as they swung into North Audley Street.

"Nothing," replied Ash, his face impassive. "Merely a business matter."

"But what was he saying about Napoleon?" persisted Amanda.

Ash turned to her with a smile. "I keep forgetting I am betrothed to a bluestocking. You used not to be interested in any but the most inconsequential matters."

Amanda bristled. "If choosing to use my brain for something beyond my embroidery and the latest gossip makes me a bluestocking, so be it."

Ash laughed. "Very well, then. Apparently, Napoleon left Paris a few days ago and is headed for Belgium. He is rumored to have over a hundred thousand men, and more arriving daily to swell his ranks. Wellington seems to be doing nothing, and the allies are still miles away from the projected battle area."

"Yes, but—" Amanda halted.

"The feeling is growing in the City that the allied forces are going to be very badly defeated."

"Oh, no," said Amanda quickly. "Napoleon's renewed dreams of glory are doomed to failure."

"I must say I, too, am more sanguine of Wellington's chances. However, your father is greatly concerned about the effect of a British defeat on my financial status. You see, when Napoleon escaped from Elba, there was a slight dip in the Consols—government stocks," Ash explained.

Amanda nodded impatiently. "Yes, I know. But, what—?"

"Your father advised me to buy up some of the stock—in moderation. I took his advice, for it coincided with my own inclination, but I invested rather more heavily than he thought prudent. In doing so, I depleted my already meager supply of available cash, and now your father is advising me to sell."

"Oh, you mustn't!" Amanda began, but she stopped suddenly, her jaw dropping. A great light had just burst over her—and about time, she thought with a grimace. Good Lord, how could she have been so stupid? She had been racking her brains for a get-rich-quick investment scheme and it had been waiting for her all along in her memory. Quickly, she rummaged in her mind for every bit of information she possessed on one of the greatest battles in English history. Wasn't it Rothschild, the financier, who had made a killing at the time? All she had to do was to convince Ash to sink every penny he could get his hands on in the funds.

Hmmm. This might not be so easy. She would be asking him to fly in the face of prevailing counsel, all on the advice of a mere female. Ash, she thought, seemed a trifle more enlightened on the subject of women in general—at least, he seemed to regard her as a real person and not a prospective piece of property. However, advice of this magnitude might very well be received with a pat on the head and the suggestion that she not worry her pretty head over matters of which she could not possibly have any comprehension.

"You aren't going to take Papa's advice, are you?" she asked at last. "You're not going to sell your government stock?"

"No. At least not yet. I fought with Wellington in Portugal and Spain for four years, and I have a great deal more confidence in him than the self-styled military experts who are spouting their ill-formed opinions all over town. On the other hand, Wellington's army is not the same as it was in the Peninsula. Many of his seasoned troops are now elsewhere—America and India, leaving him with raw recruits and ill-trained foreigners. Still, I believe I'll keep my money on Wellington. Literally," he said with a laugh.

Amanda settled back into the curricle. She would have said more, but Ash continued, on another tack. "You and my grandmother are growing wondrous thick of late." He turned to smile into her eyes, which produced, Amanda noted irritably, the usual result of turning her knees to soup. "I'm pleased she has taken such a liking to you."

Amanda tore her gaze from his. "I like her, too," she replied thoughtfully. Almost to herself, she continued, "She's a truly remarkable woman. Did you know she has created schools for young girls of the slums—to teach them to read, and to learn useful skills in the hope that they might escape the grinding poverty that so enslaves them?"

"No," replied Ash, startled. "I did not—but I am not surprised. She has always been strong-minded and independent—to put it mildly," he said dryly. "She is the scourge of the family, and has never been bound by the restraints of custom."

"That is what I so much admire in her," said Amanda enthusiastically. "She has managed to overcome many of the stereotypes that prevail here and she has maintained her own identity. She told me," Amanda continued, "of her contributions to the efforts of Elizabeth Fry."

"Fry?" Ash's brows lifted. "You mean the woman that's agitating for prison reform? Good God!" he said suddenly. "Don't tell me Grandmama has been visiting Newgate."

Amanda giggled. "No, she is quite incensed that Mrs. Fry will not take her."

"Good God," murmured Ash again. He cast a sidelong glance at Amanda. "Uh—do you have any plans to attach yourself to Mrs. Fry and her movement?"

"Would you object if I did?" asked Amanda with a smile that was tinged with sadness. The question was purely academic. If all went as she planned, Ash would soon be marrying a woman who would no more consider espousing an unpopular cause than she would walk naked down Piccadilly. To Amanda's surprise, Ash appeared to consider her words seriously.

"I don't know," he said slowly. "God knows our prisons are a national shame. Not that we don't need to do something about our other inequities. I've always thought that if and when I get things squared away at the Park, I'd become more active in the House of Lords."

Amanda stared at him, listening to her heart break into great, jagged pieces. She had not realized how empty her life was in the twentieth century until she had come to know a man who would have filled it with joy and love. Unfortunately, that man had been born almost two hundred years too soon, not to mention the fact that he was in love with another woman.

"That's very commendable," she said shakily. She turned away, swallowing the tears she thought would choke her. It took all the self-control at her command to chatter brightly until they reached Gloucester House, where the marbles were currently being displayed.

Amanda had visited the British Museum on the first day of her arrival in that fair April of 1996. The Elgin Marbles were among the first items on her prioritized list of "things to see in England." She had dutifully admired them, trying as she always did with such objects to visualize them as they had originally glowed in the sunlight of Athens over two thousand years ago. She had as little success at this as she did now, standing next to Ash.

"They're very large, aren't they?" she said at last.

"Mmp," grunted Ash in agreement. "The women look as though they could wrestle bears."

"Still, they are quite magnificent, are they not?"

"Quite. Or at least they would be if they still retained all their body parts. That fellow shaking his spear over there would be much more threatening if he weren't missing his head. How long do we have to stay here?" he asked plaintively.

Amanda laughed. "I shall take pity on you. If you will take me to Gunter's for an ice, we may leave right now."

"Done!" said Ash with alacrity, propelling her toward the exit.

Later, at the famous pastry shop, Ash having gone inside to procure ices for himself and his lady, the two sat in the curricle, companionably nibbling the famous delicacy under the trees that shaded Berkeley Square.

"Thank you for taking me to see the marbles," said Amanda at last. "You have truly performed above and beyond the call of a fiancé this last week."

"I should rather think so!" exclaimed Ash, much struck. "I cannot think of another man of my acquaintance who have made such a cake of himself—swanning about London like the veriest gapeseed. First there was the menagerie at the Tower, then the Egyptian Hall, and Westminster Abbey after that. I almost drew the line at Hampton Court Palace, only my staunch sense of duty—"

"All right, all right," said Amanda, lifting a hand in protest. "You have my profound thanks for so lowering yourself."

At that moment, Ash reached to brush a stray tendril of hair from her cheek. "It has been my pleasure, my dear," he said in all seriousness. "For I like the bluestocking much better than the empty-headed butterfly I used to think you. I wonder now how I could have been so mistaken. Or were you going about in disguise?"

Amanda, shaken, took refuge in a bantering tone. "It was simply that you never took the time to know the real me, sir. I have always been as you see me."

Which was perfectly true, of course, in a manner of speaking, but mostly it was decidedly untrue, a fact of which Amanda was only too aware.

                              *   *   *

The news from Belgium continued unpromising, and two days later on a quiet Sunday afternoon, a grim Jeremiah once again summoned Ash to the Bridge home. Amanda greeted him at the door and stood by his side as Jeremiah, hurrying from his study, spoke harshly, without preamble. "Wellington has gone down to defeat."

"What?" exclaimed Ash.

"The news has been pouring in all day. The Prussians were routed at the outset of the confrontation between Boney and Wellington, and Boney followed up with one of his lightening strikes. Wellington had to fall back beyond the River Sambre."

"Are you saying that Wellington has retreated?"

"No, you idiot, I'm saying that your precious Wellington has been beat, foot, horse, and artillery. We might have known," he concluded bitterly, "that he could not win in a face-to-face confrontation with Napoleon."

"But, how do you know all this?"

"It's common knowledge in the City. Bonaparte is in Brussels right now, dictating terms."

Amanda, watching Ash's white-faced reaction to Jeremiah's words, slipped her hand in his. She felt his fingers tighten around hers.

"There's complete panic in the City," continued Jeremiah. "Every jobber in the place is rushing around trying to sell, and that's what I've done, too. Took a gawd-awful loss, but I've got my fingers in a lot of pies and I can stand the blunt. My advice to you, young feller," he continued, jabbing a finger into Ash's cravat, "is to sell your stock as well. We'll use Gliddings, my man of business. He'll get you the best possible price." He pulled Ash toward the door. "We must go now. If we leave it any longer you'll have a disaster on your hands."

Carefully removing Jeremiah's hand from his sleeve, Ash shook his head. "I have not yet decided to sell, Mr. Bridge. Should I do so, I'll get my own man to handle the transactions."

"You fool!" shouted Jeremiah. "Don't you understand what's going on?"

"I think perhaps it is you who does not understand," replied Ash coolly, "However, I promise I shall give serious thought to your advice."

He turned to go, and Jeremiah, after one or two incomprehensible utterances, bellowed after him, "Just don't count on me to save your groats on this, Ashindon!" Then, throwing up his hands, he swung about and stumped back to his study.

Amanda followed Ash, still clasping his hand.

"What are you going to do?" she asked quietly.

He smiled somewhat painfully. "Despite what I just said to your father, I think I shall have to sell. I still believe in Wellington, but I cannot afford to lose everything. Your father has promised to restore my—our home, but I'm determined to get back on my feet on my own. The thought of being eternally beholden to that man—I'm sorry, Amanda, I know he's your father, but . . ."

His mouth tightened and Amanda longed to lay her fingers along the rigid line of his jaw.

"But, you mustn't sell, Ash," she whispered, her voice rough with intensity. "Wellington is winning. I tell you, within two days Napoleon will be skulking back to Paris with his tail between his legs."

Ash's expression relaxed a fraction. "Your patriotism is commendable, my dear, but in this instance you are delving into matters of which you have no knowledge." He placed his curly brimmed beaver hat atop his head, pushing it into a jaunty angle. "I must be off to, er, save my groats," he said, with an effort at lightness that was painful to behold.

"No!" Almost dizzy with the conflicting thoughts that raced through her brain, Amanda clung to his sleeve. Dear God, if only she had more time to think! Pausing for the merest instant to collect herself, she came to a decision.

"You must not sell out of the funds." When Ash's mouth opened in protest, she continued hurriedly, "I must talk to you, in private."

Ash shook himself from her grasp in some irritation. "I don't have time for a tête-à-tête right now, Amanda."

"Ash, this is important. Wait right here."

She whirled about and ran up the stairs to her room, returning a few minutes later garbed in pelisse and bonnet. "Now," she said breathlessly, "take me someplace where we can talk, privately and without interruption."

Ash opened his mouth to speak, but staring down into her eyes, he caught himself. He said nothing, but ushered her from the house. Fifteen minutes later, his curricle swung into Green Park, from whence he proceeded to the leafy glade where they had conversed on Amanda's first day in Regency London.

"This is a good as place as any. Now, what is it, Amanda? I really must not stay long."

Amanda drew in a long, shaky breath.

"Ash, you have commented several times on the change you have observed in me since—since my little debacle in Grosvenor Chapel."

"Yes," he replied, his voice tinged with impatience.

"There is a reason for that." Amanda paused for a moment before continuing. "My Lord Ashindon, allow me to introduce myself. My name is Amanda McGovern and I was—will be born in the year nineteen hundred and sixty-eight."

Chapter Nineteen

For a long moment, Ash simply stared at her, his eyes wide with shock. "Amanda," he said at last, taking her hand in his. "Amanda—"

"No—please. Let me finish. It all started on a day in April of 1996. I was sitting in Grosvenor Chapel when I met this strange man . . ."

Her story did not take long in the telling, and when she was finished, Amanda sat back, her hands folded, and watched Ash expectantly. Her heart sank when his only words were, "Amanda, my dear, I had no idea you were so ill."

She sighed. "As in bonkers, you mean. I guess I can't blame you for coming to that conclusion. I thought the same thing at first. I thought I was hallucinating, and it was days before I realized that I had actually, er, traveled through time," she finished lamely. It seemed like such a lunatic fringe sort of thing to say. "Look," she continued hastily as Ash opened his mouth, "you have remarked frequently on the abrupt change in my personality after my supposed elopement attempt. The way I spoke, for example. In fact, I think you said specifically that I was a different person."

"I meant that you *seemed* a different person. Merely a figure of speech."

Amanda paused, as a thought struck her. "You also thought I was faking amnesia. Ash, do you think I made up the story I just told you?"

His answer was oblique. "It did not take me long to realize that your amnesia was genuine—although now, I suppose you will say it was not amnesia at all. Frankly, I do not know what to think now, except that I believe you think you are telling the truth. As I said, you are obviously suffering from some sort of mental aberration." The concern in his eyes took some of the sting from his words, and Amanda exhaled a sigh of relief.

She grinned determinedly. "Let us shelve for a moment the subject of my general dottiness. I have in my possession something that I think will convince you that what I claim is true." She ran her finger beneath the lace at her throat and pulled out the little gold pendant that she had placed in her dressing table drawer on that morning so many weeks ago. Passing it over her head, she handed it to Ash.

"What's this?"

"It's something I brought with me from the twentieth century. I was wondering why it came with me, when nothing else did, but now I understand. Whoever, or whatever brought me here figured I might need proof at some point. Look at it, please."

Ash examined the coin curiously. " 'In God we trust,' " he read. "Who is the bearded gentleman?"

"His name is Abraham Lincoln, the sixteenth president of the United States of America. He was—will be—assassinated in 1865, shortly after the Civil War. Yes, we had one of those, too," she added. "The date, Ash—look at the date."

" '1989,' " murmured Ash wonderingly. "Where did you get this?"

Amanda stiffened. "I did not have it made up myself during the last few weeks, if that's what you're implying."

"No," said Ash, still turning the coin in his hands. "It looks undeniably authentic, but I don't understand—"

"From—from a friend. Ash, this is currency. It was—will be—minted in 1989, just as it says. Don't you see what that means?"

"Of course, I see what it means," growled Ash. "I'm just saying there has to be some other explanation." He turned the coin idly in his fingers. "Who is Derek?" he asked abruptly.

"Der—? Oh. He—he's someone I used to know."

"It sounds as though you must have known him rather well." Ash's tone was light, but contained an underlying edge.

"Ash, I do not wish to talk about Derek right now. There will be time enough later to tell you about the life and times of Amanda McGovern. Right now, we have other things to discuss. As it happens, I have a good reason for divulging my recent, ah, adventures.

Ash said nothing, but lifted his brows once more.

"You see, I am in a position to do you a spot of good."

"Oh?"

Amanda clenched her hands at the skepticism in Ash's voice.

"Yes," she said curtly. "You must not sell out of the funds, Ash. In fact, you must try to buy even more, for right at this moment Wellington is defeating Napoleon in a terrible battle near a little village called Waterloo."

"I never heard of it," said Ash, the disbelief in his tone undiminished.

"I daresay. It's about ten miles south of Brussels."

"Mmp."

"Anyway, the price of government stock will continue to fall until by tomorrow afternoon you'll be able to scoop up shares by the bucketful for practically nothing. All the next day, a pall of gloom will hang over the city, but late on Wednesday, the twenty-first, a carriage will be sighted leaving St. James's Palace. It will drive up St. James's Street, past the gentleman's clubs, and then to Grosvenor Square and there will be French Eagles sticking out of the windows. Shortly afterwards, the official announcement of the British victory will be made, and *voilà*! Stock prices will soar and you will have made a lot of money."

Ash said nothing for a long time. He continued to gaze at her with eyes like liquid smoke, finally falling once more to the coin in his hands. Amanda took it from him.

"Do you have a penknife?"

Wordlessly, he fished in his waistcoat pocket and, producing a small, ivory-handled blade, handed it to her. In a moment, having pried the penny from its gold shell, Amanda gave it back to him.

"'United States of America,'" he read from the reverse. He glanced up quickly. "That is where you live?"

Amanda nodded.

"'E Pluribus Unum,'" he continued.

"That means, 'One From Many,'" said Amanda helpfully.

"I know what it means," snapped Ash. "I took a first in the classics. What's this building with the columns?"

"The Lincoln Memorial. It's in Washington, D.C."

"Mm, yes, the new capital. I hear it's nothing but a noisome swamp."

Amanda smiled. "I guess you could say that—in more ways than one." She stopped. "But I do not think this is the time to go into all that, Ash. I realize I've given you a great deal to think about, and I think you ought to take me home now."

Ash said nothing, but after a moment set his horses in motion.

"Where in America were you—or will you—be born?" Ash asked after a moment.

"A little town called Custer, South Dakota. I was born there in 1968. I am twenty-eight years old."

Amanda went on to tell him of the accident that had disfigured her and the—

"Car crash?" he asked.

"Yes, although the proper term is automobile—a, er, horseless carriage. It runs on gasoline. That's a by-product of oil," she added.

"Uh-huh."

Amanda continued as though unaware of his continuing incredulity, telling him of her later life in California, then in Chicago.

"Are you saying," he demanded, "that in the twentieth century females teach in universities?"

"Yes." She bridled. "In my time females even vote. We have women governors of states and they serve in our legislatures. We can even—" She was about to launch into one of her favorite subjects, that of the advancement of women, when Ash interrupted.

"The men of your time must be witless weaklings," he snorted.

"No more than those in any time," she retorted. "We have a long way to go, but we're certainly better off than we've been in any other period of history."

After another brief silence, Ash spoke again. "Why?" he asked.

"Why what?" she said blankly.

"Why were you chosen for this singular undertaking? At least, I assume it's singular, since one doesn't hear of similar occurrences. Why should Amanda—McGovern, is it?—be sent on such a fantastic journey?"

Amanda regarded him soberly.

"I have wondered about that, too. I'm not sure I'm the only one to whom this has ever happened. However, in this instance, I believe Amanda Bridge was supposed to live a full lifetime. Instead, something went wrong in her brain—something fatal.

"Someone, or something, took steps to remedy the situation. That—person—encountered me—me with my knowledge of English history and a life that was less than perfect—and, I think, suffering from a similar malady. We shared the same first names and even, as I recently discovered, the same birthday. Perhaps that was all coincidence, or perhaps it was part of some impenetrable cosmic plan, but I think it was decided that I was the perfect candidate to live out Amanda's life. I don't know if it was coincidence that I arrived in Grosvenor Chapel on the same day in 1996 that Amanda was to meet her untimely end there on the same date a hundred and eighty-one years earlier, or it may have been arranged by some supernatural—arranger. At any rate, there I was—and there I went. I don't have any idea—"

She halted suddenly, for the curricle had swung into Upper Brook Street, and a few seconds later Ash drew the vehicle to a halt outside the Bridge home.

He walked her to the door, and before he departed, she reached to place her fingers lightly on his waistcoat pocket, where he had slipped the pendant. "You keep the penny," she said with a smile. "Perhaps it will help convince you that I'm telling the truth. But don't wait too long. I don't want to sound like your fairy godmother, but if you do not act tomorrow you will have lost your chance." She started to enter the house, but turned with a start. "Oh! I just happened to think. I have quite a bit of valuable jewelry. Did you notice that rock Papa gave me to wear at our betrothal ball? They would bring in—" She stopped abruptly as Ash stiffened in outrage. His eyes assumed an aspect of arctic ice.

"Why, thank you, Miss Bridge. It appears you wish me to add dishonor to the already intolerable burden of debt I owe to your family."

Amanda's eyes widened. "Oh, no, Ash, I never meant—"

"I'm sorry." Ash's expression softened minimally. "But even if I were convinced of the—the extraordinary sequence of events you have just described, the idea that I would so take advantage of our relationship is intolerable. You must see that."

Amanda's heart sank. She might have known her revelations would meet with this response, to say nothing of his stupid masculine pride in refusing her offer. Well, she would just have to see what she could do about the latter. She smiled up into his face.

"I understand what you must be feeling, Ash. I have spoken nothing but the truth, but I know how fantastic it sounds. All I can say is, just think over what I've said."

He smiled thinly, and brushing her fingertips with his lips, turned on his heel.

For an hour or so, Ash drove aimlessly over the streets of Mayfair, his thoughts in turmoil. Lord, he should have deposited Amanda directly at the doors of Bedlam instead of taking her home. How could she have formed such a farrago of nonsense in her brain? Time travel, for God's sake! Horseless carriages! And yet . . .

And yet . . . A picture of Amanda's clear, blue eyes rose before his eyes. Could a damaged mind lie behind them? She had been lucid and compelling in the telling of her story. Of course, sanity could be feigned by the insane, but surely there was no other evidence of mental aberration in her behavior—or her demeanor.

He retrieved the coin from his pocket and studied it carefully. There was an undeniable air of authenticity about the coin. It would have taken an extraordinary craftsman to create those minute letters, raised so painstakingly on the copper.

He remembered, suddenly, Amanda's deathlike aspect when he had cradled her in his arms after her swoon in Grosvenor Chapel. There had been no pulse in her slender throat, no breath from between her pale lips. Had Amanda Bridge really died in that moment, to be replaced by a woman who had traveled the corridors of time to live out the young girl's allotted span of years?

Good God.

He turned the curricle toward St. James's Street and entered Brooks's a few minutes later. The atmosphere was subdued in the coffee room, and clumps of agitated members murmured in low, discordant tones. Apparently, the news from Belgium was no better than when Jeremiah Bridge had buttonholed him earlier. The army was decimated, he heard from one gentleman. The allies had failed Wellington, reported another, and surrounded and outnumbered, he had been forced to ignominious defeat.

Ash left the club a few minutes later, and spent the evening staring at his own fire.

Good God, he thought again, he was betrothed to a woman from the future! The words clattered meaninglessly in his brain. Try as he might, he simply could not come to grips with the concept of a human being traveling through time as one might embark on a walking tour.

Yet, apparently, this is what had happened. And because of it, Amanda had assured him, his financial woes were at an end. He realized she had taken a great risk in telling him of her—adventure, for she must have known it might have resulted in her being committed to an asylum. He dared not contemplate the implication of this act of trust on her part.

His thoughts muddled beyond reason, Ash took himself off to bed at last, only to lie staring sleeplessly at the ceiling.

Chapter Twenty

It was just a little before noon on Wednesday, the twenty-first of June, when Mr. James Wincanon, in the act of pulling on his boots, was informed by his valet that a young woman was awaiting him in his sitting room.

"Eh?" he asked startled.

"Yes, sir," replied Symonds austerely. "She speaks well enough and looks to be gently bred, but I can hardly imagine—" He coughed discreetly.

"Quite." James, while not above a spot of dalliance now and then, was rarely visited by women, gently bred or otherwise. "You have never seen her before?"

"As to that, sir, I could not say. The female is wearing a largish bonnet and a veil I can only call impenetrable."

With this, Symonds, apparently feeling he had discharged his duty, bowed discreetly from the room.

A few minutes later, when James entered his sitting room, he saw that his man had not exaggerated. Her own mother could not have recognized the young woman who hurried to him, hands outstretched.

"James! I am so glad you are in!" She threw back the veil. "I am desperately in need of a favor from you."

James gaped at his visitor. "Miss Bridge! What the devil—?"

"Oh, please, this is no time for formalities. Do call me Amanda. I know it is the height of impropriety for me to visit you in your lodgings, but—"

"Impropriety! Good God, woman, if anyone saw you enter you would be utterly ruined. To say nothing of Ash dismembering me bone by bone."

Amanda laughed. "Oh, don't be silly. That's why I wore the

veil." She glanced around. "May I sit down?" she said, taking a chair without waiting for his answer.

"Look here, Miss Br—Amanda. I don't think you should stay. In fact, I was just leaving. A portion of a Roman mosaic has been uncovered in Stepney. They were laying a foundation for a new road, I understand. There may be a whole villa there—or possibly a shrine. I really must—"

"James," said Amanda gently, "you're babbling. I am truly sorry to discommode you, but this won't take long. Now, if you'll sit down, we can get this over with and you can be off to, er, Stepney."

James sat.

"Now, then," continued Amanda, "I have a simple request. I want you to buy as many government shares as you can with this." She reached into her reticule and to James's disbelieving stare pulled out a thick roll of bills.

"But—where—what—?"

"I want you to buy them in Ash's name. I have advised Ash to buy as deeply as he can—you should do the same, by the way— and I offered to give him additional funds—beyond his own—to do so, but he refused."

James, not to put a fine point on it, goggled.

"I cannot believe this," he said at last. "My dear young woman, I can't imagine where you got the idea that investing in the funds at this time is a good idea, for, in fact—"

"I know all about the drop in stock prices, but I also happen to know that tomorrow, as news of Wellington's victory spreads, the prices will soar again."

"How could you possibly know anything of the sort? No, never mind," he said hastily. "I don't want to know any more about this. Even if I were to bow to your no-doubt superior judgment on the matter, I could not go behind Ash's back. He would be furious if he knew you had come here."

"Well, I intend to tell him, of course, but not until he has had the opportunity to realize that I—that I'm right about this. Please, James," she said pleadingly. "You must know how desperate his situation is. If you will only do this small thing, you will help him get on his feet again. You will help free him from his obligation to my father."

James gaped at her. "Why the devil are you doing this? What can you know of Ash's feelings about being forced—that is, about Ashindon Park?"

"How could I help knowing how he feels? He carries his pride like a damned banner. For God's sake, James, I want to see him free of our betrothal, for I know he was forced into it."

James eyed her shrewdly. "Are you saying you do not wish for this union?"

Amanda dropped her gaze. "I know you will consider me stupid and naive, but I do not wish to enter into a loveless marriage."

James said nothing for a long moment, and when he spoke his tone had softened. "But to invest in the funds at this moment is nothing short of an exercise in futility, my dear."

Amanda lifted her head. "As to that, I know you to be wrong, but even if you were right, this is my money I'm asking you to invest. I'd do it myself, but I have no idea how to go about it." She laughed. "I had a hard enough time selling the jewels."

"Selling the jewels?" breathed James, fascinated.

"Yes, I asked Hutchings—my maid—and she advised me to go to Harper's, in Conduit Street. She said they would not likely be too nice in their dealings. I brought her with me, by the way, as well as a footman. They are out in the carriage, so I did not come out alone and defenseless into London's wicked streets. Anyway, when I told the man at the jewelry shop what I wanted, I thought he would call the police or something, but I told him I was a widow who has fallen on hard times and he was very sympathetic. The whole transaction only took about half an hour, and look!" she exclaimed, waving the roll of soft. "I have over six thousand pounds! The gentleman said he was fortunate he had that much on the premises, but he had just completed a big sale." She uttered a small laugh. "I suppose they are worth more than twice what I got, but I'm not complaining."

"Indeed," said James faintly.

"You can do this, can't you?" Amanda asked. "I mean, it's legal to buy stock in someone else's name?"

"Oh, yes. I am acquainted with Ash's man of business. I'm sure he will be—"

"Well, then, there should be nothing to it."

Amanda rose and moved to lay the money in James's lap. When he recoiled, she frowned slightly.

"James, please. I know I am flying in the face of a masculine bulwark of convention, but please help me to help Ash."

James rose to stand close to her. "I could almost believe your only motive is in helping him."

"Good Lord, why else would I be doing this?" she cried in exasperation.

James shook his head. "I do not know. Perhaps to place him under a truly iron-clad obligation to you. Forgive my candor, but it has been my experience that females rarely act so altruistically."

Amanda opened her mouth in protest, but he smiled suddenly, and Amanda was astonished at the change that came over his rather forbidding features. He was much younger than she had thought, and really rather handsome.

"I do not know about your experience with females," she said simply, "but I want very badly to help Ash, and since you are his friend I thought perhaps that would be your wish as well. As for placing him under an obligation to me, I intend quite the opposite. Once he has sufficient funds to accomplish the tasks he has set for himself, he will no longer need me." She said the words unthinkingly and almost gasped at the pain they caused.

The silence in the small sitting room was deafening, and Amanda felt she was choking on her heart, which seemed to have lodged in her throat.

"All right," said James at last, an indecipherable expression on his features. "I'll do it."

"Oh, thank God!" exclaimed Amanda, weak with relief.

The visit concluded a few minutes later with mutual expressions of goodwill and Amanda sped home to spend the rest of the day in a state of expectation bordering on panic. Had she done the right thing in telling Ash her extraordinary story? He had made it perfectly obvious that he thought her little more than a lunatic. And how could she blame him? Perhaps she was. Maybe the person she believed to be Amanda McGovern had never existed and the whole time-travel thing was a figment of a profoundly disturbed mind. It seemed to her that if one's mind were that messed up one would be somehow aware of the disturbance, but her experience with mental derangement was limited. Dear God, suppose Ash took her advice and was brought to ruin because Wellington had actually gone down to defeat against Napoleon.

She took a deep, steadying breath. No, she was completely sane, and if Ash had only taken her advice, all would be well.

Whereupon she sat down, and with great precision began to pull all the threads from the embroidery piece she had started several days ago.

Ash, meanwhile, sat in a small coffee shop in the City, sipping from a small cup of the steaming beverage and unmindful of the chatter that rose and fell around him like ocean waves. He felt light-headed and rather empty, as though he'd been fasting for several days. In his mind, the scene in the office of his man of business replayed itself endlessly.

Mr. Shaffley had handled the affairs of the Wexford family for all his adult life, as had his father before him. It was he who had first brought Jeremiah Bridge to the attention of his impecunious client, and at Ash's entry into his office he greeted the earl with an understanding sympathy.

"I have been expecting you, my lord. The news of Wellington's misfortune is all over the City. I must say I was dismayed when you invested so heavily in the funds after Napoleon's escape from Elba. It is unfortunate that you will have to take so great a loss now, but I believe I shall be able to get a fairly reasonable price for them. If you will just—"

"But it is not my intention to sell. I wish to buy."

"What!" exclaimed Mr. Shaffley. "But—but—my lord—"

"I know it must seem the sheerest lunacy to you, sir, but the news to which you refer is only speculation, and I believe the reports are false. You must agree, that if Wellington is indeed victorious, now is the time to buy."

"Indeed, my lord, but have you the wherewithal for further investment?"

"I have a few resources left, and"—Ash braced himself—"I plan to mortgage the Yorkshire estates."

"My lord!" Mr. Shaffley could not have looked more shocked if Ash had proposed to sell himself into slavery.

"In addition," said Ash, hurrying on, "I have borrowed a sizable amount of money from my bank." He smiled sourly. "They were not willing to lend me a nickel a few months ago, but becoming Jeremiah Bridge's prospective son-in-law has increased my market value to a prodigious degree."

Mr. Shaffley sat down rather suddenly behind his desk. "I do not know what to say, my lord. Is there nothing that can dissuade you from what I am persuaded is a disastrous course of action?"

Ash smiled. "I've been trying to do that all night, with absolutely no success."

Mr. Shaffley had a good deal more to say on the subject, but of course he was obliged to capitulate in the end. With a great deal of head-shaking and tsk-tsking, Mr. Shaffley at last saw Ash from the door.

Ash's first inclination on reaching the street was to hasten to the Bridge home and tell Amanda what he had done. He had already slapped the reins against his horses' backs when he changed his mind.

The fact that he wanted to see her so badly was enough to tell him that he should not. In any event, it would be better to wait until he had some definite news to tell her. When her predictions came true there would be time enough for mutual rejoicing.

Turning the curricle toward his lodgings, Ash sighed. Please God, Amanda was not the victim of a horrible aberration. Again, he withdrew the coin from his pocket and clutched it as he would a talisman. Please God, he was not mad as well to have taken her tale seriously. The papers he perused after he got home did nothing to disabuse him of this notion. Column after column of newsprint detailed Wellington's retreat across the River Sambre, the continued nonappearance of the allies, and Napoleon's increasing troop strength.

It was the longest day he had ever spent, and at the end of it he was no more sanguine of the success of his venture than he had been at its start. He went to bed wondering if Ashindon Park would be lost to him forever, for surely, in case of failure, Jeremiah Bridge would see Ash's refusal to take his advice as a breach of contract—or at least a sufficient reason to hold up any more monies.

The next day was no better. The urge to go to Amanda was almost overpowering, but he steeled himself. Time enough to celebrate with her when her prophecy was vindicated.

Finally, late on Wednesday afternoon, he strode to Brooks's. It seemed to him that the same crowd of members he had beheld two days before stood about muttering in dire periods and shaking their heads. Dear God, he wondered, had he done the right thing? There had still been no official reports from Wellington's headquarters. Surely, such an absence of news could signify nothing but disaster.

He moved into the bar, feeling that the bottom of his stomach was falling away, piece by piece. The uneasiness that had pursued him ever since he had left Mister Shaffley's office descended on him now in a thick, black cloud of despair. What had he been thinking? Why had he not simply taken the Brass Bridge's advice and gotten out while the getting was good? He must have been mad!

The last empty chair in the room stood at a table occupied by a man approximately his own age. Moving toward the table, Ash lifted his brows questioningly, and at the man's assenting nod, sank into the chair. Unlike the others in the crowded chamber, the gentleman had nothing to say until he roused from what appeared to be a reverie and turned a rather grim smile on Ash.

"The news doesn't seem good, does it?"

"No," replied Ash, and the conversation, such as it was, flagged. After another interval, Ash continued. "I don't believe a word of all this talk of defeat."

At this, the gentleman's smile grew a shade warmer. "Nor do I. I served in the Peninsula, and—"

"So did I!" Ash interrupted eagerly. "I was with the Light Bobs."

"Ah." The stranger's lips quirked mischievously. "A decent bunch of lads. Can't hold a candle to the 95th, of course."

"Lord!" exclaimed Ash. "Were you at Badajoz?"

"Yes." The response came curt and flat, and another long silence ensued. When the stranger spoke again, his tone had lightened somewhat. "I'm Lynton, by the by."

"I'm pleased to make your acquaintance. I'm Ashindon."

Lynton nodded. "Nice meeting you, Ashindon." He rose and smiled painfully. "Let us hope our faith in Old Hookey is not misplaced. I have rather a lot riding on the outcome." So saying, he moved away, and Ash noted that he walked with a slight limp.

Ash smiled wryly. Whatever Lynton had riding on the outcome of Wellington's battle, it could not compare with his own hopes.

Ash remained in the bar for another several minutes, sipping absently at the drink brought to him by a passing waiter. At last, wondering what the devil had prompted him to come here in the first place, he rose to make his way from the room. He had just passed into the club's reception hall with its graceful staircase, when he became aware of a buzz of excitement rising from the subscription room. Following the sound, he observed Lord Lynton standing at the forefront of a crowd that had surged to the window. Lynton was slapping the shoulder of the elderly gentleman next to him, and in a moment he had moved toward the door.

"What is it?" asked Ash, intercepting him. "What has happened?"

"A carriage," said Lynton in an odd voice, "trundling up the street toward Picadilly, and there are three French Eagles thrust out of the window." Breaking into a wide grin, he gripped Ash's hand in a crushing handshake, and a moment later, had left the room.

Ash leaned against the doorjamb, suddenly dizzy. Wellington had won! He listened to the huzzahs that rose about him like banners, and thought he might explode from sheer exultation. He had done it! The Park was safe, and he was no longer dependent on the patronizing whims of Jeremiah Bridge! He could marry Amanda with a clear conscience and live his life according to his own plans. He could . . . He shook his head, overwhelmed by the sense of release and joy that swept over him.

For a few more minutes, he listened to the hubbub around him, exchanging shouts of triumph and expressions of jubilation. Then, quietly, he left the club. The only company he wanted in the world right now was Amanda, but he had vowed he would not see her until he could give her a concrete estimate of his profit, which he would not know until sometime tomorrow. Once more, he turned his feet toward the solitude of his lodgings, but in this he was thwarted. Men poured out of the door behind him, as did many others from White's and Boodle's, farther up the street, and in a few minutes the thoroughfare was thronged with men exchanging bits of news as they filtered up from the palace. It was not until he had almost reached Picadilly that Ash caught the word, "Waterloo."

When he reached his lodgings, his thoughts were in such a muddle he felt himself no longer capable of coherent thought. He refused Minchin's offer of "a little something to eat" and proceeding directly to his room, he drew off his boots and undressed, flinging his clothes to the four corners of his bedchamber. He envisioned another sleepless night, for he had even more to think about than the night before. Not only had he seen the lame horse on which he'd wagered his last farthing come round the bend to finish first, but despite all rational thought to the contrary it appeared Amanda had told him the truth about her fantastic journey through time.

He climbed into bed and closed his eyes, prepared for yet another onslaught on his sanity by thinking the unthinkable thoughts that swarmed in his brain. He opened them again, seemingly a few moments later, to observe the late morning sun slanting through a crack in his window hangings. An unfamiliar sense of well-being swept over him, and after the several moments it took to identify its source, he threw back his covers, calling loudly to Minchin.

In little more than an hour later, he presented himself at Mr. Shaffley's door and was greeted with felicitations and expressions of amazed gratification. Ash was ushered into Shaffley's office and settled with great ceremony into the chair opposite the huge desk that occupied the greater portion of the room.

"I must confess, my lord," began Mr. Shaffley, steepling his plump fingers before him, "that I was somewhat dismayed by your order to buy."

"Were you, indeed?" inquired Ash dryly.

"Yes," replied the gentleman obliviously, "for it seemed the height of injudiciousness. However, your acumen has certainly proven itself. My lord," he continued in a hushed whisper, "I believe you will realize not a penny less than forty thousand pounds when the market settles down again."

"Forty thousand pounds," echoed Ash dazedly. "My God." His expression grew beatific, for it seemed he heard the words repeated by a heavenly choir.

"I cannot believe that the money I invested should bring such a staggering return," he continued.

"Well," said Mr. Shaffley thoughtfully, "fortunately, you had some resources left to you, and with the money you were able to borrow." He hesitated for a moment. "Then, there was the other . . . "

"Other? What other?"

Mr. Shaffley shifted uncomfortably. "I don't think I am supposed to tell you this, my lord, but it is you who are my client, not—" He paused again. "Tell me, are you acquainted with a Mr. James Wincanon?"

Chapter Twenty-one

Amanda felt as though she might, at any moment, simply fly apart in all directions, scattering arms and legs and other body parts in gory profusion all over the expensive Brussels carpet in her bedchamber. It was Thursday morning and she had not heard a word from Ash since their conversation the previous Sunday. What the hell was he doing? The household had been filled with nothing but chatter of Wellington's victory ever since Jeremiah had come banging into the house the night before, big with news.

Was Ash even now crouching in his lodgings, suicidally depressed because he had sold all his holdings and was facing ruin? Or was he roistering in some club somewhere, celebrating his newfound wealth because he had taken her advice? She was torn between fury at his inconsiderateness in not notifying her one way or the other and profound desolation that he did not think enough of her to share either in his despair over his misfortune or his joy over his windfall.

In was not until luncheon, when Serena proposed a shopping expedition in Bond Street, that Amanda bethought herself of a promise she had made two days earlier to visit Grandmama Ashindon that afternoon. She had never felt less like exchanging mindless bits of gossip over tepid cups of tea, but she did look forward to seeing Grandmama. She felt very much in need of the old lady's astringent company, and, besides, she could not possibly sit around chewing her nails for another interminable day.

Thus, fortified by an almost painfully smart ensemble of twilled Italian silk, trimmed with three tiers of rouleaux around the hem, she bundled herself into the Bridge town carriage for the short journey to Grosvenor Square. She had just alighted before Grandmama's house when she was hailed by a melodious masculine voice.

"Cosmo!" she said in surprise, turning to greet the slender figure that hurried toward her.

"Yes, it is I. No, you need not turn away," he continued with great dignity as Amanda pulled her hand away from his. "I shall not importune you. Indeed"—his full lips turned up in a smile of smug satisfaction—"you must allow me to inform you that there will soon be an interesting announcement made concerning myself and a certain Miss Hester Giddlesham."

"Ah." Amanda grinned. "Another heiress, Cosmo?"

Mr. Satterleigh flushed, but said nothing.

"And one with a less perspicacious father than mine, I take it. Never mind," she added as her erstwhile swain opened his mouth indignantly. "You have my heartiest congratulations and best wishes for your future prosperity. Now, if you'll excuse me . . . "

She smiled and continued on her way toward the dowager's house. Once inside, she discovered to her surprise that, besides Cousin Emily Wexford, Lianne was among those present. Amanda had not seen the young countess since the house party at Ashindon, and she was additionally surprised at the cat-in-the-cream-pot expression that spread over her lovely face as she greeted Amanda.

An unpleasant twinge made itself felt in Amanda's interior. Lianne could look this pleased for only one reason. No wonder Ash had not put in an appearance at the Bridge home. He had been visiting his love!

Of course, she thought bitterly. To whom else would Ash turn in his hour of need—or of bliss—whichever the case might be?

"Well, come in and sit, gel," barked Grandmama from her chair. "And I hope to God you have something else to talk of besides Wellington. I'm heartily sick of the man's name already, and I know it will be a great deal worse in the days to come."

Amanda pinned a smile to her face. "But he is a hero, Grandmama."

"Yes," echoed Lianne. "He has vanquished the Corsican Monster!"

"Well, let's hope they keep a better watch on him than they did last time," said the dowager with a grunt. She turned to Amanda.

"How do the wedding preparations progress? I spoke to Serena the other day and it seems your father's plans grow more grandiose every day. I expect to hear that by now he has decided you must be married in Westminster Abbey."

"No," replied Amanda calmly. "St. George's will do for Papa." She seemed unable to keep the rigidity from her voice as she continued. "It is natural that he would wish for everything to be perfect for his only daughter."

"Only daughter, indeed," snapped the old lady. "If this isn't all to the glory of the one and only Jeremiah Bridge, I'll eat my best bonnet. The man has the ego the size of one of those balloon things people are riding around in these days."

Amanda stiffened. "Grandmama, I am sorry that you and Papa have not hit it off very well, but I will not sit here and listen to you insult him."

Emily gasped and Lianne tittered nervously, but the dowager remained unfazed.

"No need to take a pet, gel. I'm only speaking the truth, after all. But now that I think of it," she added as Amanda opened her mouth, "he ain't such a maw-worm as I first saw him."

With that, Amanda supposed she would have to be satisfied.

The conversation turned once more to the subject of Waterloo and the magnificent victory won by Wellington and his allies.

"Of course," remarked Amanda, "the casualties were catastrophic—at least, so I've heard. The lists will be posted soon, I suppose."

"Oh, yes," said Emily, dabbing at her eyes. "I understand the Bellinghams have a son in Belgium, and Mrs. Gellis's husband, too. You remember him, Lianne. They had only been married a few months when he went off."

Lianne nodded sadly. "It always infuriates me when men talk of the glory of battle, when it is the women who must stay home and suffer when their men are taken from them."

Amanda nodded silently, startled at this rare expression of depth from the young countess.

"As to that—" began the dowager, but she was interrupted as a tall figure strode into the room.

"Ash!" Amanda nearly dropped her teacup into her lap, and as she stared at him her heart sank. He stood in the doorway, stiff and unsmiling, and in his hand he carried a small parcel. His eyes glittered darkly in the pallor of his face. He did not, in short, look like a man who has just realized a marked improvement in his financial situation. After a mechanical greeting to the other ladies present, his gaze swung to Amanda.

"Ah, Miss Bridge." His voice was flat and unemotional. "I have been searching for you. When I went to your home, I was told that you had come here. I wonder if I might have a moment of your time." To the dowager, he said, "Is there a place where Miss Bridge and I might be private for a few moments?"

"Good God, boy, what are you about?" The old lady bristled. "This is most irregular, and I will not—" She stopped abruptly, eyeing her grandson intently. "You may go into the Blue Saloon."

Dazedly, Amanda followed Ash. He said nothing as they left the room, progressing down the corridor until he turned into another chamber nearby. Ash strode through the door and placed the parcel on a table.

"Ash, for heaven's sake, what is going on?"

He turned to her and gestured toward the parcel. "This is for you, Miss Bridge."

"Ash, I don't understand—"

"Just open it—please." In the chilled metal of his tone, Amanda caught an undercurrent of barely leashed tension, and without saying more, she picked up the package and tore off the wrappings with trembling fingers. Her jaw dropped as she realized what she held in her hands.

"It's—they're—my—"

"Yes, Miss Bridge, your jewels. Please examine them to make sure they are all there."

Amanda set the jewel box down on the table as though it had bitten her. "Ash, what is this? How did you come by them? For God's sake, tell me what this is all about?"

"It's quite simple. I discovered your efforts on my behalf and went round this morning to purchase the jewels back from Howard's. It was necessary to borrow the funds from my man of business to do so, but that was a trifling thing, surely. You need not consider my embarrassment over the matter, just as you did not consider the humiliation of having my fiancée busy herself in my financial matters—particularly after I had expressly refused your extremely generous offer not three days ago."

"But, Ash—!" cried Amanda, appalled.

He continued as though she had not spoken, still in that voice of deadly calm. "You see, Miss Bridge, I did take your advice. I sank every penny I could scrape together into government funds and borrowed more besides. As you can imagine, then, I went to the office of my man of business this morning in a high state of anticipation. My hopes did not go unrewarded, for Mr. Shaffley informed me that my returns will be nothing short of munificent."

"I am so very happy for you, Ash," said Amanda on a sigh of relief, "but—"

"Mr. Shaffley then pointed out that my good fortune had been augmented by the infusion of an extra spot of cash, donated anonymously. I will admit I had some difficulty in absorbing the fact that apparently my unknown benefactor was none other than a man I considered my best friend. When I went to said friend, he informed me that it was my very busy, very rich fiancée who had, in a spurt of nobility, sold her jewels."

"I meant to tell you," said Amanda, bewildered. "After the dust had settled. You were being so absurd about the jewels—for which I don't care a jot."

"Apparently not—nor do you seem to care for the fact that you had no right to sell them."

"But they're mine! Papa gave them to me."

"Perhaps, having condescended to grace our backward period in time, you are unaware of the fact that you do not own anything. Everything belongs to your father, whether it happens to be in your possession or not."

"But that's positively feudal!" exclaimed Amanda, passing for the moment on this evidence that Ash now believed that she had come from the future.

"Perhaps, but that's the way it is. Thus, I am pleased to be able to return the, er, merchandise—just in case your papa might not understand your generous gesture."

"Well—thank you—I guess. But, why are you so angry?"

Ash took a step toward her, and for the first time the icy calm seemed to crack.

"*Why?* My God, what kind of man do you think I am that I would take charity from the woman I am supposed to marry? You certainly cannot plead ignorance of our provincial little customs, for I told you very explicitly that I did not want you to interfere."

"But," murmured Amanda, "I only wanted to help."

"Is that what you call help? I suppose you consider that you have made a great sacrifice, all for—no, not even love, is it? Did you think that having instructed me on the possibilities for gain, I would be incapable of making a rational decision on my own? Apparently so, for you gathered up what is most precious to you in the world, your jewelry." Ash had gone even more pale as he spoke, and his eyes were hard and bleak as a November rain. "The fact that your papa would be happy to replace it with baubles even more blindingly expensive would not, of course, have influenced you in this noble gesture."

Amanda stared at him, her breath seeming to have left her body. "Is that what you think of me?" she whispered at last.

"I don't know what to think of you. I thought I did. I thought I had come to know Amanda Bridge. Now, I have discovered you are someone else altogether—an oddity from some other dimension who seems as thoughtless as she is beautiful."

Without another word, Ash turned on his heel and left the room.

Amanda sank into the nearest chair, and for a long time simply crouched there, her arms wrapped around herself as though she had sustained a physical blow. How could he have said those things? How could he have so misinterpreted her action? He had spoken as though he hated her, and perhaps he did. She grimaced. For so long she had wished to confide her situation to him, and now that she had, he'd made it plain he considered her some sort of freak.

She tried to tell herself that none of it made any difference. Ash had his salvation in the form of a fistful of pounds, and she need not be bound by her father's promise that they wed in a year's time. She was free to return to her own place in the cosmos at a time of her choosing, and that time would come very soon if she had anything to say about it, leaving Ash free to pursue his true love.

A consuming ache rose in her like a bitter tide, and though the June breeze whispered gently through the curtains at the window, she had never felt so cold.

At last, she rose wearily and made her way from the Blue Saloon. As she walked down the corridor, a murmur of voices came to her from a chamber that lay ahead, and glancing in as she passed, she caught her breath.

There, before a pair of French doors, stood Lianne, wrapped in Ash's embrace. As Amanda watched in stony silence, Ash brought one hand around to cup Lianne's chin. He bent his head—but Amanda did not stay to observe what she knew would happen next. Closing her eyes on a sight that she knew would stay with her through the centuries, she swallowed the sob that had risen in her throat and made her way unsteadily along the corridor. Reaching the hall, she called for her pelisse and bonnet and her carriage.

"Please apologize to her ladyship for me," she said to the hovering butler, pleased that her voice contained no hint of the turmoil churning within her. "But I must return home at once."

Turning, she almost ran from the house on legs that barely held her upright.

Back in the small saloon, Ash released Lianne from his embrace.

"I wish you all the very, very best, my dear, and I'm honored that you told me first." The smile he bent on her was warm, if somewhat crooked.

Lianne stepped back and grinned mischievously. "We shan't announce it until we've set a date." She laughed aloud. "I am pleased you are happy for me, Ash, but you needn't look downright relieved. No, no," she added as a halfhearted protest formed on his lips, "I know I've been behaving like the veriest limpet, clinging to a love that never really was. It took me a long time to admit it to myself, but we are simply not suited. I know very well that I am a shallow butterfly who needs to be pampered, and—"

"And Reggie Smythe-Wolverton will pamper you till your eyes bubble," Ash said, the smile widening. "God knows, after those years of marriage to Grant you deserve some of that, but"—he gazed seriously into her jeweled eyes—"do you truly love him?"

"Yes, I do. Not wildly and with the consuming passion I felt for you, but with something that will develop more deeply, I think. He will make a good husband—and I will be a good wife to him." She hesitated a moment before continuing. "I do not think I have ever wished you happy with Amanda. You are lucky to have found your love, as well."

"I?" asked Ash, startled. His lips thinned. "You mistake the matter. The marriage of the Earl of Ashindon and Miss Amanda Bridge will be strictly one of convenience."

Lianne chuckled, her piquant features alight. "Tell that to someone who might believe you. I've seen the way you look at her. You're head over tail in love with her, Will Wexford."

Ash stared at her, bereft of speech. The chill emptiness that had settled in the pit of his stomach since his discovery that morning of Amanda's perfidy seemed to expand and engulf him until he felt himself the center of a dark, whirling, and unbearably lonely void.

"I—" he began, only to be interrupted as Emily bustled into the room.

"There you are," she said breathlessly. "Grandmama sent me to find you. She said this is getting to be like that story of the explorers who keep tramping out into the jungle one by one and never coming back."

Upon returning to the dowager's august presence, Lianne made her farewells. When Ash declared his own intention of leaving, the dowager held up a thin veined hand.

"You stay," she ordered, having subjected him to an intent scrutiny. "I wish to speak to you." She dismissed both Lianne and Emily from the room with a distracted wave. "Now then, I want you to explain yourself."

"I beg your pardon?" Ash lifted his brows in puzzlement.

"I want you to tell me why you look as though they just hanged your best friend."

Ash laughed shortly. "Considering my feelings toward my best friend right now, your comparison is singularly appropriate. Actually," he continued. "I take leave to tell you that, contrary to your belief, I am in excellent spirits, just having made a killing, as I believe the saying goes, in the stock market."

"Eh?"

Briefly, Ash related the details of the successful risk he had taken. He included Amanda's belief that Wellington would defeat Napoleon, but not her reasons for this certainty.

"Well! That is splendid news. You'll be free from now on of the Brass Bridge's golden fetters, if not from the bargain you made with him."

"Um," said Ash.

"What I do not understand is why you aren't dancing in the streets, adding your huzzahs to that mindless mob out there instead of moping about here wearing that tedious Friday face."

Ash moved to the window, where he stood staring sightlessly into the dowager's small garden for several moments. He turned, finally, and related the story of Amanda's clandestine contribution to his good fortune.

"I could not believe she would so plot against me, Grandmama. Nor that James would go behind my back in that fashion. I tell you, I came within Ames Ace of planting him a facer when he admitted what he'd done—without so much as an apology, mind you."

"But, why should he apologize?" The dowager returned his incredulous stare with one of amusement. "He had merely done a favor for his best friend's fiancée, knowing that there was no harm and a great deal of good might come of it."

"Grandmama!" Ash gaped, unbelieving. "She stole her father's jewelry! She meddled in my affairs when I expressly told her not to! Do I strike you as the kind of man who would allow a female to bestow trinkets on him like a—a pet pug?"

"What I think," retorted the old lady, "is that you are a complete fool."

Since this statement jibed so precisely with what James had said to him a few hours earlier, Ash blinked. "But, see here, Grandmama—" he began.

"I take it," said the dowager, paying him no heed, "that you have already spoken to Amanda about this wretched tendency to do you kindnesses. This no doubt accounts for her abrupt departure from my home without even the courtesy of a farewell. I will tell you to your face, boy, that if you have hurt that gel, you will have me to answer to."

"I cannot believe what I am hearing," said Ash. "Hurt her? What about what she did to me?"

"As far as I can see, the only thing she has been guilty of is trying to see you through a very trying time. Do you think she does not know how it galls you to accept Jeremiah Bridge's iron-clad benevolence? She was trying to save your pride, you looby, not destroy it."

By now, Ash was beginning to feel as though he was losing control of the conversation. It was not a feeling to which he was accustomed, and he found that he did not like it above half. He drew in a long breath.

"Grandmama, I am to marry her. I cannot have her flouting my wishes and attempting to manage my affairs. Our marriage may be one of convenience only, but—"

"Pfaw! Don't you marriage-of-convenience me, you young

twit. As if anyone with the meanest intelligence cannot perceive that you are besotted with the chit."

"What!" The room began to reel about Ash. First James, and then Lianne, and now his own grandmother—Had everyone of his acquaintance gone mad?

He opened his mouth and then shut it abruptly. The room stopped reeling and proceeded to drop away from his vision altogether. All he perceived was the dowager's bright, shrewd little eyes staring at him.

No, they had not all gone mad, had they? he thought, sitting down very slowly. It was he who seemed to have lost his powers of reason. How else could he account for the fact that he had been in love with Amanda Bridge—or McGovern—or whatever the devil her name was—for some time and had not even known it?

From a great distance he heard his grandmother's rusty chuckle. "It's perfectly understandable, boy. You've been adrift for so long in that absurd infatuation for Lianne that you did not recognize the real thing when it was right under that beaky nose of yours."

Ash did not reply. He was lost in the revelations his heart was making to him. Memories of his time with Amanda overwhelmed him. Amanda laughing with him in the park—and waltzing with him, her satiny curls brushing his chin—Amanda's lips, warm and pliant under his—the magical, companionable hour they had spent on a quiet riverbank.

Good God, he thought suddenly. He had just insulted her cruelly. She had given him all she had to give in order to help him out of his difficulty, and out of his stupid pride he had repaid her generosity with a lot of pompous prating. Would she now make good on her promise to end their betrothal? She had hinted that she might return to her own time. He felt cold, suddenly, and turned to the dowager.

"I must go after her," he said simply.

"That's the first sensible thing I've heard you say for a long time." The old lady cackled. "Be off with you then, before she flings herself into the arms of Cosmo Satterleigh again."

Ash paused in the act of hurtling from the room.

"Good grief," he said with a tender smile. "She won't do that. I have her word on it that she thinks him a complete jerk."

The next moment, he was gone, leaving the countess to stare after him in puzzlement.

Chapter Twenty-two

Ash found his quarry to be singularly elusive. On arriving at the Bridge home some ten minutes after leaving Grosvenor Square, he was informed by Goodbody, the butler, that none of the family was at home, the master of the house not having returned from his place of business in the City and Mrs. Bridge still out paying afternoon calls. Miss Bridge was expected home shortly, but would surely not be available for visitors at that hour because she would be making preparations for Mrs. Wiltsham's soiree, which was to take place that evening.

Ash immediately perceived the futility in simply waiting for Amanda to come home. Her parents were sure to arrive at an inopportune moment, and trying to fix the attention of a damsel in the throes of party preparations would be an exercise in unwisdom. He would see her tonight at the Wiltshams'. Granted, a crowded soiree was not the place to seek a reconciliation, but surely there would be a quiet nook in the vast Wiltsham House to which he could repair with Amanda. Containing his impatience, Ash mounted his curricle once more. Lost in thought, he directed his horses in the direction from which he had just come, toward Grosvenor Square and Ryder Street to make his peace with James.

In his preoccupation, Ash did not note his surroundings as he drove along the northern perimeter of the square, thus he did not see Amanda sitting on a bench inside the railed park, conversing earnestly with a young nursemaid overseeing a pair of lusty children.

"Are you sure you want to do this?" asked the young woman. Her small, knobby cheeks glowed as though recently polished as she pushed her spectacles up her nose.

"Yes," replied Amanda quietly. She was amazed at how quickly the personage had responded to the plea that pounded inside her brain as she hurried down the steps of the dowager's house. She had cried aloud, "Please, take me home! I must get away from here—back to where I belong!" and the next moment she had bumped into the little nursemaid grasping her charges in each hand. "Yes," she repeated. "Can you help me?"

"This is very sudden," said the young woman, her tone severe.

"I know. I had planned to stick around for a year or so, but—events have transpired that will allow me—no, make it imperative that I leave as soon as possible." She made an ineffectual effort to brush away the tears that streamed down her cheeks. "You see, this was all a mistake. It has been made very clear that I do not belong here."

"Humph." The young woman's spectacles glittered as they slid in another precipitous journey down her nose. "It seems as though it's you that's making the mistake." She sighed. "However, you have not been here long enough for the window to close—although it will be a close thing—and it is not our policy to keep people in another timeline who truly do not wish to stay."

"Then tell me how to get back," Amanda whispered, her lips suddenly dry.

"You must meet me at midnight at the Grosvenor Chapel."

Amanda's eyes widened. "Tonight?"

"Yes, it must be soon." The nursemaid smiled. "Oddly, it is true what they say about midnight being the witching hour—although that's something of a misnomer."

"But the church will be closed, and—"

"Not to me."

"Oh. Very well. Yes, tonight. I will be there."

The young woman rose from the bench. "Harold!" she called. "Arabella! Come along!" The two youngsters left their playfellows without dispute and ran to her side. As Amanda watched, the little group disappeared within a matter of moments into the shrubbery of the little park.

Amanda sat motionless for a long time, feeling the warmth of the June sun and listening to the humming of bees and the twittering of birds. She ought to feel satisfied, she mused distantly. She had accomplished her goal. She had provided Ash with the wherewithal to put Ashindon Park back on a firm footing, thus giving him the opportunity to marry Lianne. Instead, she had never known such desolation in her life.

She had known that leaving Ash would be painful, but leaving without even the consolation that they had grown to be friends was almost unbearable. She reviewed their confrontation earlier in the dowager's Blue Saloon. She should be angry. She knew it had been his pride talking, but the things he had said were unforgivable. How could he have insulted her so?

Well, she did not have to seek far for the answer to that. She had only imagined the affection that seemed to be growing between them. She had even, she admitted with a pang, begun to wonder if Grandmama were right and that Ash truly did not love Lianne. Amanda uttered a bitter laugh. The little scene by the French doors had certainly put paid to that idea. She was trying very hard to be happy for Ash, but the tears kept welling in her eyes.

"Miss! Oh, miss, there you are!"

Amanda looked up, startled to observe Hutchings bearing down on her. The maid's cheeks were flushed and her meager bosom heaved breathlessly.

"Wherever did you go, miss? I was waiting ever so long for you belowstairs." She gestured vaguely toward the dowager's house. "That persnickety butler told me you had left. Without me! I ran home, but you wasn't—weren't there, so I came back this way. I was just lucky I saw you sitting here. Why, what's happened, miss? You're white as a ghost."

With a great effort, Amanda McGovern tucked the remnants of her anguish behind Amanda Bridge's smiling facade.

"I'm sorry, Hutchings. I merely . . . " But the effort of explaining was too much, and Amanda left the sentence hanging. "I am going home now," she said simply.

She left Grosvenor Square and with Hutchings chattering away at her side made her way back to Upper Brook Street.

The hours that followed took an eternity to pass. Amanda considered writing Ash a note explaining her abrupt departure, but gave it up after several abortive attempts. In all probability he would never read the note. When Serena arrived home, Amanda was able to feign a sick headache with very little difficulty.

"Are you sure you will be all right here by yourself?" asked her mother anxiously, having come to Amanda's room to commiserate with her daughter. "I will stay home with you, if you wish, but this is the first time we have been invited to the Wiltshams', and your papa wishes to put in an appearance."

Amanda, picking listlessly at the tray just brought to her by Hutchings, smiled faintly. "No, you go on. I wouldn't want Papa to forgo this opportunity to show that he is now an accepted member of the *ton*."

Serena's lips twitched, and she said a little uncomfortably, "I suppose it is silly for all of this to mean so much to him, but . . . I am happy for him." Kissing Amanda on the forehead, she drifted from the room.

Gazing after her, Amanda was surprised at the pang of regret she felt that she would never see Serena Bridge again. The older woman had begun to make progress, Amanda felt, in releasing herself from Jeremiah's domination. Hopefully, she would continue in her own liberation.

Amanda rose and, placing the tray on a nearby table, paced the carpet in a measured tread and listened to the tick of the clock.

The house was dark and quiet when at last, garbed in a sober muslin round gown and cloak, she tiptoed into the corridor and down the stairs. Quietly, she let herself out of the house and was hurrying along the sidewalk when she was brought up short by a voice calling from behind her.

"Miss! Oh, miss, it *is* you! Wherever are you going?"

"Hutchings!" gasped Amanda. Good Lord, she had sent her maid off to bed hours ago. What the devil was she doing out and about at this hour? A glance at the figure who appeared behind her from the steps leading down from the sidewalk, that of the second footman, if she was not mistaken, answered her question. "Good evening, Hutchings," she said in what she hoped was a tone of regal dismissal. "I have come out to, er, take the air. My headache, you know."

"But surely not alone, miss."

"Yes, alone. You may go back to—whatever you were doing."

"But, where are you going?" asked Hutchings in appalled accents.

"To Gr—never mind, Hutchings. I wish to be alone."

The little maid began whimpering. "Oh, no—you're going to Grosvenor Chapel, aren't you? And at this hour! Surely you're not—Oh, dear heaven, I saw you talking to that wretched Mr. Satterleigh earlier. You—you're planning another elopement aren't you?" At this, she began shrieking in earnest, her apron flung over her head.

"Hutchings! *Will* you shut up?" Amanda frantically clutched at the young woman's arm. "I am *not* eloping." She continued in a softer tone as the maid's sobs subsided. "Now, please leave me alone. If you don't," she added in minatory accents, "you will find yourself dismissed without a character in the morning."

"Oh, miss, you wouldn't!"

"Try me," Amanda replied tersely, and with this she walked away, leaving Hutchings moaning into her apron.

She arrived at the chapel with minutes to spare. At midnight, the evening's activities in Mayfair were just getting under way, and the streets were crowded with elegant carriages carrying passengers to the various social functions that were taking place that night in the equally elegant town houses of the area. Unnoticed, Amanda crouched on the steps of the building, hidden in the shadow of its columns.

Promptly on the stroke of midnight, a figure approached, bearing a lantern and a watchman's rattle. " 'Evenin', miss,' " he said jovially. "Fine night tonight."

"Yes," said Amanda, drawing in her skirts. Then she took a closer look. Sure enough, the man wore spectacles and his cheeks protruded round and hard from beneath them. Amanda leaped to her feet. "You have come!" she exclaimed.

The man lifted bushy eyebrows in mild surprise. "Toljer I would, didn't I then?"

"Yes, of course," she replied, abashed. "But—who are you, anyway? Are you the same person in disguise, or many people— or what?"

"Yes," the man responded, rummaging in a capacious pocket.

"Yes, what? Which?"

"Both. One and many." He shook his head irritably. "Don't mean t'be teedjis, but you wouldn't understand if I explained it." He drew a key from his pocket. "Are you coming, then?"

Amanda moved to his side and he opened one of the chapel doors. Once inside, he led her to the seat where she had emerged into that sunny April morning two months earlier. Settling his bulk beside her, he turned and took her hand.

"Now," he began, "you must know that when you leave this time you can't never return. Amanda Bridge will die this night, and this time there won't be no one to resurrect her."

Amanda drew in a long breath and nodded.

"You'll be sent back to the moment you suffered that last, terrible headache, only this time it won't kill you. You'd best get to a doctor, though, missy, because the next time you'll die—and it will be permanent. At any rate, when you awake in 1996, everything else will be the same as before."

Thus, reflected Amanda sourly, she would be her old self, plain of face and flawed of form—as well as slightly warped of outlook. If it were not for the impossibility of remaining in the same plane of time with Ash, she would gladly put up with London's pollution and all the other ills, social, moral, and physical, of this time period, for the chance to live the rest of her life in the whole body she had been given. She shook herself. No, it would be too painful to exist here in such close proximity to him. Besides, having determined to break off their betrothal, what better way to accomplish the matter than by Amanda Bridge's death?

Dear God, she simply could not think about this anymore. The weight of her grief pressed on her like a stone. Lifting her head, she said in a clear voice, "I understand everything you have told me. I am ready now."

The watchman, his expression troubled, replied, "Very well, then. Hold both of my hands tightly, and close your eyes."

Amanda glanced around, listening to the dark silence that seemed to fill not only the little church, but her soul as well. Blinking away the tears that blinded her, she closed her eyes.

One of the first guests to arrive that evening at Wiltsham House was the Earl of Ashindon. Barely pausing to greet his host and hostess, he prowled one chamber after another, searching for Amanda. It was not for another two hours that he finally spotted the feathers of Serena's elaborate headdress bobbing above the crowd.

"What do you mean, she isn't here?" he snapped at her reply to his question.

"The poor child is at home with a headache. A very bad one, I'm afraid. I left her just getting ready for bed. I'm sure, though," she added brightly, "that she will be better in the morning. Perhaps you could call then, my lord."

Ash uttered a choked reply and swung away from her. A few moments later, he stood on the sidewalk in front of Wiltsham House, his fists clenched. How was he going to contain himself until tomorrow morning, for God's sake? Everything in him screamed for him to go to Amanda, to apologize for the wrong he had done her and to tell her of his love for her. Setting off for the Bridge house right now to wake her from a sound sleep was probably insane, and she would probably have him thrown out of the house. Attempt to have him thrown out of the house, he amended, his fists clenched.

Clambering into his curricle and directing his tiger to hang on, he clattered off in the direction of Upper Brook Street. He had covered less than half the distance when he was obliged to jerk back on the reins in order to avoid running over a small figure just crossing Davies Street. To his astonishment, when the frightened young woman looked up, to be caught in the light of a street lamp, he recognized Amanda's maid.

"Lord Ashindon!" she cried, lifting her arms in distress. "Oh, thank God. I was just coming to find you, my lord!"

"What is it, Hutchings?" he exclaimed, bringing his vehicle to a halt. "What has happened?" He lifted the young woman into the curricle.

"It's Miss Bridge, my lord. She's gone off again, and I don't know what to do. I can't tell her mama or papa or—"

"Yes, yes," said Ash impatiently. "Now, stop crying. There's a good girl. Tell me what's toward."

"I just told you, my lord. Miss Bridge has gone off, and I'm afraid she's eloping with that wretched Cosmo Satterleigh. I saw them talking today and—" She broke off, burying her face in her apron.

"What makes you think she's eloping?" asked Ash through clenched teeth.

"Why, what else would she be doing?" responded Hutchings. "Him and her was talking earlier—just outside your grandma's house. She's on her way to Grosvenor Chapel this very minute to meet him."

Good God, thought Ash. This could not be happening. He would have been willing to wager all he owned that Amanda was no longer in Satterleigh's avaricious thrall. "Did she tell you that's what she was going to do?"

"N-no. In fact, she said she hadn't any intention of eloping with him, but—what else would she be doing in Grosvenor Chapel?" asked Hutchings again. "At this time of night," she added severely.

Grosvenor Chapel. Something stirred in Ash's brain. Something alarming and unpleasant. He thought back to the morning he had found her there, lying still as death. Yes, she had gone there on that occasion to elope with Satterleigh, but she had said it was also the scene of her transference from the twentieth to the nineteenth century. He was chilled, suddenly, to the marrow of his bones. Amanda had mentioned returning to her own time. Was that what she was doing right now?

Dear God, please—No. He couldn't lose her! Not like this. Not when he hadn't even told her that he loved her.

He urged his horses to a speed such as he had never used in the city before, and within minutes he pulled up before Grosvenor Chapel. He leaped from the curricle and with a gesture restrained Hutchings and his tiger from leaving the vehicle. "No, you wait here," he said tersely.

The church door swung open at his touch, and once within he was directed immediately to the spot where a lantern glowed fitfully. Yes, there she was! But who was that with her? By God, if—But, no, the figure who crouched in the pew beside her was much too bulky to be Cosmo Satterleigh. To his astonishment, when he reached Amanda he saw that her companion was—a Charlie, for God's sake!

Amanda whirled at his approach and stood abruptly, just as she had that other time. Now, however, she remained upright, staring at him as though at a demon with horns and a tail.

"Ash! What are you—?" She swayed then, and catching her in his arms, he eased her back into the pew. He lifted his gaze to the Charlie, who displayed a gap-toothed smile.

"Don't mind me, gov'ner. I'll just be waitin' over yonder." He rose and shuffled into the shadows in the other side of the church.

"No!" exclaimed Amanda. "Don't go! You—I must—" But the portly figure had already disappeared into the darkness.

"Amanda, thank God I found you in time. Were you—were you going back to—?"

"Yes, Ash. I'm sorry you came because this is something I must do, and I had hoped to leave without any further—unpleasantness between us."

"But you can't, Amanda. That's why I came. To apologize for the things I said to you this morning. My dearest love, I have behaved very stupidly, but I hope you will forgive what I said. I didn't mean them. I seem to have a great deal more pride than is good for me."

Amanda smiled faintly. "Yes, I guess you could say that. But don't you see, Ash—?" she stopped suddenly. "What did you call me?"

Ash gathered her closer to him. "My dearest love," he answered softly. "It took me a long time to realize that, and—"

Amanda sat bolt upright. "But I'm not your dearest love." Her heart was pounding painfully. "Lianne is your love, and with me gone, you will be able to return to her. You have enough money now, so that—"

"My God, do you think I am concerned with nothing but money? Having the money is good, but don't you see, without you, restoring the Park—and all the rest—doesn't mean a damn. As for loving Lianne—" He slid an arm about her shoulders and began pressing small, soft kisses against her hair, her forehead, and her cheeks. "Contrary to popular opinion, my own included, I never really loved her at all. My feeling for her was a boy's infatuation to which I clung stubbornly far into the time when I should have outgrown it."

"But—today—" Amanda was conscious of a treacherous surge of hope rising within her. "You and she were—kissing."

"Anything you saw, my dearest love, was an expression of friendship. I will always love Lianne as one would a cherished childhood memory. She will always be my friend, and, I hope, yours, too. The occasion for the buss on the cheek was her betrothal to one Reggie Smythe-Wolverton."

"Oh." The hope rose higher, despite Amanda's best effort to quash it, until she could almost feel it lapping at her heart. She dared not believe that Ash did not love Lianne. Even less could she allow herself to believe that he loved her. She wanted it too much, and it had been her experience far too many times that what one wanted most in life was the least likely to be granted.

"What?" she whispered, aware that Ash was speaking again.

"I was just wondering if we could shelve the subject of Lianne for the moment. I would much rather talk about us."

Amanda's throat tightened painfully. "There is no 'us,' Ash. We agreed to a marriage of convenience, and I do not think I could bear that."

"Nor I, love." His fingers stroked her cheek, creating swirls of wanting in places within her that she had not even known existed. "I realize our relationship has been—well, stormy—up till now. For so long I thought you a beautiful nonentity, and when I discovered you were something quite different, I didn't know how to change my perceptions." He smiled wryly. "It didn't help to discover that someone quiet different turned out to be outrageously independent and irritatingly outspoken. How was I to know that, though I could not fall in love with a lovely wax doll, I'd topple like a tree for an enchanting termagant." He cupped her chin in his hand and turned her face up to his. His eyes, thought Amanda dazedly, were like mist glinting in a summer dawn. "After the things I have said, and the manner in which I have behaved toward you, I can hardly expect you to fall into my arms." He laughed shakily. "But, oh, my darling, if you knew how badly I wish for you to do just that."

"You don't think—?" She could hardly form the words. "That I—that I'm a freak?"

"Oh, my God," said Ash. "Is that what you—?" His arms tightened about her. "No, my darling. I think you a unique phenomenon, to be treasured and explored and loved."

He kissed her cheek, very lightly. Just a butterfly touch, really, but suddenly, something seemed to crack inside Amanda, like a fault line shifting deep within her. In a moment the crack widened into a veritable chasm through which bubbled a stinging warmth that flooded her throat and eyes. He loved her! Really loved *her*—not the Barbie doll who greeted her each morning in the mirror, but the flawed woman behind the blue eyes and the pink mouth.

With one hand she traced the line of his jaw and brought his face closer to hers.

"Oh, Ash, I've already fallen—so hard it's a wonder I'm not covered with bruises."

For an instant, Ash paused, and in his eyes the mist vanished, leaving only the warmth of an early morning sun. His mouth came down on hers, urgent and demanding, but with an aching tenderness that drew a shuddering response from her.

"And you will not leave me, Amanda," said Ash when he lifted his head at last. "You will marry me and stay with me and live with me and have my babies and——"

"Yes, to all of the above," she answered tenderly, and it was a very long time before anything was heard in the little church beyond the rattle of carriages outside and small, throaty murmurings that would have made no sense except to persons in love.

At last, Amanda glanced around. She peered into the shadows, but saw no sign of the watchman.

"He is gone then?" asked Ash. "Who was he?"

"I don't know, and I don't believe I ever will. It may well be that I shall never see him—her—again." Pressing one more kiss on Ash's mouth, she rose. "I think we better take me home now. If Mama and Papa should arrive first——"

Ash shuddered graphically. "I daren't consider the consequences. Why, I might be forced to marry you."

Amanda laughed. "Aha, you've fallen into my trap, you poor man." Taking Ash's arm she moved with him down the aisle toward the door.

"Do you think," asked Ash after a moment, "that your mama and papa would be amenable to pushing up the wedding date?"

"You do not wish to wait a year?" Amanda paused and turned to brush her fingertips over his lips. This action, not unnaturally, resulted in another long, sweet kiss, at the end of which Ash spoke unsteadily.

"I do not wish to wait five minutes, you unprincipled wench. However, I might be willing to compromise. How about next week?"

"Mm. I'm not sure how these things are done here, but I think a week might be pushing it." Amanda smiled mistily into his eyes. "But I, too, would like to get an immediate start on those babies."

Once more, progress to the church exit halted for some moments.

"Very well then," said Ash at last, his voice ragged. "We shall present Ma and Pa Bridge with an ultimatum. They agree to a wedding in a month's time, or risk the unscheduled and very premature appearance of their first grandchild." Dropping a kiss on the top of Amanda's head, he continued. "So, there remains nothing to discuss except our wedding journey. Would you prefer Paris or Rome? Or possibly Vienna?"

"All of them sound wonderful, but—oh, Ash, I want to go first to Ashindon Park. I can't wait to begin living there with you. And then I'd like to tour England." She glanced at him shyly. "I'd like to know more about my newly acquired native land."

"Excellent choice. I shall enjoy showing you 'this green and sceptered isle.' "

"Starting with Chawton, if you please."

"Chawton?"

"Yes, it's in Hampshire. There's someone there I'd like very much to meet."

Ash lifted his expressive brows, but said only, "Anything you wish, my love."

"Actually," said Amanda with an insouciant grin, "I plan to ensure the solvency of our descendants by purchasing first editions and stashing them in Ashindon Park—starting with Jane Austen. And, let's see—oh! Charles Dickens is three years old now. We'll be able to buy up all his stuff for future reference. As for the immediate future, I think we should invest in railroads, and—"

"I think you have much to teach me, my love," said Ash, a little startled.

"Indeed," said Amanda as the church door swung shut behind them. She raised a misty gaze to Ash. "But not nearly as much as I have already learned from you, my love."

"Indeed," said her betrothed, enfolding her in his arms once more before handing her into the curricle. "And now we shall have all the time in the world to continue both our educations."

"All the time in the world," echoed Amanda softly as the curricle rattled off into the beginning of a new day in Regency London.